# HIGHLANDER
# BETRAYED

# ALSO BY LAURIN WITTIG

*Charming the Shrew*
*(The Legacy of MacLeod – Book I)*

*Daring the Highlander*
*(The Legacy of MacLeod – Book II)*

*The Devil of Kilmartin*

*Jewels of Historical Romance, an anthology*

# HIGHLANDER BETRAYED

## GUARDIANS OF THE TARGE

## BOOK 1

LAURIN WITTIG

Montlake
Romance

Published by Amazon Publishing
P.O. Box 400818
Las Vegas, NV 89140

ISBN-10: 1477807276
ISBN-13: 9781477807279
Library of Congress Catalog Number: 2013907702

*For*
*Samantha and Alex*

# PROLOGUE

NICHOLAS FITZ HUGH COULD NO MORE IGNORE THE THICK CLUS-
ters of lavishly clothed courtiers nervously awaiting King Edward's
audience than he could the itch deep in his gut pressing him to escape the suffocating, odiferous confines of London and once more
be about the king's business somewhere else. Anywhere else.

The acrid scent of nervous sweat inexorably drew his attention
to the couple standing closest to him. They whispered feverishly
about money they had hidden from the tax collector. Reckless idiots.
It didn't require a spy's skills to take advantage of their stupidity.
There were plenty here who would make sure the information got to
the exchequer's ear. The couple would pay their taxes, one way or
another, likely with their lives.

It took little experience to know one did not cross the king.
Nicholas wanted to shake his head at their folly. Instead, he let his
gaze glide effortlessly over the crowd, studying his surroundings
even though he had no specific assignment. Taxes unpaid were of no
import to him. He traded in high treason, betrayals, collusion, and
many other forms of danger to the king's rule.

At least he did when the king had a task for him.

Forcing his breath to move in and out evenly, calmly, as he pro-
ceeded slowly through the crowd, he wanted nothing more than to
be away from this place, these people; to be taking on a mission the
king deemed only Nicholas able to accomplish. He had been waiting
nearly three months for the king to summon him. Now that he finally had, it meant there was something more important afoot than
tax evasion.

Nicholas leaned against a wall halfway down the long side of the
stuffy room and wished he could ignore those around him, but the

rich silks and velvets and bright colors worn by most of the company were designed to draw one's attention, like a peacock flaunting his tail feathers.

Nicholas closed his eyes, suddenly exhausted by how tedious this part of his life was. Petty squabbles, gossip, and the fetid stink of London were the best entertainment he could hope for at court.

"Master fitz Hugh, sir." A piping voice forced Nicholas's eyes open. A young page, not more than ten or eleven years old, bowed before him, drawing surreptitious glances from many of those gathered there.

"What is it, boy?" Nicholas said, carefully hiding the irritation of suddenly being the one watched.

"The king would see you in his private chamber, sir," the boy said quietly. "Will you follow me?"

Nicholas nodded, surprised and curious that he should be summoned to that room he had never before entered. He followed the page out a side door, down a short frigid corridor and into a marginally warmer room. The walls were draped in ancient tapestries depicting battles from the past. A large bed with thick posts of oak, carved with mythical beasts and draped in heavy aubergine curtains, took up one corner of the room, near the hearth. King Edward stood opposite the bed, by a window, his tall frame swathed in a heavy mantle of dark-blue velvet trimmed in creamy ermine. The gloomy grey light of late winter washed out his features, making him look older than his sixty-odd years.

The page melted out of Nicholas's line of sight, no doubt taking his place by the door where he would stand unnoticed until their king next commanded him to some errand.

Nicholas bowed to King Edward. A rush of excitement raced up his spine as he awaited the monarch's attention.

"Rise," Edward commanded.

"Sire." Nicholas took note that none of Edward's usual advisors was there. Whatever the task was, it was not one Edward wanted widely known. "I am your servant."

Edward's mouth tightened into a single determined line. "You have been a long time in London."

Nicholas nodded. "I have, sire."

"You have enjoyed your leisure?" the king asked.

"I have." *Not.* No matter how good of terms he was on with the king, he'd not complain about waiting for his summons for nigh on three months. No one would dare such an impertinence with this man. Nicholas smiled, his pleasure at this private audience genuine. "I am, however, as always, at your command, my lord."

The king looked at the page and with a flick of his long-fingered hand dismissed him. He waited until the door was closed, then beckoned Nicholas to approach.

"You are politic, as always, Master Spy. I know well how you chafe at lingering in my court. I have been awaiting news. When it came it was not what I wanted, so I find I have need of your very special skills. Others have failed where I think you can succeed."

A challenge indeed, but this was the sort of task Nicholas enjoyed the most—besting his fellows, an opportunity to prove once more that he was worthy of the king's great regard. Nicholas did not hesitate to let his pleasure at the king's assessment of his skill show on his face.

"I have never failed you, sire. I shall not start now."

"I expect no less." Edward turned back to gaze out the window, though he seemed lost in thought rather than drawn by the view. "It is no secret who your father was," the king said. Nicholas kept his breath even, his hands relaxed at his sides. He carefully maintained his pleased expression of a moment ago, though it did not suit this odd turn in the conversation. He did not know where the king led him, but no good had ever come from the vicious Lord Hugh of Stanwix, Nicholas's sire.

When Nicholas didn't respond, the king glanced over his shoulder and raised one grey-and-ginger eyebrow. "It is also no secret that your mother was Scottish."

Nicholas verified what the king already knew with a single nod. An English knight having his way with an unwilling Scottish lass was not unheard of, though his sire had been particularly vicious. His mother's clan had accepted her bastard bairn, even if his mother never could, though they'd never embraced him as one of their own. Later, when he'd left Scotland behind him for a new life, he'd confronted his father and learned firsthand just how brutal the man was.

Nicholas had known the circumstances of his birth for as long as he could remember and apparently so did everyone else. The only difference was that he didn't care. He'd determined a long time ago that his parents had nothing to do with the person he was now.

The king watched him for a long moment. Nicholas had seen more than one powerful man squirm under such royal scrutiny but he waited.

"What do you remember of Scotland?"

"Some, your majesty. I know it to be a backward, rough country filled with barbarians." That wasn't exactly his memory of the place, but it was the expected description. "I have not been there since I first came to my father's manor at Stanwix when I was ten and two. I have but few memories of my time there." Few he'd share at any rate.

The king ran a finger and thumb over his mustache, smoothing it in a gesture Nicholas had seen often. "Do you remember enough of the Scots to become one?" He turned to face Nicholas and captured his gaze. "I have seen you become a Welshman in the blink of an eye. Can you do the same as a Scotsman?"

Being a spy required the ability to blend in with those spied upon. The ability to throw oneself into whatever life was required, body and soul, often made the difference between success and death. Early on, when first he'd come to his father's manor in northern England, Nicholas had discovered he had a knack for going unnoticed. When his father refused to acknowledge him, Nicholas had survived by blending in with the other kitchen lads and keeping out of sight of his sire. He also began to learn how to trade in information, securing his position by such means when he had to, until he'd decided to move on to London.

The skill had served him well over the years, eventually landing him right here in the king's service.

But could he become a Scotsman?

He'd only met one or two Scots in all his travels as an adult so he reached into those childhood memories he thought he'd forgotten, only to discover they were right there, waiting for him. He remembered the sound of his mother's voice, the cadence, the way she had rolled her R's and swallowed the odd Scottish sound for what a proper Englishman would pronounce as a K. He remembered the way her sentences ended on an uplifting lilt, as if every utterance were a question.

"Well?" Edward demanded.

Nicholas reached deeper into his long-buried memories, reminding his senses of the Highland warriors he had trailed after as a wee boy. He adjusted his stance, imagining himself barefoot, clad in a length of heavy plaid he had once tried to wear when he was a lad.

He imagined a two-handed broadsword in his hands, the wind off the Highland mountains whipping his hair into wild tangles, as he remembered seeing the chief of his mother's clan once, a long time ago. He chose a name for himself that was fitting—Nicholas of Achnamara—his Scottish name given to him by a mother who did not want him.

Opening his eyes, he looked at Edward, allowing all the natural impertinence he'd carefully suppressed over the years to flood into his own.

"Aye, m'laird. I do not speak the Gaelic well anymore, but 'twould need only a wee bit of mummery to pass as a Scot long banished from my bonny Highland home."

Edward stared, silent, brooding. At last he nodded. "I do not know how you do that, but I am well pleased that you wield such a skill for England."

"I am your servant, as ever." Nicholas stood straight again, dropping the musical lilt from his voice with relief and an unsettling feeling he could not pinpoint. "I am to go to Scotland?"

"You are. This task calls for your particular skill at passing for what you are not, though in this case that is perhaps not entirely true. It calls for subtlety, for manipulation, for a greater ability to win information from unwilling sources than most spies hold. You are most skilled in all these areas, are you not?"

"I am, my lord."

Edward turned his back on Nicholas and paced away from the window. When he reached the far side of the room he turned back, eyes narrowed as if he weighed the man.

"You know the Stone of Destiny was taken from Scone, in Scotland, and brought to me."

"The coronation stone of the Scots? I do."

"It was supposed to break their spirit, make them see that I am the rightful king of Scotland, but the barbarians still refuse to give me their fealty."

Edward was not termed the "Hammer of the Scots" because he felt affection for the people there. The king had a volatile temper in the best of circumstances, and anything involving the Scots was never the best of circumstances. Nicholas said nothing and kept his expression neutral, though the flicker of pride he felt in the stubborn irascible Scots surprised him.

"It has come to my attention that there is another object that is held in great esteem by the Scots, an object with the power to protect those Highland brutes from invasion, or so says their superstitious tale." Edward strode to an ornately carved chair that sat near the hearth and threw himself into it, scraping the chair backward over the planked floor. He motioned for Nicholas to come closer.

"It is called the Highland Targe," the king said, ridicule thick in his voice and in the dismissive wave of his hand.

"A shield?" Nicholas asked, holding his hands toward the heat of the roaring fire. He'd seen targes aplenty as a lad—round, wooden shields, often with short spikes sticking out of their centers. The Scots favored them as weapons as well as for defense.

"The story is that there is a clan in the southwestern Highlands who are the keepers of this Highland Targe. Clearly it has not done its job," the king said derisively. "But the Highlanders of the area lay great store in its powers and use it as a means of rallying resistance against their rightful king.

"I want you to find this pagan idol. I want you to bring it to me so they will know they cannot keep anything from me, that anything they hold in high esteem, other than their rightful sovereign, shall be taken from them."

"Do you know more about where this Highland Targe might be, sire?" The Highlands were a wild country, vast, dangerous, and difficult to traverse. And they were beautiful in a way he'd never found elsewhere. A long-buried ache threatened to break loose within him, but he crushed it back into the darkness, as he always did.

"It seems to be somewhere in the vicinity of a village called Oban, on the southwestern coast, though my man in the area has been unable to learn anything more specific than that.

"You will make your way there as soon as possible. Move north as the weather breaks. I trust in your abilities to find the Targe from there."

"Very good." He buried the ambivalence that threatened to drown out the familiar thrill of a new undertaking humming in his veins. He had an assignment from the king and he would not let any regrets from his past interfere. "Am I to make contact with your man when I get there?"

"Aye. You know him well already: Archibald of Easton."

He did. Archie and he often worked together on the king's business. The man was the closest thing Nicholas had to a friend, but he was not the most skilled spy with whom Nicholas had worked. He tended to take short cuts and rush into things before all the facts were gathered. Still, they had had many a successful adventure on the king's business.

But . . . His mind spun quickly through various possibilities. If Archie had been unable to learn no more about the Highland Targe than its general location, the door was open for Nicholas to sweep in and work his particular brand of spying magic, especially since he had lived as a Highlander and understood them as Archie never would.

He would work with Archie, but it would be Nicholas's efforts that would make the mission a success and would seal Nicholas's place as the king's most favored spy, a position he'd worked long and hard to reach and one he would not forfeit for anyone.

Edward met Nicholas's eyes and held him in his steely gaze. "Archibald has been instructed to expect you and to share everything he has learned. The two of you may well be able to accomplish what he alone has not been able to.

"I expect you will deliver the prize by midsummer's eve. If you cannot transport it, destroy it and send me a piece of it as testament to your success. I know my trust in your abilities is not misplaced, Nicholas."

Pride filled Nicholas's chest. "I will not fail you, sire."

"I am counting on that."

# CHAPTER ONE

*Scottish Highlands, Spring 1307*

ROWAN MACGREGOR OPENED THE WOODEN SHUTTERS, LETTING the weak spring sunshine into her aunt Elspet MacAlpin's bedchamber. The large room at the top of the tower that housed the MacAlpin clan chief's family had small windows that looked both into the castle bailey and out to the glorious country that surrounded Dunlairig Castle.

Rowan took a deep breath of the air flowing in through the window. It was cool and crisp, and filled with the aromas of spring—damp earth, growing plants, new life. The freshness of it quickly overcame the heat of the room and diminished the sickly sweet smell of illness that pervaded the chamber. Briefly Rowan wished she could escape the room and take to the familiar greening slope of the forested ben outside the window. It was a small mountain compared to others that rose around them. This one, though, for all its lack of imposing height, rose steeply from the deep loch below the castle except for the large, nearly flat area the castle perched on, not too far up the slope from the loch.

She took one more deep lungful of the fresh spring air, then turned back to the chamber and the women who were mother and sister to her in her heart, if not her blood. Her aunt loved this time of year and if the fresh air enticed her out of her sickbed, even for a little while, it was worth the chill.

"'Tis a beautiful day at last, Mum," Jeanette, Elspet's blond-haired, blue-eyed eldest daughter, said, tucking another blanket around the frail woman. "Do you not want to go outside for a wee while?"

Elspet smiled at her daughter and niece, but there was a brittleness to it. "Nay. I shall enjoy it from the comfort of my bed this day." She turned her face to the gentle breeze. "Perhaps tomorrow, if the weather holds."

Jeanette shared a worried glance with Rowan. It was a measure of how far the wasting illness had progressed since Elspet first took sick in the fall that she was content to gaze out a window rather than be out in the spring air she loved so dearly.

The chief's wife had always bustled about, but in spring she would be found planting the kitchen garden, tending the herb beds, overseeing the birthings of the cows. She would welcome each wee beastie into the world with a smile, a prayer, and odd symbols made in the air with graceful movements of her hands. No one alive knew the meaning of the symbols, and yet the MacAlpin cattle prospered even in years where other clans' herds did not.

Today Elspet lay with her face turned toward the sunshine and her eyes half-closed. This year's wee beasties would have to fend for themselves.

"Where is Scotia?" she asked quietly. "I have not seen my bairn in two full days."

Rowan shook her head. Bairn indeed. At ten and eight Scotia was a woman grown, at least in body if not in mind. Scotia still seemed to think she could run amuck with no consequences. Since Elspet had become ill Scotia had gotten into more trouble in the castle than any pack of lads ever could. That she hadn't come to visit her mother in two days had Rowan muttering words only her Uncle Kenneth, the chief of the MacAlpin clan, ever spoke.

"I'll find her," she said to Jeanette and Elspet. "It will not take long." She leaned over and kissed Elspet's forehead.

"I thank you, love," the older woman whispered. "I do so worry about Scotia."

"As do we all," Rowan said. Had she ever been so wild? Though she was only three years older than her youngest cousin, the difference in their behavior made Rowan feel much older.

"You will keep her safe when I cannot, aye?" Elspet reached for Rowan, raising her hand just an inch above the blanket.

Rowan took it into her own. The strong, work-roughened hand that once guided her through her tasks was now nothing but fragile skin and bones, as if Elspet were melting away from the inside out. Rowan pressed it to her cheek, willing the heat of her own body to warm her beloved foster mother.

"I promise." She would not cry. Her place was to be the strength that Jeanette, Scotia, and Uncle Kenneth would need when the center of their family, the heart of their entire clan, left them.

"*We* promise," Jeanette said.

"She only needs a bit of guidance, my lassies." Elspet reached for Jeanette but did not let go of Rowan. "She loses her way sometimes."

Rowan couldn't help but chuckle quietly at Elspet's description of her youngest child. Only a mother could have such a soft spot for a child that was perpetually "losing her way."

"I shall fetch her." She gently tucked Elspet's hand under the woolen blanket. Jeanette followed her to the door. "She is so cold, Jeanette," Rowan whispered.

Jeanette's eyes filled with unshed tears. "I fear she will not last to see the summer," she said just as quietly.

Rowan swallowed hard around the thickness in her throat. "I shall find Scotia." She gave Jeanette's hand a quick squeeze and left to find her wayward cousin.

NICHOLAS TRIED TO IGNORE THE THORNY GORSE BUSHES THAT SUR-rounded him and his partner, Archibald of Easton, as they watched the top of Dunlairig Castle's curtain wall, keeping count of how often a guard passed by. It was work that required patience and Ar-chie was already starting to fidget.

Nicholas glanced at the man whom he'd known for more than ten years. They had trained in the art of espionage together and col-laborated often, so much so that they knew each other's strengths and weaknesses, their tastes in women, wine, and missions. This mission was just the sort at which they excelled.

Infiltration, then take and escape. Almost a simple burglary, but with more finesse, more cunning. They'd gathered enough information before arriving at Dunlairig Castle to settle on a plan, but Archie was always impatient with the reconnaissance that had to take place before they made themselves known to their targets. Nicholas had learned the need for such information the hard way long before he'd been trained as an agent of the king, and he never skipped, nor skimped on, getting the lay of the land before engaging with the targets. But they'd been watching the wall for several hours and, truth be told, Nicholas was as fidgety as Archie.

They'd arrived in this spot before sunup after Nicholas had spent almost two months traveling in and around Oban in search of information. Eventually he had gleaned bits and pieces of gossip and stories from the lasses and the drunkards, gaining their trust in a way Archie had not been able to, adding his own information to that which the other man had gathered over the long Scottish winter, to put the puzzle of the Highland Targe's likely whereabouts together.

A crucial break came when Nicholas happened past an alleyway where he'd espied a little boy playing warrior with a stick for a sword. The lad had shouted, "By the Targe" as he lunged at his imagined foe, stopping Nicholas in his tracks. Half an hour later, he and the boy were fast friends, striking and feinting with their sticks in mock battle. Distracted by the play, the boy had easily been led to talk about the Targe amidst his comments about Bossy Bess, the woman who lived across the way from his family, his little brother who scratched all the time, and the trouble his sister was in for kissing a lad.

Gently, Nicholas had learned that the Targe was something the lad's mother spoke of when times were hard. She had grown up in Glen Lairig, and the Targe had made life easier, its influence bringing bounty and prosperity to the glen even when all those around them were challenged by weather, sickly livestock, and lean harvests. Later Nicholas had discovered the glen was home to a small branch of the MacAlpin clan about whom no one seemed willing to talk.

The tale he and Archie finally pieced together was one of a shield meant to protect not only the clan but also a route into the Highlands, set in place by the same ancient people who had left behind stone barrows, stone circles, and cryptically decorated standing stones throughout that part of Scotland.

Nicholas had seen too much of the harsh reality of the world to believe the Targe of the story held any such mythical abilities, but that didn't matter—the superstitious Highlanders did. And if they believed it could protect them from the English, well, he would play his part in proving them wrong. And thus, the two of them had set off to the east to a castle called Dunlairig.

"We've seen enough," Archie whispered. "We know the guard schedule. We know where the gates are and how many men are set on a watch. It's time to get going."

Nicholas looked at his partner and shook his head, even though he agreed. He was the leader of this mission. He was the one who had found the final piece of information that had woven all the rest together to form a tapestry of myth, tale, and superstition that pointed here, to this place, this castle. And he was enjoying holding that over his partner's head simply because it irritated the man so much.

"You still lack patience, Archie. I'd have thought you'd learn some by now."

"You've plenty for both of us."

The words were light but there was annoyance in Archie's eyes that had been present in the man since Nicholas first arrived in Oban.

"'Tis a good thing, that."

Archie ran his stubby fingers through his unruly red curls. It did not matter how closely he kept his hair cropped, it still curled wildly. The man often looked unkempt and rough, but Nicholas knew Archie was more than he appeared. He could be ruthless when required, charming when called for, and he was focused on the mission at hand at all times, most especially when it appeared he wasn't. He was smart and as driven to succeed as Nicholas, and that was what made them effective, if not completely trusting, partners.

"Are you sure about your part in our plan?" Nicholas asked under his breath, stalling to goad the man.

"You doubt me?"

Nicholas shook his head, making note of a guard passing along the wall walk above them. "Just taking advantage of the time to make sure we both understand what to do."

"We met a sennight back, a sevenday, and have struck up a traveling friendship. I am a laborer in search of work, which should give me some access about the castle. I am known as Archie of Keltie, a MacGregor if anyone pushes for my clan. It should not be questioned since I'm as ginger as any of that rough lot."

"And as troublesome."

"Aye, I can be." He slanted an odd look at Nicholas that felt like a challenge. "And you are . . ." Archie crossed his arms over his chest and raised an eyebrow as if he did not expect Nicholas to remember his part in this plot.

"Nicholas of Achnamara, traveling home for the first time since I was a wean."

Sticking close to the truth was a trick he had learned during his tenure in the kitchen of his father's manor. He'd told too many different tales about who he was and where he'd come from, and when he could not keep the lies straight any longer he was nearly revealed to his sire, which could have caused a confrontation he knew would end in pain, if not worse. He'd had no choice but to leave Stanwix and start anew in London. He had never told Archie how much truth any of his guises held, and he never would.

"We met upon the road west of Loch Katrine," Nicholas said, "and have been traveling together for a sennight *or more*." He stressed the "or more" as it would be odd for a pair such as them to be so specific, something he had said to Archie before.

Archie scowled. "Or more," he said, then went perfectly still as the sound of someone hurrying toward them, scattering pebbles and stones down the steeply inclined path, had both men crouching perfectly still.

A young woman rushed past their hiding spot so quickly, all Nicholas could make out was hair so black it glowed even in the weak sunshine. When she was clear of their hidey-hole they stood, still hidden by the thorny gorse, and Nicholas leaned out enough to see the girl throw herself into the arms of a tall, skinny, fair-haired lad and kiss him as if they had been long parted.

"A tryst," he said, crouching back beside Archie. "If they do not move somewhere for more private play we may be here a while."

Archie peeked out at the couple, then sank back on his haunches next to Nicholas. "A lusty wench, that one. Perhaps I'll take her for a tumble once we are in the castle."

Irritation gripped Nicholas. "'Tis one thing to bed the whores in Oban, Archie, but not these Highland lasses. The clans do not take well to outsiders as it is, less so outsiders who dally with their daughters or wives."

"Then what of that young whelp?" Archie growled, peering out at the couple again. "He looks to be getting what he wants from the wanton."

"Aye, but even they meet in secret, well hidden from others. No doubt her father would object should he find out."

"Fine." Archie sighed and took up his place next to Nicholas again. "They are not going anywhere soon, from the looks of it. I suppose we'll have time to watch the castle a mite longer after all."

"Saints and angels!" Rowan muttered as she rapidly made her way down the tower stair, stopping on the landing to peer out the narrow window facing into the bailey. The hallhouse, serving as the great hall, had been the home of the chieftains of clan MacAlpin for too many generations to count. It stood across the bailey from the tower. Both had been fully enclosed by a curtain wall forming a modest bailey between the two main buildings. Several wooden service buildings had been built along the north and south walls, crowding the open area into an even smaller space.

And Scotia was nowhere to be seen.

Rowan made her way through the bailey, asking everyone she passed if they had seen her wayward cousin, but no one had. When she arrived at the gate, she asked the guard the same thing and finally got an answer.

"She passed through the gate a while back," said Denis, the gate guard, giving her a nearly toothless smile. She often wondered how the man chewed his food, but the generous girth of his stomach told her he had figured it out. "Not too long ago," he continued. "She went around the loch side of the castle. Is she in trouble again?"

Rowan smiled at his concern for Scotia. In spite of her hellion ways, everyone seemed to have a soft spot for her, including Rowan. "Not yet," she said. "But if she does not rabbit up to visit her mum, she will be."

The smile faded on Denis's weathered face. "How fares Lady Elspet this day?"

"She is neither better, nor worse. Even Jeanette does not know if that's good or bad." A headache started to pulse between her brows. It would be so much better if she could break down and cry as Jeanette sometimes did, or act out as Scotia did, to release the worry, but it was not in Rowan's nature to do either of those things. She held things in, close, until they beat a rhythm in her head that made her want to retch.

But she never did.

"We are all praying for her return to health," Denis said.

Rowan touched his forearm. "I know."

He nodded, then smiled again. "You'd best get after Scotia. She's got a bit of a head start on you, and you ken well how hard it is to find that one when she does not wish it."

"Aye, all too well." She waved as she left the shadowy gate passage and turned right toward the nearest corner of the castle. When she reached the top of the path that led at an angle from where she stood, crossing in front of the looming curtain wall, and continuing all the way down the slope to the loch shore, she stopped. The path was steep and rocky with dense gorse bushes, now robed in glorious golden flowers, reclaiming all but the slimmest of trails in places, making for a treacherous track to the lochside. With other easier routes to the loch, this one was seldom used. Rowan couldn't imagine why Scotia would go this way.

Rowan looked around, hoping to espy her cousin somewhere other than along this path. She judged the rock-strewn trail with a careful eye.

"Scotia?" she shouted. "Are you down there?"

She waited, listening, knowing it was unlikely the girl would respond even if she was on the path and had heard her, but it was worth a try. With a sigh, she started down at a hurried pace. She did not have to go far before she spied Scotia partly hidden by the gorse. The lass's raven hair, so different from Jeanette's pale blond tresses or Rowan's own coppery brown, glinted in the sun and shifted in the wind, drawing the eye to where she stood kissing a tall gangly lad with honey-colored hair that fell almost to his broad shoulders.

Conall.

Rowan allowed herself a few more of her uncle's favorite words.

Was the bairnie totally daft? It was bad enough that Scotia was trysting with a lad but this one had been specifically banished from Dunlairig Castle to his mum's cottage down the glen. Kenneth had found the two doing a bit more than kissing in the loft of the stable a few months back and swore he'd make her marry the lad, but Scotia would have none of it, vowing she was yet a maid and would not be forced to marry anyone. Kenneth gave in, as he often did with his youngest, but declared Conall's life would be forfeit if he caught them together again without wedding vows taken first.

Apparently the lad either didn't value his life overmuch, or he had bollocks like a bull.

Of course, it was just as likely that Scotia was the instigator of this misdeed. For a girl who swore she was not ready to marry, Rowan feared, one way or another, her cousin would find herself in exactly that state before summer's end and they'd all have to listen to her temper when that happened.

Rowan closed her eyes for a moment and rubbed the place between her brows where the pulsing was pounding. She did not have the luxury of taking to her bed as some did with such a headache, so she took a deep breath and braced herself for the coming confrontation. She closed the distance quickly, yanking her cousin out of Conall's embrace without warning.

Scotia shrieked as she swung around, landing a sharp slap on Rowan's face and knocking Rowan back a few steps. Shocked, Rowan ignored the stinging on her cheek and the rapid staccato beat in her head and advanced on her disobedient cousin, fury and pain quickly burning away the more rational irritation of a moment ago.

Conall pulled Scotia backward out of Rowan's reach, pinning the girl to him, her back to his chest, her arms caught in his embrace. A sound like an angry cat escaped Scotia's throat.

"Scotia, wheesht," he said close to her ear. "You'll only make this worse."

She struggled for a moment, then the fight seemed to drain out of her. Rowan knew better than to believe Scotia had given up, but she hoped it was the case. The girl had to grow up sooner or later. Rowan feared it would be later, though.

"Let her go, Conall." Rowan tried to ignore her throbbing cheek. She knew her words were clipped and harsh, but it was the only way to keep her crackling temper in check. Nothing drove Scotia to a shouting match like someone else's temper, and that would surely draw the attention of someone in the castle. "She'll not do that again." She held Scotia's angry gaze, making sure the troublemaker understood this was not a choice.

The lad wisely hesitated, then slowly loosened his grip. Scotia glared at Rowan but did not try to attack her again.

Rowan glared right back at her. "Are you not ashamed of yourself, cousin? It's been a full pair of days since you visited your mum and when I am sent to find you, here you are putting young Conall's life in danger because you cannot control yourself enough to do what is right."

"'Tis my fault, Rowan," Conall said. "I missed her."

"You are a true dafty, Conall, if you do not think Kenneth's threat is real. Do you know what kind of grief you will bring upon your widowed mother if you force Kenneth to act?" Rowan knew full well that Kenneth wouldn't take the lad's life—they needed every able-bodied man they had after the last few years of skirmishes and raids against their neighbors had taken so many warriors, but she doubted not that he'd take the hide off Conall's back if it came to it.

She looked from Scotia to Conall where they stood shoulder to shoulder, their hands linked. "'Tis lucky for you both that I was the one to find you, else you"—she looked at Conall—"would be dead already, and you"—she looked at Scotia—"would be locked in your chamber until Uncle Kenneth chose a suitably stern and elderly husband for you."

"He would never!" Scotia's anger snapped in her eyes like sparks off flint.

"Do not test him, my cousin. Say farewell, Conall, and this time mean it."

"You'll not tell her da I was here?"

The lad's words were more plea than question, making him sound every bit like the wean he was and not the man he thought himself to be. Scotia was clearly preying on the lad's lust, keeping his mind too muddled to think clearly about what they did. Keeping her own muddled, too, no doubt, for Rowan was sure Scotia would rather face the wrath of her father than the death of her mother.

"I will not say anything this time," Rowan said, watching as Conall let out the breath he'd been holding. "But if I ever find you two together again, I will go directly to him and you'll both suffer the consequences." She should do so anyway, but Kenneth had enough grief with Elspet's illness and she was loath to add to that burden. "Say goodbye, Conall. You, too, Scotia."

Scotia stuck her tongue out at Rowan, then turned and kissed Conall like it was indeed a final parting. The childish rebellion so quickly followed by a woman's farewell to a lover exasperated Rowan. Scotia was stuck between childhood and adulthood and did not seem able or willing to climb over that wall even though 'twas well past time to do so.

When the kiss grew more heated, Rowan was pretty sure they had forgotten she was there. She rubbed her forehead, the pain of the headache spreading from the pounding there to a growing pressure behind her eyes.

"Be a man, Conall. Go."

He broke the kiss, and stepped back from Scotia. Scotia held his hand until their arms were stretched between them.

"Scotia, I have to go."

There seemed to be genuine distress in his voice and on his face, and for a moment Rowan thought she might have misjudged the pair's relationship.

"We do not want Rowan telling your da I was here." He looked a little green, as if the thought of facing the chief was more than he could handle.

"No, you do not," she said, assured by his color that the tryst had been Scotia's idea. It was hard to say no to Scotia when she set her mind to something.

Scotia shook her head and let go of his hand and they watched Conall turn and run down the path toward the loch until he disappeared around a bend where the bushes grew high.

"I hate you." Scotia's voice cracked through the air at Rowan as effectively as her slap had.

"That's too bad since I just saved Conall's life." She crossed her arms and waited for the usual capitulation from her cousin, swallowing down the bile that rose with each pound in her head. As soon as she got Scotia to her mother, Rowan promised herself, she'd lie down in the dark bedchamber she shared with her cousins for a little while.

Scotia didn't turn around. She balled her fists and everything about her seemed taut, about to snap, like a bow pulled back too far. She whirled about, fury in her eyes.

"Why cannot everyone leave me alone?" She stomped her foot and the ache in Rowan's head ratcheted up another notch. "I know what I'm doing." The ground seemed to tremble with her words and all the birds in the bushes around them took flight. She grabbed Rowan by her upper arms, squeezing hard enough to leave bruises in her wake. "Why?!"

Every hair on Rowan's body rose with that tremble and an odd pressure pulsed under her skin. A tremendous *crack* slashed through the air, followed by an ominous rumbling, as if the mountain were speaking to them.

"What is it?!" Scotia gripped her arms even harder, as an unnatural wind pushed down the hillside and over them.

Terror gripped Rowan. As she looked up the hill toward the rumble, a horrible memory she'd buried long ago hurtled at her. "Nay," she whispered. "Not again."

Everything went silent in Rowan's head as the pain reached a crescendo. She wrenched her arms free from her cousin's grip and squeezed her hands to her scalp, her head feeling as if it was going to split asunder.

Another loud crack, as if the very ground beneath their feet was breaking wide open, though it barely trembled. Rowan looked up just in time to see the curtain wall above them burst, like heavy storm water through a dam, sending blocks of stone and rubble down the steep embankment.

"Run!" a deep male voice shouted at the same moment.

Rowan whipped around in the direction of the voice but didn't see anyone.

"Run, now!" Suddenly a stranger burst onto the path not far up the hill and hurtled down toward them.

Scotia screamed, "Which way?" but didn't move.

Rowan grabbed her skirts with one hand and Scotia's arm with the other and pelted up the path toward the stranger. The path angled back toward the curtain wall but it was the shortest way to safety.

Rowan did not want to think about what would happen to them if they were caught in the avalanche of falling stone.

Scotia shrieked and ripped her arm from Rowan's grip as they drew even with the stranger. Scotia raced past him, leaving Rowan behind as the first pebbles bounced across the path. Rowan glanced up toward the castle as she and the stranger followed Scotia. She could see nothing but a looming wall of grey dust, the sharp scent of it crowding her already straining lungs. The ground shuddered again.

Rocks the size of her fist bounced all around her, clattering against one another with a sound like heavy rain. One of them hit Rowan hard in the shin. She stumbled, nearly losing her footing, but the man running ahead of her seemed to have eyes in the back of his head. He reached back, caught her arm and pulled her upright and forward.

Massive blocks of stone tumbled past them, end over end, some launching high into the air, then falling with deadly thuds all around them. A river of gravel raced down the hillside, adding its din to the tumult while making the path treacherous and slippery. Scotia had disappeared ahead of them and Rowan could only hope she'd already made it to safety.

A sudden sharp catch in Rowan's side made it even harder to breathe but the man kept a grip on her hand and she had no choice but to keep running.

The dust cloud enveloped them, adding even more difficulty to the uphill run, making breathing more labored, and seeing almost impossible. After a lifetime of coughing and gagging on the dust, the two of them burst out into blinding sunshine where the path finally cleared the corner of the castle. Scotia stood there, bent over at the waist, her hands braced on her thighs, gasping for breath. Rowan fell to the ground, as did the stranger, their sides heaving as the last of the wall gave way, its stones thundering down the hill with a deafening roar, covering the path behind them, destroying everything in the way.

Darkness tried to close in around her but she would not give in to such a weakness. She lay back upon the ground and tried to slow her gasping breath, tried to steady her heart, tried to clear the dust from her face. As her vision cleared she gradually became aware of faraway shouts probably inside the castle.

Stunned, Rowan sat up gingerly, the pain in her side growing stronger. She winced and looked about. The wall . . . huge stones . . . destruction. Impossible. And yet, as the breeze began to clear the dust, she could see it was true.

She couldn't catch her breath. Her heart pounded in her chest, harder now than when they had sprinted to safety. Terror and relief warred with a vague sense of remorse, though she knew not why she should feel that. She closed her eyes, blocking out the sight of the ruin, but not the sound of shouting, of stones still shifting, sliding down the slope, not the sharp scent of stone dust mixed with the fresh scent of torn and bruised plants, not the pain in her side that pulsed with her heartbeat, or the barely noticeable echo of her headache keeping pace with it.

She forced herself to open her eyes. The ruined remains of the wall sat at the top of the slope and a river of rocky destruction flowed downward, leaving a harsh scar on the hillside right to the edge of the loch and beyond.

The curtain wall was down, leaving the castle, and the clan, vulnerable. Leaving them exposed.

# CHAPTER TWO

Nicholas took long pulls of fresh air into his lungs as he counted himself a fool. What had he been thinking to run toward the women? Self-preservation was rule number one in his line of work because with a certainty no one else would put themselves in harm's way to save his hide. Not even Archie. Nicholas had glanced at their hidey-hole when he ran by and Archie wasn't there. He was nowhere to be seen.

Nicholas ran a hand over his face, knocking away enough dust to create another small cloud around him. He sneezed, then looked about him from his place on the ground. Clearly Archie had not been as stupid as Nicholas. His partner had done the smart thing, running away from the danger, looking to his own safety first. After all, you couldn't finish an assignment if you were dead or maimed, but where was Archie now?

A cough gripped Nicholas, clearing more of the dust from his burning lungs. When the wracking cough subsided he took the opportunity to take stock of his situation: He was unharmed, Archie was likely fine, and he'd helped a pair of the clan's lassies to safety. Perhaps his impulsive act would smooth their way into the castle? It was an angle he was not above exploiting. He buried the grin that wanted out and made sure his face held nothing but concern before he pushed himself up to sitting.

The lass with creamy skin and hair that had glinted copper in the sunshine, before the dust had covered its wildly curling glory, sat a few feet away facing him. She had big eyes of the palest green he had ever seen, trimmed by cinnamon lashes. When she had passed him going down the hill, she had moved with grace. Her voice had been low and angry, yet it had slid over him like fine silk.

She coughed and groaned.

"Rowan?" The black-haired wench's voice was high and tight. "You are bleeding!"

Rowan slowly looked down at her leg, where Nicholas could see a bruise already spreading purple and red across the shin and wrapping around her lower leg, but he could see no blood, only a finely shaped calf.

"Where, Scotia?" she asked, her voice oddly devoid of emotion as she glanced at their companion. She touched her face but there was no blood there, either.

Scotia moved to Rowan's side. Nicholas stood and angled closer to the women.

"Do not move." Scotia's voice was still high and tight, but there was a command in it that had Nicholas reassessing his first impression of the girl. She had acted like a spoiled wean when Rowan had confronted her and the lad, but there appeared to be more to her.

Rowan froze, but there was still no emotion. Scotia lifted Rowan's left arm gently, revealing a thin shard of stone stuck in Rowan's side. Rowan's eyes went wide. What little color had remained in her face faded to grey and her breath grew even shallower than it had been. She reached for the shard as if to pull it free.

"Nay!" Scotia grabbed her arm to stop her. "You ken what Jeanette always says. Do not pull something out until she is there to tend it if it bleeds too much."

"Of course," Rowan said, her voice steady but her hand dropping to her lap. "I remember."

Nicholas crouched beside the injured lass, concerned more by her calm and glassy gaze than anything else. "Who is Jeanette?"

"My sister," Scotia said at the same time Rowan said, "My cousin."

"And she is a healer?" He looked first to Rowan for confirmation, then at Scotia.

"Aye," Scotia answered. "The best for many miles around."

"Tell me where to find her and I shall fetch her." Nicholas made note of the women's relationships. He did not yet know who they were beyond their names, but that did not mean they couldn't be useful in his task here. After all, the best information he and Archie had been able to glean was that the MacAlpins of Dunlairig, the clan that resided in this castle, were the keepers of the Highland Targe. And even though his story was good enough to gain entrance to the castle, anyone who could aid him in his endeavor was useful. Helping an injured member of that clan seemed likely to not only gain him entrance, but would make him welcome, too. That she happened to be very pretty—bonny, he corrected himself—was a boon. He smiled at Rowan.

Before she could give him directions, Scotia took charge. "You stay with Rowan," she said. "I'll send the guards out, then fetch Jeanette. It will be better if I break the news to her than if some stranger does."

Pride filtered across Rowan's face and Nicholas felt something ease in his chest as emotion began to animate the lass's face again. But the pride was chased away quickly by a grimace of pain. Nicholas fought the peculiar urge to comfort her, even though he knew her not at all.

"'Tis a good plan," Rowan said to Scotia, her voice tense but calm and the glassiness in her eyes all but gone. "Denis is in the guardhouse. He will know who to send out. Tell Jeanette 'tis nothing bad but to bring her basket with her. Kiss your mum while you are there and reassure her that I am well."

Scotia nodded solemnly and took off at only a slightly slower run than her dash up the path.

"Her mother is your aunt, aye?" he asked, lifting her hand and cradling it between his own. He had learned early in his life that such a gesture often encouraged trust in a woman, and a trusting woman was a valuable source of information. But he was not prepared for the surge of awareness that rushed through him, sending his heartbeat skittering the moment he touched her icy hand.

"Aye, and my foster mother, Lady Elspet," she said, watching him slowly chafe warmth into her hand. After a moment she pulled her hand from his.

He didn't reach for her hand again but did not back away either. "Lady" was usually reserved for the wife of the chieftain in the clans.

It seemed his luck was with him. Rowan and Scotia were kin to the chief. "Is there aught I can do to make you more comfortable until Jeanette gets here?"

She looked down the hill. "Will you help me stand?"

"I would not do that were I you," he said.

"But I must." She made to stand but a sharp intake of breath told him how much it hurt her.

"Why, lass?" he asked, helping to ease her back down to the ground.

Rowan looked down the path at the rubble-strewn hillside again. "I need to check beyond where you saw us. Make sure no one was caught in the rubble."

"Was there someone with you?" He knew there was. He also knew the lad had been out of sight before the wall fell so he was likely well clear of the damage.

She caught her lower lip between her teeth and looked him square in the face, catching his gaze with her pale eyes. His breath caught at the intensity of her scrutiny, as if she could see into him and judge his worth.

"Who are you?" She pushed a stray tendril of coppery-brown hair out of her face, but did not break her gaze.

"Nicholas"—he pronounced it as his mother had, *Neecolas*—"of Achnamara." The tendril flew back across her cheek and he could not stop himself from reaching out and smoothing it behind the shell of her ear. A shiver ran up his spine as he touched her and he thought she felt one, too.

She took a deep breath, gasping again as she did so, breaking the moment. "There's a lad I'm worried about. If he was caught in the wreckage, Scotia will be in more than one kind of trouble."

"Ah, a tryst you interrupted?" The idea of a tryst with this woman slammed into him so hard he sat back, landing hard on the ground. The image of her long, creamy limbs tangled with his sent his heart hammering, and desire to parts that should remain neutral at the moment.

"Exactly." She cocked her head at him, as if his sudden movement confused her. Voices sounded from the direction of the castle, pulling her attention away from him. A small line formed between her brows and she rubbed at it absently. "He should have been clear, but if he was not . . . well, as much as it would solve certain problems, I could not leave him there to die. Please, I need you to go quickly, and if you do not find him, pray, do not tell anyone I sent you looking for him."

Nicholas was shocked that she would trust him with her cousin's secret when she knew nothing of him except his name, but he also knew leverage when he saw it and he wasn't one to pass up such a weapon.

"As you wish, mistress," he said as he rose to his feet.

He quickly scanned the area around them, trying to see into the deep shadows of the nearby forest for any sign of Archie. Why was the man not here? Where had he got to? It would be better if one of them stayed with her, to be seen as the rescuer of the lass when her kinsmen arrived. Manipulating their way into the castle would be simple, playing on her kin's gratitude, but since Archie was choosing to remain hidden, that opportunity was slipping through Nicholas's fingers. He glanced about once more, searching for the man in the forest shadows to no avail.

"Is there someone there?" Rowan asked, scanning the forest as he had.

"Nay mistress, 'tis only a habit to keep watch about me in unfamiliar places. I would not wish to leave you here alone if there was danger about."

"I doubt there is more danger lurking than what we have just escaped," she said, the line between her brows growing deeper. "Please, go and look before we are joined by others. If the lad is there, we need to get him help quickly."

Irritation gripped Nicholas but he had no choice. Archie was nowhere to be seen, and he needed to keep the bonny Rowan in his debt. He nodded to her and moved back down the rubble- and scree-strewn hillside. Archie would have much explaining to do when he came out of hiding.

Rowan sat on the hard ground, holding herself upright stiffly. The sharp burning in her side pulsed with each heartbeat. The deep ache in her shin and the echo of her headache throbbed in time with it. A faint nausea kept her from trying to get up again in spite of her need to see if anyone else was hurt, inside or outside the destroyed castle wall.

But Jeanette wouldn't let her up anyway, so she sat, stoic, as her cousin examined her injuries. In spite of the destruction that had just occurred, the thing that should be their sole concern in this moment, four surly Highlanders stood in a ring at Rowan's back where she couldn't see them but she could feel their wariness washing over her. She knew it wasn't aimed at her but at the stranger who had helped her and Scotia escape the falling wall. Scotia stood behind her as well, but she was sure that was to avoid having to look Rowan in the eye.

Anger pushed away the nausea and dulled the pain. If it were not for Scotia's tryst, neither of them would have been in the path of the wall and all of them could be seeing to the needs of the clan right now, rather than hovering over her while her injuries were tended.

"Who is with Auntie?" she asked.

"Helen," Jeanette said.

Rowan stifled a gasp as Jeanette pulled the stone shard from her side.

"Uncle?" Rowan grimaced as she twisted to look over her shoulder at Kenneth, the glowering man she loved like a father. His hair hung to his shoulders, a hint of the jet-black he'd had in his youth peeking through the steely-grey braids at his temples. "Is anyone else hurt?"

"Hold still," Jeanette said as she tore Rowan's gown and kirtle a little more than the stone had. "You were lucky. It does not look too bad. I shall have to bind it, but I do not think you need stitches."

Her uncle suddenly moved in front of Rowan, drawing her attention with him. The three other Highlanders stepped up on either side of the chief, forming a wall of men with the women behind them. Nicholas must be returning, though she could not see around her kinsmen.

"Was anyone hurt inside?" Rowan asked again, trying to stand to see if Nicholas had found young Conall, but her head swam. Jeanette's firm hand on her shoulder pushed her back down to the ground.

"Da, if you could answer her, she might not try so hard to get your attention that she further injures herself." Jeanette shook her head and Rowan didn't correct her assumption.

"I'm not hurt that badly." Rowan tried to hide the wince as her cousin pressed a cloth to the oozing wound in her side, then began wrapping a long length of linen around her torso to hold it in place.

"No one was hurt but you," Kenneth said, but he did not turn when he spoke to her, keeping watch on the hillside. "The wall is not going anywhere. I can attend to it when I'm done with the outsider Scotia spoke of."

"His name is Nicholas of Achnamara."

Kenneth grunted but did not move. She leaned over enough to peer between her uncle and the shaggy black-haired Uilliam, the chief's best friend and Champion, catching sight of the stranger as he closed the distance between himself and the Highlanders.

She had not really looked at Nicholas of Achnamara before. His touch had played havoc with her senses, but she'd been too dazed by their near escape to truly see him. He had broad shoulders, a trim waist, and it was clear, in spite of the dust that dulled its shine, that his hair was as inky as Scotia's. But where her cousin's was smooth and mostly straight, his was wavy and a bit wild about a face that was just rugged enough to keep him from looking pretty.

"That is the man that helped you?" Jeanette whispered.

Rowan nodded but she was trying to see if he had Conall with him. He glanced down at her as he drew to a halt a man's length from Kenneth, then locked eyes with her uncle.

"I found no one below," he said and Rowan closed her eyes and gave thanks.

"Who are you?" Kenneth demanded, icy suspicion frosting the air between them.

"He's the one that saved us!" Scotia's heated words melted the cold and Rowan nodded, though she knew no one was looking at her.

"Thank you for saving my sister and my cousin," Jeanette said, standing and leaving Rowan the only one not on her feet. She pushed herself upwards, ignoring the burning in her side and the wooziness in her head. Jeanette sighed but helped her, looping her arm around Rowan's waist. Rowan leaned into her cousin.

" 'Saving' is a bit of an overstatement, mistress," Nicholas said, a smile on his face as he dipped his head slightly, though his eyes never left Kenneth's. "I *only* helped them to safety."

There was a long silence and Rowan knew her uncle was weighing each and every word the man had spoken, determining the truth or lies therein.

"Jeanette, should not you and Scotia be getting Rowan inside?" Kenneth's question was a command.

"But, Da—" Scotia complained.

Kenneth raised a hand to cut her off but Scotia paid no attention.

"—You owe him hospitality," she said. "He has done a great service to the clan this day."

Kenneth growled again. "Jeanette, get them inside."

Rowan looked straight at Nicholas, waiting for some reaction from him that would reveal something about this man, this stranger, who had appeared out of nowhere just as the wall fell, but he never took his eyes off her uncle. Canny man.

"Come on, Ro, Scotia." Jeanette took some of Rowan's weight as she turned her toward the castle gate.

Rowan looked over her shoulder at Nicholas once more. She was grateful to the man for helping her escape the wall, but there were questions that needed answering: Why was he here, and who or what had he been looking for after the wall fell?

"Come, Rowan," Jeanette said quietly, urging her cousin along.

Rowan limped where she'd been hit in the leg and took care to breathe shallowly. Scotia moved with them, trailing behind.

"Try not to injure him too much, Da," Jeanette said over her shoulder. "He did get two of your lassies clear of the wall." She winked at Rowan. "Mostly."

NICHOLAS GLANCED OVER THE CHIEF'S SHOULDER AND AN UNwanted concern further threatened his calm. The women were moving slowly toward the gate. Rowan limped and he knew the stone shard in her side had hurt, but she hadn't complained once about pain, and none of these men had offered to help her, to carry her. He forced himself to take a deep breath and look away from the distraction of the women.

But now he stared at the men who stood by and let Rowan limp into the castle with only her cousin for support. Would they have helped her if she'd cried and moaned? But she hadn't. She was strong, stoic—and yet Nicholas itched to sweep her into his arms and . . .

But he could not. He turned his attention once more back to the line of men in front of him. No matter how quickly Rowan had gotten under his skin, he had to stand here and face her scowling kinfolk.

He'd already taken the measure of the chief. The man was fiercely protective, as was his duty, and he was used to having his orders followed without objection, and yet the impertinent comments from Jeanette revealed that he must have a soft spot for his family, for she showed no fear in speaking so and he showed no anger at it. Anyone who had dared speak to Nicholas's own father that way would have regretted it quickly and painfully, as he had cause to know firsthand.

"Who are you?" the bear of a man standing to the chief's right asked. His black hair was so shaggy and his beard so wild, it was hard to see more of his face than a glimmer of eyes and the tip of his round nose.

"Nicholas of Achnamara," he replied. "And you are?"

"It does not matter who he is." Kenneth's glare grew razor sharp. "What are you doing here?"

No "Thank you for aiding my daughter and niece." Straight to the point.

And Nicholas must answer him.

"I have been traveling," Nicholas said, which was true. "I'm trying to find my way home again." Which wasn't.

"You do not ken your way home?" the bear scoffed. "Are you deep in your cups then?"

Nicholas found it interesting that the chief did not seem to mind sharing this interview with the other man, as if they had done this many times together.

"Nay, not deep in my cups." He let the tiniest sliver of irritation sharpen his words. "Lost. I was but a wean when I left my home, only ten and two. It has taken me a long time to return and I confess I do not remember exactly where Achnamara is, except that it is in the Highlands." Which was a lie. He knew exactly where it was, far away from here. "Do you ken where it is?" he asked the bear pointedly.

The man grunted. "I do not."

"Where have you been all these years?" the chief asked.

"My father's home, in the borders." Again, the truth would suffice and it would account for his rusty Gaelic.

The bear bobbed his head a little. "That explains it."

"Explains what?" Nicholas tilted his head a little to the left, trying to see the man's eyes. Did he suspect something? Did he distrust Nicholas's story? It was, so far, the truth except for the part about looking for his home. He could not return to that place.

"You are a Sassenach, no?"

An old visceral reaction to the word—Sassenach, "outlander" —fisted in his gut. Everyone was an outlander to Highlanders. "Do you have a problem with that?" Nicholas raised his chin and stepped closer to the man.

The bear stepped forward until he was nearly nose-to-nose with Nicholas. "That depends. Which side of the borders would you be from? The feckless English side, or the feckless Scottish side?"

Nicholas fought a smile. He knew this dance and had instigated it himself many a time to throw an adversary off. He pulled his shoulders back, letting his chest puff out.

"Well, your own dear da must have been from the feckless English side," Nicholas said, cocking his head as if considering an interesting bug. "'Tis a pity your mum had not the good sense to turn him and his money away before they made a great lout like you." Nicholas waited, still trying to see the man's eyes for some clue as to whether he was about to get run through with a claymore, or had interpreted the insult as the test it seemed to be.

"He'll do," the bear said to the chief and stepped back from Nicholas.

"Perhaps." The chief stared at him hard, as if weighing the truth in each word one by one and Nicholas realized how shrewd the man was. He'd let the bear goad Nicholas while he'd watched his reactions, judged him. "Where are you bound for?" he asked at last.

Nicholas looked over at the castle, then back to the man standing in front of him. "Here, if you will allow it. I have been traveling for a long time. It would be nice to bide a while in one place. Perhaps someone here will ken something of my home."

Once more he could almost see Kenneth measuring his words for lies but since it was all truth, though not all *of* the truth, there were no lies to be found. At length he glanced at the bear and they nodded slightly to each other without exchanging a single word.

"You can bide a short while here," the chief said.

Nicholas let out a slow breath and smiled but the chief's glower got darker.

"I said a short while, and you'll have to work for your keep."

"Of course." Nicholas knew there was more to come. No man invited strangers into the midst of his home so easily.

"We've been the winter without news of the world," the chief said, "and now it appears we have need of men to clear the wall."

"What do you ken of walls and their construction?" the bear asked Nicholas.

Nicholas looked over his shoulder at the rubble field and shrugged. "I know how to run away from them when they fall." A grudging splatter of chuckles ran through the two otherwise silent men. "Other than that, I've seen them built a time or two but know little of the ways of doing it."

"Do you have enough muscles to do more than run?" the bear asked.

"Enough to take you down, auld man." Nicholas grinned at him, playing the game the bear seemed to enjoy. "I have done a bit of labor in my life. I can help clear the rubble but I will be of no use building it back." Of course he wouldn't be here long enough to build it back anyway, but they needn't know that.

"Hmph," the chief scowled at him. "You shall work with Uilliam here." He jerked his thumb toward the bear. "The faster we can get the rubble moved, the faster we can rebuild the wall. You do not mind hard work, do you?"

Nicholas shook his head, but he was still trying to find the catch in the invitation, for he was sure there was one.

"And you'll not be leaving his sight"—the chief leaned his head toward Uilliam.

"Or Duncan's," Uilliam interrupted, echoing the chief's gesture by jerking his thumb at the younger of the other two men. Nicholas judged Duncan to be about his own age of a score and five or possibly a little less. His brown hair whipped about his face, making it difficult to judge either his temperament or his precise age.

"Or Duncan's sight for any reason," the chief finished.

And there it was—the catch. He'd found a way into the castle but he wouldn't have free run of it. It was good enough for the moment. Once he'd had the time to gain the trust of these men, the rest would fall into place.

The chief stepped toward Nicholas until his craggy face blocked out everything else.

"You ken that I'm granting you hospitality, aye?" He poked a sharp finger in Nicholas's chest. "And with it my protection? In case your Sassenach father did not explain your responsibilities in such a situation, let me. You will bring no harm to anyone within this castle while you bide here. And in exchange, we will make you the same pledge. No harm to you while you bide within these walls. Do you accept our hospitality?"

Hospitality. It was a Highland custom he had counted on and not something most of the king's spies would understand. Never was such a promise of safety made in the English court and yet here, in the Highlands, where the world was full of dangers from men and nature it was a grant of reprieve from all that, an offer of safety, of comfort, of sustenance, however temporary, and in exchange he must vow the same—to bring no harm to these people. He swallowed, strangely unwilling to enter into an oath he was unlikely to be able to keep.

But he had no choice. He needed access to this castle. If he did not accept he was sure he would, at best, be sent on his way; at worst, he'd be imprisoned . . . or dead.

"I accept."

# CHAPTER THREE

ROWAN GRIMACED BUT REFUSED TO ADMIT HOW MUCH THE CUT IN her side hurt in spite of the mint poultice her cousin had used to numb it. At least she had been the only one injured. And for all that it hurt, it could have been so much worse if the stranger, Nicholas of Achnamara—she liked the way his name rolled around in her head—hadn't caught her when she'd tripped, hadn't pulled her to safety.

Rowan grunted as Jeanette poked at the cut, making sure all the stone was out. "That is enough, Jeanette. I have work to do."

"She is almost done, Rowan, but you will not be seeing to any work the rest of this day," Elspet said from her bed. Scotia sat next to her with her arms crossed like armor and pique painted all over her face.

Rowan wanted to argue, but she'd not tax Elspet's fragile energy by doing so. "You know what a good hand Jeanette has for this work." Pride twined through Elspet's quiet praise. "If she says you will barely have a scar when it is healed, you ken that to be true."

Rowan didn't care about a scar. But she did care that she hadn't done her proper duty with Scotia. If she had kept a closer watch on her wayward cousin, she never would have been meeting Conall on that path and none of them would have been in danger when the wall came down.

"I'm sorry I didn't get Scotia away from there before the wall collapsed."

Jeanette looked up at Rowan, their faces so close Rowan could feel her cousin's breath on her cheek. "And what, pray tell, was she doing on that poor excuse for a path that was more important than being here with her mother?" Jeanette looked across to the bed and leveled a stern glance at her sister even though Scotia wouldn't meet anyone's eyes.

Elspet managed to echo Jeanette's question without ever saying a word. She simply turned her mother's eye on her youngest daughter—but the girl remained stubbornly mute.

The image of Scotia and Conall wrapped in each other's arms flashed through Rowan's mind, bringing the memory of the warmth and unsettling feelings that had swamped her when Nicholas held her hand in his. Remembering the heat of his touch brought with it the memory of his scent that had washed over her, earthy and fresh, like the forest she loved to wander. An unusual restlessness gripped her. It had taken more self-control than she'd thought it should to leave him to face her uncle and Uilliam.

"Rowan?" Elspet's voice wavered slightly, rising on a thin note of concern. Rowan retraced her wandering thoughts to find the question Elspet wanted answered.

"I do not know what Scotia was doing on the path." She closed her eyes as Jeanette pressed a pad of linen against her wound, soaking up the still oozing blood, thankful for the excuse not to meet her aunt's. She hated lying to her but Elspet did not need more worries, especially not where her errant daughter was concerned. "But she did not want to come away and I stood there and argued with her."

"Is this true?" Elspet had a hand on Scotia's arm. "Why would you not do as your cousin asked?"

Scotia glanced at Rowan with a look that seemed to ask for help. Rowan shifted on the bench, searching for a way to explain without actually lying.

"Be still, Ro. Scotia, go and fetch another kirtle for Rowan. This one"—Jeanette indicated the bloodstained one lying on the floor at Rowan's feet—"will have to be mended and cleaned, though I know not if the blood will come out."

Scotia didn't say anything but she did have the grace to mouth "my thanks" to both of them as she slid off the bed and made for the chamber door.

"Are you done?" Rowan asked Jeanette.

"Nay." She reached into the basket that sat by her feet and pulled out a small glass vessel. An oiled leather scrap was secured with a thong about the wide neck. She opened it and the sharp scent of vinegar mixed with something herbal made Rowan wrinkle her nose. Jeanette slathered some of the salve over the wound. As soon as the salve touched it, a hiss escaped Rowan's lips.

"That burns!"

"Aye, but auld Morven swears it keeps a wound from festering. Hold still." She blew on the cut and a cooling sensation radiated from the salve, dampening the pain. "Better?"

Rowan nodded. "Now can I dress?"

Jeanette chuckled. "I need to put a dressing over it first." Minutes later Jeanette had covered her work with a fresh linen pad and wrapped a long length of more linen tightly about Rowan's ribs to hold it in place.

Scotia came back into the room, a kirtle hung over her arm. Jeanette glanced at their mother, who had drifted into one of her many naps.

"You should be ashamed of yourself, Scotia," Jeanette said quietly, taking the undergarment from her and handing it to Rowan. "'Tis bad enough to ignore your duty to your mother, but to put Rowan and that stranger in peril, too." She shook her head at her sister. "What were you thinking?"

The stubborn glint was back in Scotia's eyes as she glared at Jeanette. "I did not ken the wall was about to collapse. How should I ken such a thing?"

The moment the wall had started to fall was etched in Rowan's memory . . . a memory that included a terrible headache that had plagued her up until that very moment.

And then it had ceased, leaving only the echo of it behind.

Another memory tickled her mind, flitting just out of reach—a terrible headache, a wall falling—but she couldn't grab the memory and pull it close.

A shiver sent goose bumps over her flesh.

"You'd have likely been crushed beneath the stones if Rowan hadn't come in search of you." Jeanette was wagging a finger, scolding Scotia, something they all seemed to do more and more of these days.

Scotia stared at her for a long moment, then huffed and quickly climbed back on the bed next to her mother, whose eyelids flickered open. "And Rowan would have never had cause to be rescued by such a braw man as Nicholas of Achnamara if she had not needed to come find me." The girl smiled like she'd eaten something sweet.

Rowan's face and the rest of her body went hot, except for the oddly still chilled wound. "Do you think Uncle Kenneth will let him stay?"

Elspet's face went from sleepy to serious. "He helped you and Scotia. I expect he will be allowed to bide a while at least, though it will depend upon what impression he makes upon the chief."

Rowan had a strong impression of Nicholas of Achnamara. He was a stranger, yet he'd done a service to the clan this day. Surely that spoke to his character. And then there was the fact that he was a strong man who looked able to wield a sword or an ax in defense of the clan. Saints and angels, they needed men for that. But there was still the lingering question of why he had been there just when the wall fell. Where had he come from? She tried to hang on to her doubts about him, to ignore the memory of him holding her hand, tucking her hair behind her ear. When he touched her, she'd gone breathless in a way that had naught to do with running up the hill.

"See, Mum?" Scotia leaned her head close to Elspet like two girls trading secrets. "Rowan's cheeks are bright. She does notice braw warriors. It is only necessary to distract her from her duties long enough for them to make themselves known to her."

Rowan scowled at her cousin until she noticed the twinkle in her aunt's eyes. She wished to see more of that familiar teasing glint.

"I will admit," she said, letting her mind wander to the man in question, "he is very well built, with hair as dark as Scotia's, but unruly." The sudden thought that it would be soft sent her stomach pitching and a new wave of heat to her face.

"Is he as braw as Rowan describes?" Elspet asked Scotia, as if they were gossiping in private.

"Och, aye. And more so. He is broad in the shoulder, narrow in the hip, and his plaid showed off his finely muscled calves. I think he may even have a dimple in one cheek"—Scotia leaned her head upon her mother's shoulder as if in a swoon—"though Uilliam had him scowling most of the time so 'twas hard to tell for sure."

"'Tis sorry I am that I have not yet had the pleasure of meeting such a fine specimen of a man." Elspet's teasing smile brightened the room and Rowan realized they were all smiling back at her aunt. A different kind of warmth infused her heart, seeping deep into her bones. What would the three of them do if Elspet didn't get better? How would they go on?

Rowan had lost both of her parents years ago and now she was faced with losing her beloved aunt, too. Grief threatened to overwhelm her but she pushed it back. There would be time enough for grieving. For now, they were here, safe, and together.

If this happy moment required that Rowan was the focus of their collective teasing, so be it, for the sunny smile that lit up Elspet's face was worth any embarrassment her impish cousin Scotia would rain down upon her.

"I notice braw men," Rowan said with a wink at Jeanette, "'tis only that I never have a chance to catch their eye before Scotia bats hers and addles their wee brains."

"I do not!" Scotia said, sitting up on the bed, ire snapping in the air between them.

"Aye, my lassie, you do," Elspet said with a more wistful smile. "You do, but this one—what did you say his name was?"

"Nicholas of Achnamara," Scotia said.

"Nicholas, he had eyes for our Rowan, aye? Only for our Rowan?"

"Nay, he did not!" Rowan said with a laugh.

Scotia gave a huge sigh. "Aye, only for Ro." She snuggled up next to her mother and laid her head back on Elspet's shoulder. "Mum, as I left to find Jeanette he knelt beside her and took her hand into his." She looked over at Rowan again, narrowing her eyes and pursing her lips. "You should have seen how startled Ro looked. Silly lass could have leaned forward and kissed him but she just sat there, staring into his eyes."

"Not all of us are used to throwing ourselves at men," Jeanette said quietly, partly teasing but clearly from her tone not entirely.

"And I was injured!" Rowan added an extra thick layer of indignation to her words.

Scotia tried to sit up again, but Elspet held her in place with a hand on her arm. "I can see why one might want to throw herself into such a man's arms."

All three girls giggled.

"What? You think me too old to throw myself into a braw man's arms?" Now it was Elspet's turn to act indignant, arching her brows at them, her eyes wide. "How do you think I got Kenneth?"

"Mum!" Jeanette and Scotia both squealed her name. Rowan leaned back carefully on the bench, resting her back against the wall. Work would wait. She'd not miss the opportunity to enjoy this rare moment.

DUNCAN HAD SHOWN NICHOLAS WHERE TO STOW HIS TRAVEL SACK and they had taken a quick meal in the great hall. Now as they made their way slowly across the cramped bailey toward the remains of the fallen wall where Uilliam had instructed them to meet him, Nicholas kept an eye out for Archie and his telltale ginger hair in case he'd made his way inside the compound. He surveyed the people moving about the cramped open space, greeting each other, hauling water from the well, on their way somewhere. He was also noting the quickest way out of the castle. Should the need arrive there was the main gate, and a small postern gate tucked between two wood and thatch buildings pent up against the southern curtain wall. And of course the rubble pile of the northern section of the curtain wall was a great gaping hole in the castle defenses and thus a good way in or out of Dunlairig Castle.

He noticed that nearly everyone except the smallest of the children carried at least one knife in plain sight. Who knew how many were concealed.

Nicholas nodded at a young woman carrying an empty bucket and tools for cleaning hearths, turning to watch as she made her way to the tower that stood to the east side. It was situated across the small bailey from the hallhouse—Duncan had called it the great hall—where they'd taken their meal.

"What is in the tower?" he asked Duncan.

"The chief's family's quarters."

"Is that where they took Mistress Rowan?"

Duncan slanted a look at him and nodded.

Nicholas had been watching the movements of the people of the castle since he had walked through the gate, taking note of any patterns he could discern, watching for any sign of extra protection that might indicate something precious, like the Highland Targe, being guarded. But he had seen nothing so far.

He turned his attention back to his surroundings, craning his neck, looking up the length of the square, grey tower. The sky was bright behind it, making it difficult to see any detail other than the dark holes that marked windows. Would the chief keep a protective talisman in the place where his family slept? It seemed likely, especially since there were precious few places to hide anything in this castle made up of an ancient hallhouse, an old tower, and a small array of sheds and huts along the less than sturdy curtain walls.

He would have to look for an opportunity to get inside the tower soon to search it. Perhaps Duncan would take him there to see Rowan? It was worth a try once he had the man's trust. For now, he'd settle for learning what he could about the wall and any defenses they might have planned until it could be rebuilt. Any knowledge could prove useful.

"Uilliam, we are here." Duncan shouted at the bear of a man standing atop all that was left of the wall. A thin cloud of dust still hung in the air, washing out the color of the man and everything around him.

"Aye, I can see that," Uilliam replied but didn't pay any more attention to them.

"Are we supposed to just stand here, then?" Nicholas asked his companion.

Duncan shrugged, but motioned to a large squared-off stone that had tumbled into the bailey instead of outside of it. The stone was easily the size of a man and made an ample bench for them.

They sat there for a long time watching Uilliam pick his way carefully over the tumbled remains of the wall, muttering to himself. He'd stop to pick up a stone now and again, only to turn it over in his hand, then toss it back onto the pile. After a while Nicholas leaned toward Duncan.

"What is he doing?"

"He told me he wanted to take it in as it lies, that the stones might talk to him. I think he is daft, myself."

"I am starting to agree with you."

Duncan actually smiled at him and they sat in silence a while longer. The sound of a door opening behind them had Nicholas turning to look toward the tower. Raven-haired Scotia stepped out of the shadowed doorway into the bright bailey, a wad of bloody material in her hands. The image of the stone in Rowan's side flashed through his mind and he found himself hoping the injury was as minor as the healer-lass had said.

Duncan waved at Scotia and she gave him a little smile and a half-hearted wave. The man smiled back and almost disguised a sigh.

Nicholas shifted his attention to his companion, watching Duncan watch the lass as she crossed to the far side of the bailey and disappeared inside a small hut.

"You sigh over Scotia," Nicholas said.

"I do." Duncan didn't take his eyes off the hut's door, clearly waiting for another glance from the lass. "She is determined to get into trouble and it is all Rowan and I can do to keep her out of it."

A weird twisty feeling grabbed Nicholas's stomach. "You and Rowan? Are you married to the lass?" The question was out of his mouth before he could stop it. There had been nothing obvious between the two of them outside the castle. Surely if she had a husband, he would have rushed to her side. If that husband was Duncan, he should be beaten for not taking care of the lass when she was injured.

Duncan stopped watching the hut and looked at Nicholas with a considering eye. "Would it matter if I was?"

It wasn't an answer so likely he was not. Nicholas shrugged. It would not do to appear too taken with Rowan when Scotia was the more likely source of information. "I could not help but notice that she is a bonny lass. It would seem likely that she is wed."

"She is not."

"So you and she are keeping an eye on Scotia?"

"Someone has to. The irritating lass can find trouble in the most unlikely of places and ways. I have known her since she was a bairn in her mum's arms. She used to be such a sweet lass. I watched over her like a big brother when she was little. But she's gotten spoiled and, since her mum's been sick, she has gone a bit wild." He shook his head. "She is fiercely good at finding trouble."

Nicholas knew an opportunity when he saw it. No matter what Duncan said, he could see the way the man's gaze kept drifting back to the door where Scotia had disappeared. He might not realize it yet, but he was taken with the difficult lass, and that might come in handy somewhere in this mission.

"You are kin?" Nicholas carefully looked away from the man, hoping he'd reveal something useful about Scotia if he didn't feel too pressed.

"Everyone who lives in Dunlairig Castle is kin at some level. We are not close kin, though. Distant cousins at best."

Nicholas leaned back on his hands, watching the enigmatic Uilliam pace along the rubble, his shadow following him as it rippled over the fallen stones. It wasn't much information, but it was a start.

"Och, you laggards!" Uilliam finally summoned them to join him on the wall.

"At last," Nicholas said, noting Duncan's quick glance back at the hut where Scotia had disappeared.

The two of them made quick work of climbing the pile to join Uilliam at the top.

"It looks as if it burst from within," Duncan said as they arrived at the highest point of the rubble pile.

Uilliam didn't look at Duncan, but he nodded. "Aye, it does. It is almost as if something trapped inside the wall forced its way out except for this part here, where it looks as if something pushed back, keeping the wall from falling outward or inward. It collapsed on itself. 'Tis a good thing, too, for look—" He pointed down the embankment toward the area where Rowan and Scotia had been standing when the wall went down.

"It would have crushed them," Nicholas said quietly.

"Aye, it surely would have. 'Tis dumb luck that this part did not tumble down the hill as the rest did. If it had I do not think we would have Rowan or Scotia, or even you"—he nodded at Nicholas—"still with us today."

"Has this happened before?" Nicholas pretended to examine the remains of the wall, but he knew nothing of building or masonry so it was really just a show of interest.

"Nay. It has stood nigh on twoscore years." Uilliam shook his head. "I ken not what is wrong. Perhaps when we remove the rubble it will become clear."

Nicholas turned his attention to the stones beneath his feet. "Is there a burn that runs beneath here?" He lifted a stone as if he spied something.

"Nay, the rock ledge is dense and stable." Uilliam sounded like he spoke to himself. He pulled on the right side of his night-black beard as if that helped him think. "There is a wee bit of a slope to this area, but nothing that would cause the wall to topple."

"I felt the ground tremble before the wall exploded." Nicholas was trying to remember exactly what order things had happened.

"Are you sure? I did not," Uilliam said.

"'Twas slight. I do not think 'twas enough to topple such a wall. You are sure none of your enemies have sabotaged it, or weakened it by attacks?" Nicholas asked.

"I suppose that is possible. We will see."

Nicholas considered the wall, or what was left of it. "Are you a mason, then, Uilliam?" he asked.

"Nay, but I expect we will learn something as we clear the rubble. We shall build it ourselves, anyway. No reason to spread the word that our wall is breached. The damn Diarmids would leap upon that news like hounds on a bone."

As would King Edward. Perhaps Archie was already on his way to their contact in Oban to send word to England. That would explain his disappearance, though Nicholas thought it would be better to wait until they had the Targe. It would be better if Archie had stayed here and stuck to their original plan.

"Is there another way to shield the bailey from this direction?" Nicholas let the words hang in the air for a moment, letting the idea of a shield wiggle its way into Uilliam's thoughts even as he might learn about some other defense this clan had that would be of use to the king.

Uilliam cast him a sidelong glance, his eyebrows drawn down so low his eyes were but a dark pool beneath them. "Why?"

"It seems likely word will spread, though you are isolated here so it may take a while, but all it will require is one person passing by. 'Tis not as if you can hide a missing wall."

"Are you going to be the one to spread the tale?" Uilliam stepped close enough to Nicholas that Nicholas had to look up, but only a little.

"Nay, not me," he said, raising his hands palms out. "I plan to stay right here for a while. I will not be spreading tales to anyone." Not if Archie was taking care of it, at any rate.

"Good." Uilliam stepped back from Nicholas and turned his attention back to the rubble pile. "We'll figure out a way to protect the castle and the clan, never you worry." Uilliam's face was like a thundercloud, the black hair and beard sheltering eyes that crackled like lightning. "Never you worry."

Nicholas had no wish to antagonize the man, so he turned his attention to the task before them.

"Well then," he said, "no matter why this fell, or when word gets out, it wants cleaning up."

He gazed to the outside of the wall, looking out toward the azure loch far below, keeping a lookout for a shock of ginger hair in case Archie hadn't gone back to Oban and was still out there. At the same time he wondered how they could clear the debris when the hillside dropped off so close, and so steeply just beyond where they stood. He looked left toward the gate and the corner of this wall that still stood, then to his right toward the tower and the other corner of the ruined wall, which was still standing. Just past that corner, outside the standing wall and beyond the rubble field he spied a rough meadow, less pitched than the hill, with a lone flowering tree in its midst, and dotted with rusty-colored shaggy cows. It was the most likely place to take the remains of the wall.

He would get little opportunity to watch the activity in the castle while hauling rubble to that pasture but it would give him ample time to win the trust of Uilliam and Duncan and then it would be easier to slip the leash and search the castle for the prize.

"Duncan," he asked, rubbing his hands together as if he was anxious to get to work, "where can I find a cart?"

Rowan stood in the window of Elspet's bedchamber, looking down on the three men gathered atop the rubble, trying to distract herself from the burning in her side and the ache in her shin. She rubbed her arms, trying to chase away chills that raced up and down them. Pressure had started to build behind her eyes again, setting up a rhythmic throb, subtle but there, as if beating her up from the inside out.

But she didn't know why. She was rarely ill and never could she remember more than the odd headache on a trying day. This one seemed to have set up house in her head. Perhaps she should ask Jeanette for some willow bark tea.

She watched Uilliam inspecting the wall, or at least the odd part of it that had not tumbled down the hillside. It was as if something had kept that section of it from moving over the lip of the embankment.

It didn't make any sense, especially since that part of the wall was closer to the edge than the rest of it. A crawling sensation joined the throb in her head, sending out itchy tendrils along the inside of her skull. She couldn't shake the feeling that she should know something about the wall, almost as if she had something to do with it. But that kind of thinking was daft. Or she was.

The memory that had burst upon her when she realized the wall was falling had receded just as rapidly, like a dream that quickly fades upon waking. It fluttered deep in her mind, teasing her into chasing it, all the while keeping just out of her grasp. But it was there, haunting her.

Haunting. Aye, that was the feeling. As if that memory haunted her, ghostlike in her mind, there, but not solid enough to bring into the light.

Perhaps Elspet would know what bothered Rowan, for she knew there were pieces of her life she could not remember, but the very thought of asking had her heart tripping over itself. Her palms grew damp, and her breath was held hostage in her chest.

"What ails you, my lassie?" Elspet's raspy voice was filled with concern and Rowan felt the rare prick of tears in her eyes.

"I do not ken, Auntie. I feel . . ." She did not know how to put what she felt into words, so she shrugged and shook her head.

Elspet carefully levered herself up to sit, leaning against the massive wooden headboard. "Come here, Rowan," she said, slowly patting the bed beside her.

Rowan's body was doing everything it could to make her bolt from the room but she knew, deep in her bones, deep in her heart, that she had nothing to fear from Elspet, so she slowly forced her feet to carry her to perch on the side of the bed. Elspet took Rowan's hand between her cool palms, stroking the back of it as if Rowan were a spooked calf that must be gentled.

"I have not seen you thus in a long time, lassie. It is the wall that frightens you, is it not?"

"Aye, but there is . . . more."

Elspet nodded slightly, and kept stroking her hand. "Close your eyes. Calm yourself. I think perhaps it is time for you to remember."

"Remember what?"

"Close your eyes and let it come."

Rowan tried to do as her aunt instructed, once more endeavoring to pull the memory into the light. She knew the castle wall falling had triggered the memory, so she turned her thoughts there, to the moment she had looked up and seen the stones tumbling toward her. Something flashed through her mind, as if she looked at two walls falling simultaneously.

Panic clutched her, like a hard band squeezing her chest so tightly she could not breathe. Cold sweat burst out all over her. She leapt to her feet, shaking her throbbing head. The fire in the hearth popped, making her gasp as if it had been another wall falling, and she knew that whatever the memory was, it was not one she wanted to face.

"I must go," she said, not daring to look at her aunt, afraid she'd see disappointment there, or blame for Rowan's being too much of a coward to remember whatever it was she couldn't—*wouldn't*—remember. "I shall send Scotia to you," Rowan said as she fled the chamber.

# CHAPTER FOUR

Two days after the wall fell Jeanette told Rowan they were to take their evening meal in the great hall. Elspet was chafing that no one had properly welcomed their visitor and she wanted a report on him that went beyond Kenneth's terse "He can haul a lot of stone."

Relief leaped through Rowan at the instruction, followed quickly by guilt. She loved her aunt but every moment Rowan had spent in Elspet's chamber for the last two days, Elspet had watched her, tracking her movement about the room, until she felt like a mouse about to be pinned by a hawk. Rowan had caught her several times, and each time Elspet had given her a questioning look. Rowan felt like a coward, turning away each time to busy herself with the fire, or the soup, or anything she could think of. But she refused to return to their aborted conversation. For reasons she couldn't fathom, the very thought of it sent flashes of terror through her.

Now, sitting at the high table, Rowan was about to enjoy a good meal and good company. And, if a certain braw stranger happened to attend the meal, who was she to complain about the distraction? She shifted in her seat, trying to ease the itching of the healing cut on her side. Jeanette said itching was a good sign and there was no festering, thank the angels. The bruise on her leg bothered her less. It was a lovely combination of greens and purples but was concealed easily by her gown. As long as she was careful not to bump it against something it was fine.

Rowan looked down the length of the great hall with its large hearth along the right-hand wall and six long trestle tables set up end-to-end in two rows. The low hum of happy conversation ran like quiet music through the small knots of people seated there, disrupted now and then by the discordant rise of a worried voice, or the happy squeal of a bairn.

Scotia slid into the seat on the other side of Jeanette, who sat next to Rowan, just as Duncan entered the great hall. Scotia had chattered endlessly today about Nicholas of Achnamara, about how his muscles flexed as he loaded stones into a cart, and how his midnight hair ruffled in the spring breeze as he worked clearing the wall with Duncan and Uilliam and all the other lads called in to help, including Conall, in whom Scotia suddenly had no interest.

Rowan found her cousin's fickleness difficult to understand, though she understood why a certain man would draw her attention. It was hard not to notice him, even when she tried not to on her trips through the bailey. Rowan found herself watching him work from her aunt's window and now she watched the far door, hoping that Nicholas of Achnamara would follow Duncan in.

She could not get the man out of her mind despite spending a short time in his company. First he had kept her awake and then he had invaded her dreams.

Foolishness.

That the braw and mysterious Nicholas had dominated those dreams last night was her own doing, even though in truth she could not remember any of the details. But the restlessness left behind by those dreams? That she was more than willing to blame on the man.

As if summoned by her thoughts, Nicholas came through the far door into the hall at that moment, followed by Uilliam, who stood by the door, clearly keeping watch over their guest. Nicholas's hair was wet and so black it had hints of blue in it. His chiseled face was tanned, freshly washed, with a day or two's beard softening his square jaw. He moved into the hall smoothly, his plaid barely stirring with his strides, as if he took care not to leave any sign of his passing, or sound of it, unlike most men who seemed to take great delight in stomping about as much as possible. He caught her watching him and smiled.

"Did I not tell you he is beyond compare with any of the lads in the castle?" Scotia whispered.

"Aye, you did, several times." Rowan silently cursed the heat rising in her cheeks but she could not make herself look away from him.

Duncan called out, catching Nicholas's attention. Rowan took advantage of that moment to escape the trap of his dark eyes and beguiling smile. She trained her gaze on the trencher of food in front of her and gave thanks for Duncan's distraction. And yet, even though she wasn't looking at Nicholas anymore, the restlessness grew like an itch she couldn't pinpoint but that was slowly driving her mad. She squirmed in her seat and peeked at him through her lashes as he moved quickly and efficiently to a seat across from Duncan, where he piled roast boar and onions onto his trencher as if he hadn't eaten in days.

Rowan forced herself to look away again and take a bite of her own food. Maybe her injury had been worse than she thought? Maybe she'd been hit in the head with a falling piece of the wall and didn't remember? Maybe she was addled by the memory of him crouched beside her, holding her hand so carefully that she felt both fragile and protected. It was not a sensation with which she was familiar, and though she would have denied it even a few days ago, she had to admit, at least to herself, that it had been nice to be treated so, even if it was only for those few moments.

She was as bad as Scotia, it would seem, her head muddled by a braw man, but Rowan would not follow in her cousin's ways. She did not have the luxury of setting aside all responsibility and duty to act upon attraction and impulse, especially with Aunt Elspet so sick.

"Why do you stare at our visitor?" Jeanette tried not to smile as she spoke, but the teasing gleam in her pale blue eyes gave her away.

"I do not," Rowan pulled her attention back to her trencher again, not even aware of when it had drifted back to the man.

"Aye, you do." Scotia leaned forward so she could peer around Jeanette, a smirk on her face. "He is a braw lad with that mysterious look in his eye and those broad shoulders. I think his hair is near as black as mine. We'd make beautiful bairns."

"Scotia!" Rowan knew she glowered at her cousin who only grinned back at her. "I doubt a grown man would have aught to do with a wean like you."

"I am not a wean anymore, just spirited." Scotia lifted her chin. "There are men who like me well enough."

Rowan rolled her eyes. "There are men who like you a wee bit too well." She lifted a slice of boar from the platter in front of her and dropped it on her wooden trencher. Jeanette leaned back in her chair between them and silently watched the two. "You would be wise to keep . . . them . . . at arm's length."

"Is that why you were below the wall, Scotia?" Jeanette asked. "Pray, tell me you were not meeting with Conall again."

Shock coursed through Rowan's spine. "Again?" It was her turn to look from one cousin to the other. "This was not the first time you have gone against your father's command?"

"I told you, I am not a wean anymore. I am a woman, with a woman's desires."

"And a wean's discipline." Rowan threw herself back in her chair and looked over the gathering, wondering if perhaps Kenneth really would kill the lad. More likely he'd force the two to wed. "You do ken the troubles you chance bringing down upon your heads if you keep seeing that lad?" She leaned across Jeanette toward Scotia, her voice barely above a whisper, even though neither Kenneth nor Elspet were in the hall. Gossip had a way of scurrying through the castle like rats before a flood and this was something she did not want spreading to Kenneth's ears. "If you love him, how can you place him in the path of your father's wrath, and then talk of no one but Nicholas?"

"You shall never understand, Rowan," Scotia hissed at her, her eyes snapping with anger.

Rowan pushed her trencher away. Scotia was right, she'd never understand what drove her. It was hard to take her seriously when the lass flirted with every man she met and fell in love with more than a few of them. Conall was only the latest in a long line of lads Scotia thought she loved. Perhaps it was good Scotia was so distracted by Nicholas that she had all but forgotten poor Conall. The way they had been going, Scotia would find herself married to the lad by summer's end if she wasn't careful and Rowan feared that would go ill for everyone. She shook her head at her cousin's inconstant nature.

"Is it really so much to ask that you put the future of your family and your clan before your own daft notions of love and desire?" Rowan asked.

"Daft?!" Scotia turned beseeching eyes to her sister. "You understand, do you not Jeanette? You have been in love before."

"I have, and I do not." A sad smile dimmed the light that was usually Jeanette. "Da has enough cares right now without you adding to them. 'Tis time you recognized that and took responsibility for your part in keeping this clan safe. Do not stir up trouble. Think before you act, especially with the lads."

Tears trembled on Scotia's inky lashes, but Rowan knew from long experience that they were not tears of grief, nor contrition, they were tears brought out by temper. Scotia was used to getting her way and on those rare occasions when she didn't she retaliated first with tears, and then with silence. Rowan preferred the silence.

To her credit, Scotia didn't let the tears fall.

Jeanette sighed and returned to her meal.

Rowan hated arguing with either of her cousins. She owed much to them both. They had accepted her into their family without question or jealousy. And while she had fully intended to speak with Scotia about her folly, she had not wished to do it here, not now, and not in such a contentious way. Someday the lass would settle down and not be so distracted by every eye-catching man that crossed her path. With luck that day would come soon.

She cast a quick glance at the man who had begun this irksome topic, only to find him watching her. Their eyes met and he smiled again before turning back to his nearly empty trencher. An odd fluttering in her stomach accompanied a quickening of her heart's pace as she pondered the muscles and dark hair that Scotia had been praising for days. At least her cousin had a good eye for the handsome lads.

Handsome, indeed, but what sort of man was Nicholas of Achnamara really, and why did he have this mesmerizing effect on her? She pushed away from the table and her half-eaten meal and stood before she even realized she had decided to do so.

"Rowan?" Jeanette regarded her. "You have not finished your meal."

"I am not as hungry as I thought. Since Auntie cannot act as hostess I think I shall make sure our visitor is finding his stay with us satisfactory."

"But that is my responsibility, cousin," Jeanette said, that gleam once more alight in her eyes.

"True, it is, but I shall take that responsibility this night." She made an exaggerated sigh and let her hand flutter to her chest. "It is the least I can do when you have so much work running the castle."

Rowan and Jeanette laughed while Scotia sat back in her chair, her arms crossed in front of her, shaking her head. Rowan found herself grateful to Jeanette for easing the tension that had hummed through her bones with her gentle teasing. She kissed her cousin's cheek and went to learn what she could about Nicholas.

Nicholas watched Rowan at the head table, noting well that she kept glancing at him. He'd been unable to take the seat he would have preferred, with his back to the wall and a good view of the entire space but at least he'd sat so the dais with its long table was easily in his line of sight even if the entire hall lay between him and it. The three women sitting up there were all pretty in their own way, but Rowan was the one who drew his eye. The distraction she posed was a welcome rest from his increasing frustration.

All day Nicholas had been trying to find out something, anything, about the Highland Targe but no one was talking about anything but the fallen wall and their ailing Lady.

Nicholas had looked about for any clues to the Targe's existence as best he could today but he always had Duncan or Uilliam on his heels so he hadn't gotten further than what could be seen from the bailey or the pile of rubble.

At least Uilliam had stopped following him at the door, though the man had positioned himself at the far table behind Nicholas. He wasn't subtle, but then he probably didn't intend to be. But Nicholas could be subtle, more subtle even than he had been. Perhaps he should be so subtle in what he actually wanted that they would think he was after something completely different. Scotia did not seem as likely a mark as he had thought. Perhaps the bonny Rowan would prove more receptive.

If he could learn nothing of the Highland Targe from Duncan at least he could tease some information about Rowan from the man.

"I see Mistress Rowan is better," Nicholas said as casually as he could.

Duncan glanced at the dais and bobbed his head.

"How is it that such a striking lass is not married?"

"She does not seem much interested in the lads."

"Scotia seems to be interested enough for herself and Mistress Rowan."

"Aye, that one is too interested as you have discovered." Duncan chuckled. "You handled her quite well this afternoon."

Handling Scotia's flirtatious advances had been nothing compared to his experiences with the courtesans in Edward's court. He had managed to flirt with her without promising anything more as she'd walked beside him and his cart to the meadow and back several times. His subtle questions and not-so-subtle charm that normally had women telling him whatever he asked should have opened the door to the Targe but they were deftly turned back on him until he had, at last, given up, realizing that despite the girl's behavior she was smarter than he'd thought. Surprisingly so. Duncan, bless the man, had finally suggested she was needed by her mother and freed Nicholas from the girl's grip.

"I think 'twas you who handled her well," Nicholas said, his eyes still on Rowan. "I was caught fast in her web."

Duncan looked up at him and nodded slowly. "It is rather like a sticky web, is it not?"

Nicholas took a teasing tone with Duncan as he watched Rowan rise and give Jeanette a kiss on the cheek. "Sticky for most of us lads, but you slipped clear of it without effort."

"Years of practice. That one was born flirting."

"But not Rowan?"

Duncan looked at him, all seriousness now. "Rowan is cheerful, takes care of anyone and everyone. She clearly loves her cousin, but she worries over Scotia's obsession with the lads. We all do." His eyes narrowed for a moment, as if he concentrated. "I cannot say I've ever seen her attempt to gain a lad's attentions for herself, though she's good enough at gaining it when there is work to be done."

They fell silent while they turned their attention back to the excellent meal.

Duncan's insight shed light on Nicholas's brief experience with Rowan. He had found her to be loyal to her cousin. Protective, even when it appeared her protection was not wanted. Brave. Stoic. And she had sent him to be sure Scotia's trysting lad had not been harmed when Rowan could not go. She had trusted him with Scotia's secret even though she had no idea who he was. He did not know whether that showed great insight on her part or great naiveté. Yet when he had taken her hand, she had seemed at a loss for what to do, and when he'd touched her, smoothing that errant lock of her amazing hair behind her ear, her breath had caught as if no man had ever done such a thing before.

Just as his own breath caught as he watched her move gracefully through the hall toward him. His gaze traced the long line of her back as she leaned down to speak to an older woman, the gentle curve of her breasts against the pale golden-yellow of her gown as she stood again, the subtle sway of her hips as she once more moved in his direction. She was beautiful, all the more so because she looked perfectly at ease, as if she belonged here and knew it deep in her bones. He'd never known that feeling, that sense of belonging, even after the king had taken him into his service.

But now that he knew what it looked like, almost without thinking he took note in case he ever needed to simulate such a thing. Mostly, he simply enjoyed watching her.

Nicholas didn't even try to take his eyes off her as she arrived at the end of the trestle table. Conscious that all eyes in the hall were upon them, Nicholas smiled at her, trying to exude benign trustworthiness in his posture and countenance.

"Duncan. Nicholas." She nodded at both of them, a hint of a smile softening her full lips.

"Will you join us?" Nicholas motioned to the place beside him on the bench. Rowan took the seat across from him, next to Duncan.

She leaned close to Duncan and said, just loud enough for Nicholas to hear, "I see he is not a god after all, but only a man. Scotia had me doubting my memory."

Duncan glanced at Nicholas, mischief alive in his eyes. "Pray, what did she say?"

Nicholas leaned in, ready to be teased by this striking woman.

"Only that he had the strength of ten men," Rowan said, sighing with great drama as Scotia must have done, "and the shoulders of a god. That his hair . . . well, she has a weakness for hair such as his."

Duncan stifled a snort. "Aye, she certainly does."

"Long?" Nicholas played along with the teasing by flagrantly twitching his almost shoulder-length hair out of his face.

Rowan grinned and it was as if the world were new and bright. "Just hair. She does not fancy bald men."

Nicholas laughed and was delighted by a husky chuckle from Rowan.

Duncan shook his head and smiled as he looked from one of them to the other.

"My aunt regrets that she has not been well enough to do her duty as the chief's lady and properly welcome you to Dunlairig, so I am here in her stead." The formal words, so at odds with the teasing of a moment before, lent credence to Duncan's description of this woman.

"I am sorry your aunt is ill. I wish her a quick recovery."

"Thank you. Duncan has got you settled, then?" she asked, clearly determined to do her duty in this task.

"Aye."

"If there is aught you need, you have but to ask."

He needed to see her sunny smile again, to see the twinkle in her eyes as she teased him, to hear that husky chuckle that sent blood rushing where it should not.

"I have shelter, food, and work to earn my way." He held her gaze with his, struck by the seriousness that had replaced the play in her pale green eyes. "There is nothing I need, mistress." He needed naught, 'twas true, but what he wanted . . . that was something entirely different.

He took a bite of the boar, swallowed it half-chewed, and changed the subject. "Your injury is healing well?"

She startled, as if pulled out of her thoughts. "Oh, aye, well enough."

She leaned in toward him, a soft smile on her face now that the formalities were done, so he leaned toward her, happy to be close enough to catch a whiff of her fresh scent. It was not lavender. It seemed all the ladies at court smelled of that at one time or another. Perhaps it was heather, or the clear mountain air clinging to her.

"It itches something fierce," she whispered, and for a swift moment he had lost the momentum of their conversation, distracted by her nearness. "The cut," she added when he had paused too long.

"Wounds often do. I'm told it means they are healing well. Perhaps you need something . . . or someone," he smiled at her and didn't even think about what he wanted to convey in the smile, "to distract you."

Before she could reply, a small boy with white blond hair and bright blue eyes pushed between Rowan and Duncan, reaching for a wooden tray of honey cakes. Mischief sparkled over Rowan's countenance once more as she scooped the tray up, holding it over her head.

"Give it!" the boy squealed. "Give it!"

"That is no way to ask for something, wee Ian," she said with barely suppressed laughter.

"Give it to me!" The boy stood back, planting his fists on his tiny hips as if he were a fierce Highland warrior already.

Rowan turned away from him, lowering the tray enough to peer at its contents but not so low the boy could snag it with a quick lunge.

"Oh my," she said, letting a smile light up her face, "there are only three here. One for me, one for Nicholas, and one for Duncan."

"Nay! S'mine!"

The lad couldn't have been more than five winters old, yet he mimicked a Highland warrior in his stance and attempted severe expression. Recognition slammed into Nicholas like a fist to the gut. Five winters. Was he himself this fiercely a Highlander at five? He certainly had been at ten and two when he'd reluctantly left the Highlands behind him.

"I might consider sharing one," Rowan said. She winked at Nicholas and his momentary melancholy was wiped away. "Would that merit a proper request from you, wee Ian?"

The lad stood there glaring at Rowan for a long moment. She picked a cake off the tray and took a slow bite, closing her eyes as she let out a low "mmmmm." The boy's fierce look turned quickly to pleading, and Nicholas knew he would plead, too, if her teasing were aimed at him. He tried to suppress his grin.

"Please? Please, Rowan?"

"Oh, you are asking nicely now?" She slowly licked the sticky honey from her lips and heat began to build in Nicholas's belly.

She was not an exceptional beauty, and yet there was something about her that he couldn't quite name that drew the eye more strongly than even the most admired ladies attending the king's court. He could not take his eyes off her mouth.

"Please, may I have a honey cake, Rowan?" wee Ian finally managed to get out, his hands folded and tucked under his chin as if in prayer.

Rowan seemed to consider the request for a long moment.

"Do not torture him for his ill manners too long, mistress," Nicholas said quietly. "There is only so much we lads can take from a bonny lass."

Pink tinged her cheeks even as she raised one auburn brow at him. Rowan lowered the tray so wee Ian could see the prize that awaited him.

"Only one," she said. "Remember how your tummy hurt when you ate too many last time."

The boy considered the remaining cakes carefully, grabbed the largest one and scampered away with a gleeful shout of triumph.

"But now we are one cake short," Nicholas said to Rowan. "Whatever shall we do?"

She rose from the table, reached through the people sitting at the next table down and snagged a cake.

"There are always plenty of honey cakes," she said, looking him in the eye. "One only needs to ask nicely." And she dropped the cake on his trencher.

Nicholas laughed and she smiled back at him. He picked up the offered sweet and took a large bite. "Mmmm," he said, his eyes on hers.

"Good, aye?"

"Very." The easy banter disarmed and charmed him. There didn't seem to be any ulterior motive on her part, no seduction in spite of the lust that flooded through him. But perhaps a small spark of interest? A spark that, if fanned, might aid his cause.

She took a bite of her own cake, a look of pure pleasure lighting up her face.

A horn sounded mournfully from the bailey. Once, twice, thrice. Silence fell around those still lingering over the evening meal and they all rose, the loud conversations and laughter of a moment ago replaced with a quiet murmur.

"What is that?" he asked.

"We are called for a blessing," Rowan said, the fun and ease of a few moments ago gone, the formal tone once more in place. "She should not be out of her bed."

"Who?" he asked, but Rowan was already heading for the stair that led to the bailey. He turned to Duncan. "Who should not be out of her bed?"

"Lady Elspet. It is she who makes the blessings." Duncan stuffed the last of his dinner in his mouth, snagged the last honey cake and motioned for Nicholas to follow.

Curiosity had him hard on the man's heels.

# CHAPTER FIVE

A LOW RUMBLE OF MUTTERINGS PASSING FROM PERSON TO PERSON accompanied Rowan out of the hall and into the bailey that was growing more crowded by the moment. People streamed in the gate, adding to those who had clearly been within the castle confines when the horn sounded. What was Elspet doing? She didn't have the strength to be out of her bed, never mind the strength to perform a blessing.

Rowan tried to find Jeanette or Scotia in the crowd but it was too dark and there were too many people. How had they all arrived so quickly? She skirted the thickest part of the gathering, moving easily through the open space between the large knot of people and the wall toward the tower, but was stopped by a warm hand on her shoulder.

Nicholas stood behind her. He dropped his hand and was about to say something when the sound of the tower door opening sent a complete and sudden hush throughout the gathering.

Kenneth filled the open doorway, his arm wrapped around the waist of the striking, but very frail, Elspet. Rowan noted that despite her aunt's faded hair and gaunt and deeply lined face, it was as clear as ever that Jeanette was her daughter, for they favored one another strongly.

The couple made their way slowly through the bailey, the crowd parting to ease Elspet's passing. When Kenneth reached the nearest part of the destroyed wall he tried to stop, but his wife said something to him. He quietly argued for a short moment before capitulating to his lady's wishes. Rowan's heart warmed. Most thought of Kenneth as a hard warrior, a strong chief to his clan, but only those closest to him—and she was glad to count herself amongst them—knew of the soft place he held in his heart for his wife. He had an exceedingly hard time saying nay to anything Elspet truly wanted.

Keeping his arm about Elspet, he helped her not only to the center of where the wall once stood, but up on one of the larger stones that had not yet been moved. She tried to step away from him, but he refused to take his arm from around her waist, and in this she yielded with a gentle smile.

Elspet seemed to gather herself carefully. She pulled a small ermine sack from a fold of her arisaid and held it cupped in her hands. She cast her gaze across the entire gathering, nodded her head as if something satisfied her, raised her hands with the white furred sack in them heart-high, and then she began what felt like a prayer, though it was not in a language anyone understood. It was the strangest combination of musical and guttural sounds, as if they fought each other to escape on Elspet's voice. Rowan always thought them beautiful. Her aunt swished her hands through the air as she spoke, leaning heavily against her husband while she did so. Kenneth looked grave, but did not stop his wife.

"What is she saying?" Nicholas whispered to Rowan.

"I ken not. No one does," she said just as quietly, "but it is a blessing of the old ones, the ones who came before. It has been passed from mother to daughter over many, many generations."

"Does she ken what she is saying?" Nicholas leaned so close she could feel his breath on her ear, sending shivers over her skin that had nothing to do with the temperature of the air.

"I asked her once," she said, her feet rooted to the spot in spite of her urge to move closer to the compelling Nicholas, "when I was a wean. She told me she repeated what her mother taught her, understanding the intent, but not the meaning." She shrugged. "She said the meaning had been lost over time, but it was a blessing."

Elspet's voice suddenly rose, raspy but stronger than Rowan would have thought possible. She placed the sack at her feet, then raised her hands and began waving them almost violently through the air, the motion at odds with the normally graceful and peaceful blessings her aunt gave. An unfamiliar sensation began in Rowan's feet, climbing up her legs in time with her aunt's frantic hand motions, almost as if water filled her, pressing against her skin from the inside, pushing, pulsing to get out. The pressure built as Elspet's words became something not benign, soft, reassuring, but powerful, with a force that washed out over the bailey like a punishing wind before a summer storm.

The hairs on Rowan's arms rose as an unnatural wind whipped around her, calling to the pressure inside her that pounded in her head and pushed almost painfully against her skin. She gripped her head lest it explode. She doubled over as her stomach roiled, the deluge of pressure overwhelming all her senses until she could neither see nor hear nor feel anything of the world around her. She tried to cry out, but could not draw enough breath to so much as whimper. Her knees went weak under the assault but she did not fall.

"Rowan? Rowan! What is it, lass?"

She reached for the voice like a lifeline and slowly began to pull herself out of the maelstrom. She heard her name again and realized it was Nicholas calling to her. His hands gripped her shoulders, steadying and supporting her. The hard plane of his chest was solid against her back. She pulled those sensations about her like armor, shielding herself from the confusion and fear she would not give in to.

"Lass?" Worry laced through the single word and Rowan opened her eyes, only then realizing that the world hadn't gone black. Torches still beat back the night, flickering in their sconces along the standing part of the wall.

"I am fine." She tried to pull away from him, but he held her there, gently but firmly. She sank back against him, leaning into his strength, grateful he had not released her, grateful that all eyes remained upon her aunt.

Elspet repeated the last words of the once more soothing blessing, letting them drift over the silent gathering as gently as a morning's mist. With the last graceful movement of her hands she crumpled into the waiting arms of her beloved husband.

"It is done," Kenneth's voice boomed. He held Elspet in his arms, cradling her like a sleeping bairn, her head tucked into the hollow of his shoulder. "The blessing is made, even if it is late, and not in the usual way. I shall hear no more about evil spirits and witches from any of you. The wall fell. We will discover the reason for it, but it is not an omen of ill and your lady has blessed us *and this place*. Nothing can harm us while we rebuild the wall." He stepped off the high stone with care and took his wife back to the tower. Jeannette and Scotia separated themselves from the crowd and followed in their wake.

The crowd stood still and silent for the longest time and when Rowan tried to push away from Nicholas again, he still tethered her in place with his hands. Finally, as if there had been some signal that she did not hear, everyone began to disperse at the same moment.

Tentatively, Rowan pushed away yet again and this time Nicholas released her. She tensed, wondering if it was his touch that had chased away the panic or if Elspet's completion of the odd blessing had released her from its grip.

When the barrage of debilitating pressure and fear didn't return, she swallowed hard and only then realized that her face was wet, the cool breeze tracing the tear tracks on her cheeks. She wiped them away, then headed toward the tower where her family had disappeared.

Nicholas grabbed her arm and gently pulled her around to face him, stopping her from retreating, which should have panicked her more but oddly calmed her.

"What happened?" Worry made him look older than she'd thought him to be. Concern and curiosity swarmed in the dark depths of his eyes and the urge to lean into him again, to let him support her with his strength and comforting touch, to confide in him exactly what she had experienced, was strong.

But she didn't know what had happened to her. Never before had she felt such a thing during a blessing, or any other time for that matter, but then Rowan had never seen a blessing like the one tonight. Nay, Nicholas was a stranger here and she had no reason to trust him, especially where her aunt was concerned, even if she could find the words to explain it.

Rowan looked around for Jeanette before she remembered that her cousin had returned to the tower with her parents. Had she felt anything during the blessing?

"What happened?" Nicholas repeated his question.

She looked at his hand upon her arm, his grip strong and gentle at the same time. She could feel his concern, his curiosity, but she dared not tell him. She shook her head, the only answer she could give, then quickly turned away before she changed her mind.

NICHOLAS FISTED HIS HANDS TO KEEP HIMSELF FROM REACHING out to Rowan again. She didn't want to tell him what had happened and he couldn't force her to. All he could do was watch her walk away from him, her shoulders set in a rigid line. Stoic.

But something had come over her during the blessing. Hell, he'd felt something wash over him, as if Lady Elspet had sent a warm river of energy coursing through the bailey, swirling around everyone gathered there.

But where he had felt only the passing of the sensation, Rowan had reacted as if she'd been punched in the gut. She'd staggered, gripped her head and he could not stop himself from reaching out and steadying her. He'd been surprised when she leaned back against him and he had fought the urge to wrap his arms around her, compromising by keeping his hands on her shoulders, holding her upright when her knees threatened to buckle.

He turned his attention to the crowd still lingering around him, scanning the faces for any hint that someone else had felt what Rowan had. But none appeared particularly disturbed by the proceedings.

He thought back to his impressions during the blessing. It was nothing like a blessing from a priest—words, a cross drawn in the air, with no physical impression that anything had changed. But

Elspet's blessing was made of words no one understood and undecipherable symbols drawn upon the air . . .

It was palpable. Powerful.

Rowan would have been knocked from her feet had he not steadied her. And he had sensed something, like an unseen river flowing through the crowd, filling the bailey, silent, untouchable, yet carrying something in its current, something . . .

His mind went back and forth between a priest's blessing and Elspet's. Elspet's and a priest's. They served the same purpose: to protect the clan and the castle.

Like a shield.

Impossible. It could not be. And yet he could not deny the witness of his own senses, of Rowan's reaction, or of Kenneth's words. The chief had assured the clan that they were protected and everyone here gathered had accepted his proclamation without question.

All of this pointed to the stories Nicholas had collected of the Highland Targe, an ancient shield that protected this route into the Highlands from invaders. Had he truly just witnessed the shield being set in place? And if so, was Elspet the shield, or could it be something so small it would fit in the sack she had raised to the sky?

Nicholas shook his head. Logic told him none of this could be true, but his instincts screamed otherwise. The Scots were a superstitious lot. Highlanders believed in second sight, in healing with a touch, in selkies, brownies, and the sidhe, the fairy folk who stole human children and left their own changelings in their place. They believed in sacred healing wells, and that they were the makers of their own destiny.

His own upbringing, those precious years amongst his mother's kin, had taught him that sometimes superstition was less than truth, but sometimes it was more. He had seen enough of these things as a lad to know there was more to this land and these people than the English would ever believe.

He watched the people about him in the bailey, gathered in small knots, chattering away, but there was a calmness to them that hadn't been there before, as if they believed deep in their bones that they were protected from whatever evil had toppled the wall and threatened their security.

A calmness that wasn't shared by Rowan. She had been shaken by the blessing, as confused as he had been, but also physically affected. Was she a part of the Targe or was there something else happening that he did not understand?

He whipped back to where he'd last seen Rowan and after a moment spied her on the stair that led to the rampart. Checking the groups still lingering in the bailey, he saw Uilliam-the-bear and Duncan deep in conversation with several other men, their attention elsewhere finally. Not wishing to draw anyone's notice, especially his keepers', he moved slowly toward the rampart stair.

When he reached the top he stepped into a shadow, letting his eyes adjust to the darkness. After a moment he spied her not far down the wall walk, leaning out over the wall as if she was trying to escape . . . or fly.

"Rowan?" he called as quietly as possible, not wishing to startle her. She pulled herself back fully inside the wall and turned to him.

"You followed me." She closed the distance between them, stopping just out of reach. "Why?"

"I was worried about you." He stepped closer, wanting her to reach out to him.

In the faint glow of the torch light from below he could see her wrap her arms around her torso as if she were cold, or perhaps she was keeping herself from touching him. He preferred that explanation.

"Are you well, lass?" he asked, keeping his voice pitched low and filling it with concern that was only partly feigned.

"I will be fine." She turned back to the wall and leaned her elbows there. Nicholas matched her stance but stood close enough so he should have felt the heat of her, but he did not.

"What happened?" he asked, taking care not to look at her, but exquisitely aware of her every movement. Her breath hitched at his question and she leaned a little farther over the wall again.

"Nothing."

He allowed that word to drift between them, waiting for her to fill the silence, but she seemed content to let it remain empty.

"It did not look like 'nothing.'" He turned to face her, leaning his hip against the wall and cocking his head to try to see her expression. But she actually looked away from him as if she knew what he was up to, the minx.

"It looked like you got punched in the gut," he continued. "You went ghostly pale. You stumbled backwards into me. You did not answer me until the fourth time I spoke your name. It did not look like nothing."

She turned to face him, her hip against the wall and her arms once more across her torso. "And I am fine now, so it was nothing."

They stared at each other for a long moment and Nicholas became aware of a shimmer in her eyes. The lass valiantly fought tears and his respect for her strength of will grew.

He reached across the space separating them and let his knuckles slide over the soft plane of her cheek, unaccountably pleased when his touch drew a faint smile to her lips. "You do not have to be strong all alone, lass."

She swallowed and notched up her chin. "I do."

"Nay, you do not." He took her face gently between his palms, drawing her close. He dropped his voice to a whisper, "You leaned on me a little while ago. You can lean on me now." Her eyes were fixed on his, her breath feathering across his skin as he lowered his mouth to hers, unable to resist the lure of her strength and sweetness any longer.

At first she stood perfectly still, as if he had startled her, but she did not pull away. He shifted the angle of his head and kissed her again, lingering a little longer over her lush lips, letting himself get a little lost in the faint taste of honey and the scent of fresh mountain air and heather that surrounded him.

"You can lean on me," he whispered against her mouth.

Tentatively she leaned into the kiss and he barely contained a groan at her acceptance. Her hands came to rest lightly on his chest, heat radiating from the contact. He slid his hands into her hair, pulling her a little closer still. She sighed against his lips, as she parted hers, accepting his deeper kiss. Desire punched into him, sending his body in directions he wasn't prepared to follow. Not yet.

And yet he could not step away . . . not yet.

He let himself revel in the softness of her lips, the silkiness of her hair, the scent that reminded him of a Scottish forest, losing himself for long moments, forgetting everything but this moment, this woman, this kiss. And when the need to take the kiss further almost overwhelmed him, then he pulled himself back to his senses, gentling the kiss, nibbling at the corner of her mouth. Finally he forced himself to pull away, just far enough to break the kiss before he completely lost himself in her softness and the scent.

She opened her eyes and dropped her hands from his chest. Confusion had taken the place of the shimmer of tears. Confusion was better.

"Why did you do that?" she asked.

Without thinking about his answer he said, "Because I have wanted to since first I saw you." He stroked her cheek again, unable to resist the soft, creamy feel of it and realized he'd spoken the truth. "Can I do it again?"

"Nay." Her reply was quick and sure. "You should not have followed me up here."

Disappointment caught him by surprise, quickly followed by a strange flash of pride in her and a certain amount of annoyance that she had not succumbed to his attentions as most lasses did. He stepped back far enough so that he could not feel the heat of her anymore and tried to remember why he had followed her here.

"Perhaps, but clearly something happened to you during the blessing, lass, and I cannot in good conscience let you be alone until I am sure you are recovered completely. Can you not tell me what disturbed you so?"

She didn't meet his eyes. "I do not know what it was. It happened so fast, and then . . ." Her voice trailed off into nothingness.

"Then?" he asked.

She looked at him out of the side of her eyes. "Then it was gone, over, whatever. Perhaps I had something for the evening meal that was off? Maybe the honey cake wasn't any good?" She shrugged but it felt contrived, as if she did it for his benefit.

"Perhaps."

She smiled at him then and it was as if the sun broke through the night sky. "I do thank you for catching me, for letting me lean on you." She looked down and he'd swear she was embarrassed.

He watched her take a deep breath as if she fortified herself from something. Him? Perhaps he had muddled her emotions more than she was letting on.

"You are most welcome, mistress, for both." And the odd thing was that he really meant it. As he watched her go he realized that she had deflected every question he had asked. She was as adept as he was at avoiding saying what he did not want to say. He chuckled. Perhaps this mission wouldn't be as easy as he'd thought, but it would certainly be interesting.

His thoughts turned back to that kiss and the way Rowan had softened under his lips, as his had softened against hers, and he realized that he would have to tread carefully with the lass lest *she* charm the truth out of *him*.

As Rowan moved through the following day her thoughts kept returning to those few moments over the evening meal, laughing and teasing with Nicholas. Her body heated all over again every time she remembered the feel of his lips on hers, the hard plane of his chest under her palms, the feel of his heart hammering as fast as hers.

Rowan slowed her pace as she descended the stairs from the great hall into the deeply shadowed bailey. She needed a moment to regain her equilibrium before she returned to her aunt's bedside.

Never had she reacted to a man the way she did to this stranger. Nicholas. Just the thought of his name sent a little thrill over her skin, heating her cheeks as if she were a lass caught up in her first flush of infatuation.

His bravery in helping her cousin and herself escape the collapsing wall, his willingness to keep Scotia's tryst a secret, his laughter over wee Ian's antics, and his gentle caresses and unexpected kiss had filled her up as if she had been an empty ewer. The closeness of his body as they had stood on the ramparts had warmed her in ways she wasn't prepared for and didn't completely understand.

Longing echoed just behind her heart. She had not thought herself wanting in any way and yet it had taken Nicholas of Achnamara only a pair of days to leave her feeling as if she'd been missing something important in her life.

She stopped at the tower door, her hand on the cold iron handle, letting the reality of the situation settle around her. She was daft to let Nicholas make her feel this way. She was sad over Elspet's failing health, her uncle's barely contained worry, Scotia's childish ways, and the heavy responsibilities that would soon fall on Jeanette's shoulders. And then there were these headaches, the memory that she couldn't quite grab but that left her panicked anytime she tried to even think about it, and the odd reaction she had to the blessing. Nay, it was not surprising that the diversion of a man with warm brown eyes and an easy laugh should lift her out of that sadness and confusion for a few moments.

That was all she was feeling—relief, however brief, from the burdens that lay upon them all. She was not lacking in anything. She was loved, respected, needed. She wanted for nothing and yet, as she lifted the latch and pushed the door inward, she couldn't help but wish for one more kiss from Nicholas.

Folly. She was not Scotia, losing all sense because some braw lad smiled at her . . . or kissed her. It was nice to be distracted from her panic and everything else that was happening to those she loved, but that was all. She took the stairs two at a time, stopping at the top of the tower to peer in Elspet's chamber to the right.

"Come in, niece." Elspet's weak voice drifted through the darkness.

An unwelcome urge to pretend she had not heard held her still for a moment before she pushed it away. "You have slept a long time, Auntie," she said, moving quickly to the hearth to stir the fire back to life. "Are you hungry?"

"I did not mean to sleep."

"Then you should not have taxed yourself with the blessing." Rowan winced at the harshness in her own words. She took a breath to quiet her mind and stirred the kettle of broth that hung over the fire. "Is there aught I can get you?"

A quiet sigh. "Do not fash yourself."

"Auntie, that is what I am here for. You have taken good care of your own daughters and me these many years. It is our turn to take care of you."

"Nay. You should not have to."

"But we want to."

"Contrary, as always." Elspet's laugh was little more than a wheezy breath. "'Tis what your own sweet mother said about you when you were but three."

Rowan quickly rounded the bed, laying a hand upon Elspet's forehead. It was cool for a change, but the wheezy laugh was now a quieter, but still wheezy, breath. "Would you take some broth?"

"Is it here?"

Rowan was so happy to hear her interested in broth that one would think her aunt had declared herself cured. "Aye. It has gone a bit cool but I have roused the fire. It shall be warm again soon." She adjusted the woolen blanket around Elspet better as the topic foremost on her mind begged to be broached.

"Auntie, may I ask you something?"

Elspet tried to smile, but it was mostly in her eyes. "Of course, my lassie."

"You are not too tired?"

"Ask me now. The morn is far away."

Rowan swallowed. More and more, Elspet spoke as if her time were only in the here and now, not in the future.

"Have you ever felt . . ." Rowan tried to find words to describe what had happened to her during the blessing. "Have you ever felt something odd," she began again, determined to continue this time, "when you made the blessing? I felt something this time that I never have before."

Elspet's eyes narrowed and she tried to sit up in the bed. Rowan helped her, noting that only yesterday her aunt had the strength to sit up on her own. Rowan settled an arisaid around Elspet's narrow shoulders and the blankets over her lap.

"Tell me what you felt," Elspet said. Her voice surprised Rowan in its intensity.

Rowan sat on the bed next to her aunt. "It was like a stream was rising through my legs and trying to push its way out of my skin, a pressure, a pulsing." She almost added that Nicholas had had to keep her from falling but she didn't want to share that part for some reason, not yet at any rate. She rubbed that spot between her brows that had started to ache again. "Do you ken what it was, Auntie?"

"Were you the only one to experience such a thing?"

Rowan shrugged and rose from the side of the bed where she had perched. "I did not see anyone else who seemed . . . uncomfortable. I have not spoken of this with anyone, though." She moved back to the hearth to stir the broth that was not yet warmed. She placed another peat on the fire and knelt down to blow on the embers. "What do you think it was?"

"What do *you* think it was?" Elspet asked quietly.

Rowan swallowed hard and sat back on her heels. "I do not ken, but it raised a panic in me the like of which I have never experienced." She stopped as that elusive memory skittered through her mind, once more slipping out of her grasp. Something about that memory was connected to what had happened to her in the bailey . . . and to the curtain wall falling toward her, as if both things were familiar.

She closed her eyes and forced herself to remember the moment when she knew the wall was falling toward her. The pounding in her head had grown stronger and stronger, pulsing just as it had during the blessing in the bailey, just as it was now.

She rubbed the spot between her brows where the pain always seemed to gather and tried to settle her mind, to think, to be ready to grab that memory and drag it into the light.

The wall falling... The pressure building... Her head pounding...

The image of a wall falling, hurtling toward her, burst behind her eyes. Fear writhed in her stomach. Guilt strangled her heart, and grief . . . so much grief. She groaned and gripped her head, pressing against unbearable pressure.

"Do you remember?" Elspet's voice was quiet and commanding. Like a knife, it cut through the rising panic, grounding her here in this place with this woman who had always kept her safe. "Think, Rowan."

"Another wall falling? Not the curtain wall. I cannot say where or when. And grief—devastating grief. And fear. And guilt."

Elspet was quiet for a long time and Rowan was almost afraid to ask her anything else. She wasn't sure she really wanted to know what had happened to her. Eventually, when her breath had calmed and her hands no longer shook, she looked over her shoulder at Elspet sitting in the gloom, her fingers plucking at the blanket in her lap, her brow furrowed in deep thought. Rowan filled a small earthen bowl with the tepid broth and brought it to her.

"Auntie, what does it mean—falling walls, pressure beyond comprehension, searching for a way out of me, and blinding panic?" The question was out of her mouth before she could stop it, as if it would not be suppressed.

Elspet reached out for the broth, taking the bowl with trembling hands. "I do not understand," she mumbled, as if to herself. "How?"

"What?" Rowan asked, not understanding.

Elspet waved one hand and soup sloshed from the bowl over her lap but she didn't seem to notice. "Fetch Jeanette. I need to speak to Jeanette." Her words grew more agitated as Rowan tried to steady the bowl. Elspet shoved the bowl at her, sloshing the rest of the broth over the edge of the bed where it dripped to the floor. Rowan grabbed the bowl, setting it on the table, then began to pull the wet blankets from her aunt's lap.

"Nay, leave that. It is not important. Get Jeanette!" she said, her voice forceful even as it trembled. "Please, get my *daughter*!"

The words sliced through Rowan. Never had Elspet made such a clear distinction between her niece and her daughters as she did in that moment. She struggled to swallow the lump that clogged her throat, hating that whatever had overtaken her during the blessing, whatever a falling wall meant, had caused her aunt such turmoil. How could it be anything but evil?

"I'll fetch her immediately, aunt." Rowan set the bowl down on the foot of the bed and left the chamber in a rush.

# CHAPTER SIX

ROWAN CROUCHED BY THE SIDE OF A RUSHING BURN, HER BODY SO tense she ached everywhere. She crushed her hands against her ears and she hummed loudly to herself trying to drown out . . .

Yelling. Angry, hurtful yelling.

She hummed louder, a tuneless effort to keep the words from getting into her head. She must keep them out of her head.

But she couldn't. They grew louder and louder until, with a shriek, they took form, pummeling her with wind, with noise like the world was ending. She looked up to find huge stones hurtling toward her. Fear shattered inside her—

"NAY!"

A crash woke Rowan suddenly from the nightmare. She was sitting straight up in her narrow bed, her arms flung forward as if she'd pushed something away from her. The ewer that usually sat on a small table near the door lay shattered on the floor.

The chamber door flew open and Jeanette stood there, her blue eyes wide as she took in the room. She moved quickly to Rowan's side, and perched next to her.

"What happened?" she asked, gently pressing Rowan's arms down from their outstretched position.

Rowan shook her head. "A dream. A dream." Panic still gripped her hard and she dared not even blink for fear whatever she had dreamed of would return as it had each night over and over again since the blessing.

"Do you remember anything of it?" Jeanette asked.

Rowan tried to grab hold of the wisps of dream that lingered. "I was afraid. So afraid. And then . . ." She tried to find words to describe the feeling, for that was all that remained of the dream, the fear so much greater than anything else she had ever experienced. She shook her head again. "It is gone."

"Perhaps for good," Jeanette said, rising and moving to the shattered ewer. She picked up the largest pieces, looking at them, then at the table. "Curious."

Rowan rose from her bed and began to dress, pulling her gown over her kirtle as she tried to shake off the remains of the dream.

"How fares my aunt this day?"

Jeanette collected the rest of the ewer pieces, setting them on the table. "She is agitated." She dusted her hands off. "I was on my way to my still room to get more of the herbs for her sleeping draught when I heard you cry out, and the crash of the ewer. How do you think it fell?" she asked, once more pondering the broken crockery.

"Fell? Scotia probably left it too close to the edge of the table, as she is wont to do."

"Aye, that is the likely answer, but I heard you cry out almost at the same moment I heard it crash. I was sure you had hurt yourself and dropped something."

"Nay. I was abed, dreaming of . . ." The dream was like that elusive memory that had plagued her all her waking hours since she'd questioned Elspet about the blessing two days past—disturbing but always slipping through her grasp before she could see it clearly. "Has Auntie asked for me?" She belted her arisaid in place and drew the ends up over her shoulders, pinning them securely with her mother's ancient broach.

"In a way."

Rowan whirled to face her cousin. "What does that mean?"

Jeanette paused for a long moment, chewing her bottom lip, a sure sign she was worrying. "She wants us to take her to the wellspring, Rowan."

At the word *us,* hope surged, but she quickly damped it down. "She has not been there since this illness overtook her."

"She has not had the strength. She has been fretting about it for a while, but for the last two days it has become an obsession. She does not seem to think she will overcome this illness, Rowan. She says it will set her mind at ease if she knows one of us has taken her place."

"You."

"Or Scotia."

"It will surely be you. Scotia is too . . ." She could not find the word to explain, but Jeanette didn't need her to. They both knew that Scotia was not the one.

"Mum wants you to come, too."

The knot in Rowan's chest loosened. "Of course. And Uncle Kenneth?"

"She does not think he will let her go so we are not to say anything to him."

The knot tightened again. "She is that determined?"

"Aye. She is adamant that we must go immediately." Jeanette's breath hitched. "I do not think she believes she will be with us much longer."

"Nothing is sure." Rowan grabbed Jeanette's icy hands in hers, squeezing them and wishing she could keep the impending grief from her cousin, from all of them. "It never is."

Jeanette closed her eyes, and squeezed Rowan's hands.

"When does Auntie wish to go?" Rowan asked quietly.

"Soon. She is making an effort to eat, though I think she truly does not have much appetite. She sips on broth all day and when she is awake in the night. It has helped strengthen her. As long as the weather holds she should be able to travel very soon."

"Truly?"

Jeanette was the one with the healer's touch but Rowan knew she had been unable to find any infusion, anything of any sort, to aid Elspet, and neither had Morven. She could not believe something as simple as sipping on broth had helped her aunt so much. She did not think it could, but she would not tell Jeanette that.

Rowan knew that what had happened during the blessing had shaken her aunt. That was what drove her in this quest. She was sure of it. Elspet knew something that she was not telling her, and Rowan was determined to learn the truth.

"So she has not asked for me." She swallowed a lump in her throat that wanted to block not just her voice, but her breath, too.

Jeanette sighed. "Nay, she has not, and I find that very odd. She was quite agitated when you fetched me the other night." She looked at her cousin with determination in her eyes such as Rowan had never seen before. "What passed between you?"

"She did not tell you?" Was that possible?

"Rowan? What happened?"

"I asked her a question she either could not, or would not, answer."

Jeanette's lips flattened at the lengthening silence. She put her clenched hands on her hips and cocked her head. "Well? Are you going to tell me what you asked her?"

"How is it that she did not tell you?" Hope that Jeanette might have some answers drained away. "Jeanette, I never would have asked if I thought it would upset her so."

"I ken that. You love her as if she were your own mother."

"I do, and I thought she loved me as a daughter."

Concern flashed across Jeanette's features and she closed the small distance between them, laying her hands on Rowan's forearms. "She does, Rowan. You ken that. This is but a temporary rift between you. Can you not tell me what caused it? Perhaps I can help?"

Jeanette's caring dulled the pain of Elspet's distance a little and Rowan suddenly found herself unwilling to chance Jeanette reacting the same way.

"'Twas nothing important, Jeanette. I think I must have caught her when she was too tired and she did not have the strength to deal with my impertinence in her usual gentle way. 'Twill pass and all will be well."

"Are you sure?" Jeanette asked.

Rowan smoothed the scowl she could feel on her face. "Do not fash over me. Let us get Auntie as strong as we can and take her to the wellspring. If that can be resolved 'twill ease her mind and she will rest easier, regardless of what the future holds." And if Rowan's question was the thing that spurred her aunt to want to get to the wellspring as fast as possible, then perhaps, if she were lucky, the answer to it lay in that sacred place.

Nicholas stood under the shelter of an overhanging outbuilding roof near the ruined wall. He watched Rowan dash across the bailey from the tower to the great hall, her arisaid pulled up over her head as protection against the sudden downpour of cold heavy rain. Nicholas let out a frustrated sigh.

He'd been watching Rowan for two days, but she would only glance at him, then hurry away the minute he moved in her direction. The urge to hear her husky laugh again was chafing at him, never mind the need that surged through him every time he thought of the kiss they'd shared.

He pulled the old plaid he'd acquired when first he arrived in the Highlands more firmly about him, using it as a cloak to shut out the bone-deep chill that came with the torrential rain, but the only thing that seemed to warm him was remembering the slide of her palm against his chest and the faint honey taste of her lips. It was daft. He was no besotted lad untutored in the effect a pretty young woman could have upon him, yet he could not remember the last time he'd been as taken with a woman, as distracted by her. He'd found himself looking for Rowan again and again as he moved through the last two days of endless toil.

But he couldn't let her distract him any longer or he'd never complete this assignment—and that was not an option.

Duncan, of course, stood next to him, seemingly unaffected by the weather except that he leaned against the wall of the outbuilding in the shelter of the overhanging thatched roof.

"The rain is different here than in the borders," Nicholas said when the silence began to grate on him. "'Tis harder, like the land itself."

"Is it?"

"Aye." There was a long silence between them until Nicholas asked, "Do all of the women go up to the shielings for the summer pasturage?"

"You mean will Rowan go?" Duncan slanted a grin at Nicholas. "I've seen the two of you watching each other. Perhaps." He looked back out at the rain, his expression sobering. "I suppose 'twill depend upon Lady Elspet's health."

"She looked very frail the night of the blessing."

Duncan nodded his head slowly. "She must be very ill. I had not seen her in nigh on a month before that. She did not even leave her chamber for the Beltain festival, nor the blessing of the beasts. I cannot remember a time she did not attend those." The man's whole countenance fell and his shoulders drooped when he talked about Lady Elspet.

"Her lasses must be very concerned about her. Kenneth, too."

Duncan nodded slowly, casting his gaze toward the rubble or what was beyond it.

Nicholas took a long, deep breath, taking in the rich earthy smell of mud, the fresh scent of the rain, and the tang of wet granite, savoring them. This was what his home had smelled like. Here, a person could breathe. For the space between one heartbeat and the next he let himself imagine what his life would have been like had he never left the Highlands. He scraped his fingers through his hair, and shoved the thought away, though the image of a sweet-faced woman with riotous coppery-brown hair and eyes of palest green would not be banished.

He glanced toward the dark doorway where Rowan had disappeared a few minutes ago. "Duncan, it looks as if it will rain for a long time yet. Do you not want to get inside?" Nicholas pointed at the open door to the great hall's undercroft, forty feet away from them.

Duncan leaned out from his place against the wall far enough to observe the sky beyond the eaves. "'Tis settled in, to be sure." He leaned back against the building. "There shall be no more work on the wall this day."

Nicholas quirked an eyebrow at the man who had yet to answer his question.

"You wish to see Rowan."

It was true, though Nicholas could not account for why this lass had so captured his attention.

"We shall get drenched," Duncan grumbled as he pushed off the wall, "but at least there is ale and a fire to be had."

"And more bonny company than you, lad." Nicholas grinned and took off at a careful trot across the muddy bailey.

ROWAN SETTLED HERSELF ON A BENCH ALONG THE WALL OPPOSITE the great hall's hearth, a basket of wool by her side and plenty of room to work her spindle as Scotia arrived, quickly followed by Duncan and Nicholas. Scotia made her way past the older men, before pausing to banter with the younger men. Nicholas nodded at the gathering as he passed them, but made his way directly across the large chamber to where Rowan sat. She was vaguely aware that Duncan followed Nicholas and that Scotia followed them both like a duckling followed its mother.

"May I join you, Mistress Rowan?" Nicholas said as he took the seat next to her. Duncan waited for Scotia to sit, then sat beside her some little way down the bench.

"I am glad you did not leave before I could say good day," Nicholas said.

She grabbed another tuft of wool and sent her spindle spinning as she slanted a glance at him. A smile creased his cheeks, not quite deep enough to make dimples, but creating a striking sharpness to his face that was handsomely set off by the soft waves of his hair. She could not help smiling back at him before turning back to her thread.

He leaned toward her, their shoulders touching, and studied the spindle as it spun between her knees. "Do you ever just sit, or are you always busy at some task?"

"There is always work needs doing," she replied, grabbing another handful of wool and feeding it into the lengthening thread.

Nicholas was quiet but he did not lean away. Rowan sighed and leaned into his warmth and weight. The contact was both comforting and disturbing, sending flutterings through her stomach and heat and restlessness to places lower.

"Do you have nothing to do but watch Rowan spin?" Scotia leaned forward so she could see around Rowan.

"Nay, mistress, I do not. There are stones to be moved, but it is not safe work in such a downpour."

Scotia looked at him for a moment and Rowan knew the lass was considering the best way to catch Nicholas's attention.

"Then you must earn your keep another way," Scotia said, mischief clear in both her voice and the glint in her vivid blue eyes. "Tell us about yourself. Why do you not ken where your home is?"

"Scotia, 'tis rude—"

Nicholas laid a hand on her arm, stopping her admonishment. "Do not fash yourself, Rowan. Scotia is right. I must earn my keep and this rain is not showing signs of letting up." He gave her arm a slight squeeze before releasing her. He leaned forward again, elbows braced on his knees, angled a little toward the prying Scotia and the silent Duncan.

"There is not much to tell. I was raised amongst my mother's kin until I was nearly ten and two. My mother was not well so I went to my father at that point, near the border. I did not wish to leave for, I dearly loved my life in the Highlands, but 'twas for the best."

Rowan watched as he told this tale, held still by the wistfulness in his words.

"Why did you not return to Achnamara when you were old enough to?" Scotia asked, taking the question directly from Rowan's own thoughts.

Nicholas smiled. "'Tis not as easy as that, lass. I had a life in the borders—"

"A wife maybe?" Scotia asked.

Rowan's spindle dangled in her hands, slowly unwinding her thread. She could not look at Nicholas.

"Nay, I have never been wed."

Rowan let out a breath she had not realized she was holding.

"Just a life that kept me busy."

"So why are you here?" Rowan asked, her eyes on her spindle but her attention on his response.

"That life was not enough anymore."

Silence hung between them.

"I wanted to see where I came from," he finally added. "See who my mother's people were."

"You have not seen your mum in all these years?" Scotia asked.

Nicholas shook his head and leaned back against the wall, his hands clenching his knees. Rowan scowled at Scotia, who did not seem to notice the strain her questions had caused. She leaned her shoulder against his this time and was gratified to see his hands relax.

"I have not seen my mum in more than ten years," Rowan said quietly. She probed the memories like a sore tooth, happy in an odd way that there was still pain there, that she hadn't become so accustomed to her parents being gone that she didn't feel the loss anymore. "She died when I was ten, along with my da. I still miss them very much." She set the spindle in motion again. "You must miss your mum."

"I miss her family. My mum never had much care for me," Nicholas said.

Rowan didn't know how to respond to that quiet confession. How could a mother not care for her child?

Raucous laughter burst from the cluster of men gathered around a table near the hearth, breaking the quiet moment.

"Duncan, you have not got your ale yet," Nicholas said, rising from his pensive place at Rowan's side. "Shall I get us all some?"

Rowan shook her head but Scotia accepted. Duncan did, too, though he scowled at Scotia, then looked to Rowan for help.

"Scotia, do you not have to get back to your mum?" she asked, all the innocence in her voice she could muster.

"Jeanette told me she was fine for a few hours. I have not been here that long. I'll have an ale," she said to Nicholas, rising from her seat and touching Nicholas's arm. "I shall even help you fetch it."

Duncan rolled his eyes as the girl smiled up at Nicholas as if he were a god, not some laborer who'd happened by their castle as he wandered lost in the Highlands. Rowan kept her smile to herself. Duncan had such high expectations of Scotia, yet she let him down again and again without even realizing it. Maybe someday Scotia would grow up enough to realize Duncan's gruffness with her hid deeper feelings. Just how deep, Rowan didn't know, and perhaps he did not either. But Scotia would test the patience of Job and Duncan was the closest they had to that man.

Rowan sighed.

"You like him," Duncan said, sliding toward her on the bench until only the basket of wool separated them.

"You do not?" she asked, sidestepping the answer that seemed all too obvious.

He considered her question for a long moment, then, in his understated way, dipped his head. "He'll do. Do you trust him?"

It was Rowan's turn to ponder the question. The truth was, she did, but she couldn't say exactly why. Did she trust him only because she wanted to? The man affected her like no one she'd ever met before, making her feel cared for, protected, desired even when she had not known she wanted to feel those things.

He made her blood sing with kisses and smiles. He had lifted her from worry and care more than once with something as simple as a smile or a gently teasing remark. And then there was the pleasure of looking upon his fine countenance.

But did she trust him?

"I want to. My instinct is to trust him, but I fear I know too little about him to truly do so. Does that make sense?"

"Aye. I have the same thought. He has done naught to keep me from trusting him, but that in itself makes me wonder if he is trying too hard to win my trust."

Rowan laughed. "So you would rather he create a little mischief in order for you to trust him?" Nicholas and Scotia were returning from the far end of the hall, laughing at something as if they were boon friends. "If he is not careful, Scotia will insure he tests your trust, Duncan."

"She does have that impact on a man, but to my mind he's got his eye set on another."

Rowan almost dropped her spindle but caught it deftly. She kept her head down as Nicholas handed a tankard to Duncan, then slid between Rowan and Scotia, who'd taken a new seat far away from the once more scowling Duncan.

"Nicholas," Scotia said, "did I not tell you he'd be scowling when we returned?" She nodded at Duncan.

"Aye, you did, minx. I suppose I shall have to dance with you next time the opportunity arises."

"That was the wager."

"You wagered I'd not be scowling when you got back?" Duncan said to Nicholas, shaking his head. "Where this one is concerned, it is my most common expression."

Nicholas laughed and Rowan rolled the new thread on her spindle and tucked it into a fold of her arisaid. "'Tis the common expression of everyone where Scotia is concerned, except for her mum."

Scotia stuck her tongue out at Rowan and they all laughed at her childish response.

"You need something to keep you busy," Scotia said to Duncan. "Then you could keep that sour look off your face."

"You keep us all busy enough. This one, too." He jabbed a thumb in Nicholas's direction.

"I have not given you any trouble, have I?" Nicholas asked. "Except that you would have preferred to stay outside in the rain when I wished to come inside."

"Duncan! You would keep our guest out in the rain?" Rowan feigned disappointment in her voice.

"It was not my—"

"He is a hard-hearted man," Scotia said, mocking him, too.

"Och, lasses, do not be too hard on the man. He has been greatly busy making sure I am not trying to bring harm to the clan or the castle, though I am encouraged to harm that damn pile of stone as much as I like."

The three of them were chuckling and giggling at Duncan's spluttering defense of his actions.

"Fine. Yes, I had no care for this rogue who is sure to bring the castle and all of us who live here to our knees. And Scotia is exactly the minx he deems her to be, requiring constant vigilance lest she join forces with the English to conquer the Highlands one man at a time. At least you, Rowan, cause me no suffering."

His comments had Scotia's face red, her ire clear in the icy glare she aimed at him. Nicholas had gone oddly silent, too, so only Rowan was left quietly chuckling.

"That will teach the two of you to poke a quiet bear." As much as she was enjoying the teasing and the company, she had things that needed tending. She tucked the wool basket under the bench and rose, bending to give Duncan a quick kiss on his bristly cheek. "You do a fine job of watching over all of us. I thank you as I know Uncle Kenneth does, too, else he would not give you such arduous chores. Scotia, I am going to get dinner for Auntie Elspet and Jeanette. Shall I bring enough for you, too?"

"Nay. I shall eat here. Perhaps Nicholas will keep me company?"

Nicholas laughed. "You shall have to ask Duncan if that is acceptable."

"At least I can keep an eye on both of you at the same time that way. I suppose 'tis acceptable."

Scotia smiled, transforming herself from childlike to a glowing, beautiful young woman. Rowan was always stunned by that transformation and knew that if Scotia were aware of it, she'd shed the childish behavior and would have even more men at her feet. The poleaxed look on Duncan's face confirmed it. She looked to see if Nicholas was equally enamored, but found him watching her.

"May I help you take the meal up to your aunt's chamber? With Duncan's permission, of course."

She sought out Duncan's gaze, raising her eyebrows, their brief conversation now being tested.

Duncan nodded. "You shall return here directly. Do not make me come looking for you, Nicholas."

Nicholas grinned. "I would not, Duncan. Will Uilliam or the chief give you trouble for it?"

Duncan shook his head. "They trust me."

The implication was clear in Duncan's voice and Rowan wondered if he was giving Nicholas room to prove himself untrustworthy.

# CHAPTER SEVEN

NICHOLAS FORCED HIMSELF TO MOVE MORE SLOWLY THAN HE wished as they gathered Lady Elspet's meal. He was sure Duncan's sudden test—for there was no doubt in Nicholas's mind that this was a test—was in some way Rowan's doing. Was it that because she trusted him, so Duncan did as well? It should not matter why she had convinced Duncan he was trustworthy. He should not care what her motivations were, merely that he was achieving what he had set out to do, but he did care. She was not another in a long line of women to be manipulated, used. She was strong, loyal, and kissed so sweetly.

He clenched his fists hard enough to feel the bite of his nails against his palms. He couldn't care. She could be no more than any other woman to him, a means to an end, no more. He was a fool if he let her mean more than that. And he was no fool.

Rowan quickly assembled a fresh pot of broth and a bit of meat. She handed bowls, spoons, and a small basket of bannocks to Nicholas, then led the way across the sloppy bailey, thick with frigid puddles and sucking mud. Keeping everything as dry as possible in the still heavy rain was a challenge. They stopped just inside the tower while Rowan took off the cloak she had snagged from someone in the kitchen and hung it on a hook near the door.

She turned back to him and his heart almost stopped at the sight of her fresh-faced beauty, so different from the women at Edward's court.

The curve of her cheek and her long lashes, darker now that the rain had wet them, were accentuated by the flickering torchlight. The rain had her hair wilder than usual with the damp. It clung about her face, adding lacy embellishments to her pale skin.

He stepped toward her, only then remembering that his arms were full with dinner. Perhaps he was a fool. He gave her a wry smile.

"We should get this to the Lady while it is still hot."

Rowan swallowed. "Aye. Follow me."

She led him up the turnstile stair, passing a landing on their way. He tried to look down the short corridor as they passed it but could not linger to take stock of what he saw.

At the top floor he followed Rowan into a large room that should have been used as a solar, but there was a large bed on the opposite wall. Lady Elspet slept in the midst of it. She was covered with several blankets and was so frail she looked more like a child than the wife of the chief. Jeanette rose from a stool set near the bed and took the provisions from him.

"Thank you for helping Rowan bring the meal," she said, casting a questioning glance at her cousin. Rowan and Jeanette quietly arranged the food near the hearth. They exchanged a few whispered words that he could not make out, but if the looks that Jeanette kept sending his way were any indication, he was the topic. He smiled at her but she looked away.

As they returned to the door Jeanette said, "Where is Scotia?"

"She was in the great hall when last we saw her, holding court as best she could with the auld men and boys," Rowan said.

"What are we to do with her? She shall get herself in trouble that even we cannot get her out of if she keeps on the way she has."

Nicholas agreed, but did not say so.

"I cannot promise to keep her in line," he said, "but have already offered Duncan my help in keeping an eye on her. He worries, too."

Jeanette looked to Rowan for a decision.

"Duncan has always had a soft spot for Scotia, ever since she was a bairn, but he cannot keep an eye on her all the time any more than the rest of us can," Rowan said. "Thank you. With Auntie so ill, we are all distracted from our usual tasks."

"Like minding your cousin." He shook his head. "I do not think she appreciates how much you all watch over her."

"'Appreciate' would not be the right word," Jeanette said with a rueful smile. "Detest? Hate? What do you think, Ro?"

"'Hate' seems right, but she tolerates Duncan and she might well welcome braw Nicholas's attention." Rowan was teasing him again and he felt a pull between them that was not overtly sexual, but was compelling nonetheless.

"I'll watch my step, and hers."

Jeanette placed an oddly calming hand on his forearm. "You are a good man, Nicholas of Achnamara." She smiled at him. "I think 'twas a good wind that brought you to Dunlairig."

Nicholas swallowed. She would not think so when he had finished his task.

AS THEY REACHED THE BOTTOM OF THE STAIR, ROWAN REACHED for her cloak at the same moment Nicholas did, startling at the touch of his hand upon hers.

"Let me," he said, plucking the heavy wool cloak from the hook and settling it on her shoulders with a flourish. He reached for the ties and tugged her close with them. The heat of his hands resting under her chin reminded her of when she was a child and Elspet would tie her cloak for her.

"She is as much your mother as theirs, is she not?" he asked, his head ducked so he could catch her eye.

"Aye. She has been my mother longer than my real mum was." She allowed herself to rest her chin against his hands, stopping just short of rubbing against them like a cat.

"You lost both your parents at the same time?"

"I did. I do not remember much about that, though. I am told Kenneth found me wandering in the woods near our cottage and brought me here, but I do not remember any of that." And no one had ever explained what had happened, not specifically, and she had only asked once. "I am told 'twas an accident and I was spared."

He let his thumb run along her jaw and she could tell he watched the movement. "You were so young, it must have been hard to come here all alone."

"You were young when you left your home, too. You ken how hard that is."

"Aye," he smiled but it was wistful and he looked as if he was seeing something other than Rowan, as if he looked back at that time. "'Twas the hardest thing I had ever done."

"Exactly, but everyone here was very kind to me. Elspet and Jeanette especially, but it was Uncle Kenneth who tamed me."

"Tamed you? I cannot imagine such a need."

She laughed a little at the memory and he smiled so wide the creases in his cheeks showed deep. She reached up and ran a finger along one of them and he closed his eyes and leaned into her touch. A thrill ran through her. Here was a strong man who gentled to her touch like the mousers that lived in the stable. It was not something she could have imagined, nor the feeling of power that accompanied his reaction.

His hands still held the ties of her cloak and with them, he pulled her gently closer, until she was so close she could lean slightly and rest against his chest, which she did, letting the strength and heat and scent of him surround her. All thoughts left her mind as he leaned down, kissing her as he'd done before, gently, as if asking for permission. She closed her eyes and sighed, and he took advantage, sweeping his tongue into her mouth. Instinct took over as she followed where he led down a sensuous path filled with the heat of his body, so close to hers, the taste of him, and that earthy scent that now spoke to her only of him.

An unfamiliar need raced through her and that same restlessness that had followed her out of her dream of him had her wanting more even as he gentled the kiss. He nibbled on her lips for a moment, then leaned his forehead against hers. As soon as his lips left hers, she became aware of the rapid beat of her heart and a sense of having been taken out of her body, then dropped back in, a different person than when she had started.

"I am sorry, Rowan." His voice was raspy. "I should not have done that, but I could not keep myself from it." He ran his thumb over her bottom lip and she couldn't stop herself from following its path with the tip of her tongue.

Her mind was racing. He was not the first man who had stolen a kiss from her, but never had she experienced a kiss that shook her so. She could not manage to speak, nor did she move. Why didn't he move if he was sorry for kissing her? And it was then that she realized she had a firm grip on both of his arms. She took a deep breath and released him, stepping back until there was more space between them than she wanted.

"I am not sorry," she said. She looked at the floor between them for a long moment. "I have been hoping you would do that again."

She glanced up to see his reaction to her confession, only to find him grinning like a fool.

"You were, huh?"

She nodded quickly and knew her pale complexion was giving away her embarrassment. He stepped close again but didn't touch her this time.

"So you might let me do that again?" he asked, the grin still on his face, but a more sober hopeful look in his eyes.

"Aye."

He touched her cheek, running a finger down it as she had done to him, leaving a trail of sensation in its wake she would not soon forget.

"I would like that very much." Her voice was breathless even to her own ears.

"As would I," he said as he brushed her lips with his own one more time, lightly. "But I fear we must return to the hall before Duncan sends a search party after us." He sighed and quickly tied her cloak, his knuckles sending ripples of joy against her skin. A smile played about his lips, lips that had been so soft against hers, lips that had roused such heat deep within her. And that damned restlessness.

"We should get back," she said, looking deeply into his dark-brown eyes. Neither moved for a long moment, awareness crackling between them, until they both sighed and headed back into the rainy bailey.

THE NEXT MORNING, JUST AFTER SUNRISE, NICHOLAS SAT ON THE damp rubble amidst muddy puddles left from yesterday's downpour. He hadn't slept much, tossing and turning the night away. When he did sleep he dreamed of Rowan, of her soft skin and silky hair. In his dreams he kissed her, laughed with her, made love to her. In his dreams he betrayed her, and King Edward killed her and all the good people of the castle. In his dreams what started with kisses and passion ended in rivers of blood.

He thrust his fingers into his hair, scraping it back savagely from his face, and turned his thoughts away from his fractured dreams to the cause of them. Today the sun shone and Duncan had loosened his leash enough to give Nicholas a sense of freedom, though he knew it was only a pretense. He could see neither Duncan nor Uilliam but he'd wager a king's ransom he was still being watched.

He'd finally gotten a look inside the tower last night. He'd spent much of the night, when he wasn't dreaming, going over everything he'd seen, making sure he had a map of it firmly etched into his brain, for he had to return there, had to find that pouch that Lady Elspet had at the blessing. It might not be the Highland Targe, unless his prize was not an actual shield. He wouldn't know until he got a good look at it.

This would be a good time for Archie to return, offering some distraction, and cover as a new stranger in their midst, to be watched, but the man wasn't here, at least not inside the castle.

A commotion at the stable drew his attention away from his musings and the unexpectedly strong kick of his conscience over the consequences of completing his mission. A lad Nicholas had not met led a shaggy, saddled Highland pony to the tower door. The stable-boy stood there, talking to the pony and scratching its forehead for long moments until finally the door opened. Scotia led the way. Next came Jeanette with Lady Elspet. Her great frailness gave harsh evidence of her ill health. Pale Jeanette held her mother, one arm wrapped around the woman's waist, the other cupping her elbow, as if Lady Elspet would shatter should she so much as stumble.

Just as he began to wonder where Rowan was, she came out of the tower. She looked tired, or maybe it was concern that laid the shadows under her eyes. She whispered something to Jeanette and Lady Elspet. Jeanette looked at her mother, but the Lady shook her head and nodded at the pony. Rowan squared her shoulders, her eyes snapped with anger but her chin quivered—perhaps with sadness, or perhaps with pique, he could not tell, but it made him want to pull her into his arms and kiss away whatever bothered her. The passion that had started with their kiss in the tower and then built in his dreams slammed into him and he fought the need go to her and kindle that fire again. His body rebelled, but this wasn't the time.

There might never be a time.

He was surprised by a deep sadness that threatened to swamp him at that realization. There might never be a time, and it would be his fault, his responsibility, his treachery that made that true.

As he watched the women clearly preparing for an outing, he pushed away the distracting feelings seeing Rowan raised in him and focused on what the other women were doing.

He could not fathom where Lady Elspet would be going in her state of illness. She had clearly been overwhelmed from performing the blessing and had not left her solar since. He leaped off his rocky perch and strode over to the women, carefully *not* looking at Rowan lest his desire outwit his need for information.

As he arrived, the stable lad set a step next to the pony, and Jeanette and Scotia helped Lady Elspet to mount. Her cloak snagged on the back of the saddle long enough to reveal a quick glimpse of the ermine sack. Black-tipped white tails that hung from the mouth of the pouch flashed in the bright sunlight, a detail he had not noticed at the blessing. Jeanette quickly arranged the cloak around her mother, tucking it about her legs. Whether she did so to keep her mother warm or to keep him from getting a closer look at the pouch, he couldn't say, but she accomplished both.

"Off so early in the morn?" he asked.

"We are off to visit Mum's cousin," Jeanette said, but she didn't look him in the eye and Rowan busied herself with the plaid she carried, shaking it out before she and Jeanette settled it around Elspet. The three young women positioned themselves protectively around the Lady's mount and moved slowly toward the gate.

The urge to reach out and touch Rowan's hand, to hear her voice again, confounded him. He was no lovesick boy, but a man well used to the wooing of women without the trouble that came with having true feelings for them. But he could not shake the desire that threaded through every thought he had, every dream he'd had of Rowan.

Against his better judgment, he stepped forward to follow the women just as Rowan glanced back over her shoulder at him, her auburn brows drawn down into a deep vee over her pale leaf-green eyes. She shook her head slightly, but the message was clear. Where they went, he was not to follow.

Nicholas stood in the middle of the bailey, frustration drumming through him as the women and the ermine pouch headed through the gate. He took a step to follow them, then stopped, taking a deep breath to calm his thoughts. He could not act without a plan no matter how torn he was between the itch to follow them and perhaps get his hands on that pouch, and the need to invest in Duncan's trust by staying put.

He looked once more at the gate, then at the tower, then back at the gate. The urge to follow was strong, but the women were moving slowly and would not be hard to track if he could find a way to leave the castle without causing himself trouble. He turned away from the gate, his mind quickly running through ideas and just as quickly discarding them as unworkable.

He was moving toward the steps to the rampart, thinking at least to determine which direction the women were going, when the tower door opened and a buxom brown-haired woman of indeterminate age stepped into his path lugging a heavy bucket of ashes. Not one to miss an opportunity to ingratiate himself to someone who might have information he needed, he postponed his trip to the wall and gave her his most winning smile.

"May I help you with that, mistress . . .?" He lifted the bucket from her hand before she could decide.

"Helen," she said, deep dimples appearing in her round cheeks. "You would be the new man working with Uilliam and Duncan."

"I am. Nicholas of Achnamara, at your service." He carefully did not accompany the familiar words with the equally familiar flamboyant court bow. "Where shall I take this for you?"

"Over this way," she said, leading him around the corner of the tower and to the ashbin.

He flirted with her as he dumped the dusty ashes on the pile, handed her the bucket back and watched the sway of her hips as she returned to the tower. He mulled over how he might use Helen to gain legitimate access to the tower.

"You need not leer at the lass, cub."

Nicholas wasn't really surprised to find Uilliam leaning against the base of the curtain wall not far away and was very glad he'd followed his instincts to help Helen, rather than to watch the women leave from the ramparts. It would not do to give away his interest in what they were about this day.

"I do not think the lass minds me watching her walk away," he said, raising his eyebrows in a teasing challenge, but Uilliam said nothing. Nicholas looked back in Helen's direction as she disappeared through the tower door, then back at Uilliam, whose attention was as riveted to the lass's hips as Nicholas's had been. Interesting . . .

An idea, oft used and nearly always successful in one way or another, presented itself, wrapped up like a present in the guise of Helen. Perhaps, if he played this right, there was a way to follow Rowan and the other women.

"Is there something you need of me?" Nicholas asked as he moved toward Uilliam.

"Nay," the bear said, not taking his eyes off of where Helen had gone.

"Duncan said 'twas too muddy to move more of the wall today," Nicholas said. "Is there aught else for me to do?"

"Nay, not for you."

Nicholas nodded, letting the silence spin out between them as they both kept watch on the tower door.

"Are you here to keep an eye on me in Duncan's stead then?" Nicholas asked.

Uilliam grunted in answer. Perhaps Uilliam or Kenneth hadn't been pleased with Duncan's decision to allow him to accompany Rowan to the tower last night.

Nicholas leaned his back against the cool stone wall next to Uilliam. He cast his gaze out over the bailey, watching as the castle came to life and people wandered toward the great hall to break their fast. Nicholas waited for the other man to relax, just slightly, before he spoke again.

"Do you have a problem with me helping Helen?"

Uilliam glared over at him. "Should I?"

Nicholas worked hard to keep from smiling. "If I fancied the lass, you should."

"She would not go for the likes of a wandering Sassenach."

"Really? Not even a braw Sassenach like me?"

"Definitely not." Uilliam said. "And do not try to change her mind, either."

"So you have no issue with me helping her, only with me helping myself to her?"

A low growl rumbled through the man, not unlike the sound of the bear he so resembled. Nicholas held up his hands as if surrendering his position. "She is a bonny, happy lass, Uilliam, but my eye goes more for tall, auburn-haired lasses."

Uilliam stared at him for a long moment as if gauging the truth of Nicholas's words.

"Which reminds me," Nicholas added, pushing away from the wall, "do you ken where Rowan has gone?"

Uilliam shook his head, but Nicholas didn't think it was in answer to his question.

"Duncan says you have already caught her eye." He glared down at Nicholas. "Hurt her in any way and I guarantee you shall regret it."

Nicholas's conscience kicked him but he ignored it. A conscience had no place in a spy's life.

"I have no intention of hurting her." It was the truth, though some things were out of his control—like the passion that flared every time they kissed, or the reason he was here in the first place.

"Kenneth cares little what your good intentions are. Actions are what he is looking at. Do not let the chief down by dallying with his niece."

Nicholas nodded. Oddly he did not want to promise this man something he could not. "So you do not ken where the lasses and Lady Elspet have gone this morning?"

"Lady Elspet has left the castle?" He pushed off the wall, rounding on Nicholas.

"Aye, with her daughters and Rowan. They said they were off to visit a cousin but I thought it very odd, given how frail the Lady seems."

Uilliam's shaggy brows drew so low his eyes disappeared. "'Tis not your place to question Elspet. If the lasses are with her, she will be fine. Jeanette would not let her go anywhere if she thought 'twould harm her."

Nicholas thought Uilliam underestimated his Lady's will, but it was not his place to tell him so. Time to divert the man's attention again. "Well, since I have naught else to do this day, perhaps I shall see if Helen needs more help. 'Twill keep me out of trouble, aye?"

"Stay away from Helen, mon."

"I only mean to help the lass."

"She shall do fine without it."

"I do not know. If I cannot find Rowan," he grinned, "perhaps I shall have to see if I can woo Helen's attentions away from—"

"Rowan is gone from the castle. If your interest is so easily turned to another lass you should stay clear of her."

Nicholas laughed at the man's blustering. "I am but teasing you, Uilliam."

He humphed, crossing his massive arms over his barrel chest. "Rowan is bound to be gone most of the day, but 'tis sure I am that she shall be back in time for you to test your smile upon her at the evening meal."

Nicholas grinned. "So you think she has not gone far, then. Perhaps I could catch up with her?"

"You probably could, but clearly you were not invited, so do not go where you are not wanted."

"Are you saying the lass does not want me?"

"Aye, 'tis exactly what I'm saying."

"I cannot believe it." He feigned disbelief for he knew otherwise.

"Rowan has no interest in you, nor does any other lass here, even if you see behavior to the contrary. They only want you to feel welcome, 'tis all."

Nicholas decided to stop tormenting the man. Perhaps he was ready to be rid of the annoying Nicholas now.

"Is the fishing any good in the loch?"

"Aye."

"Unless there is aught I can do here for you . . . or Helen . . ." He slanted a sly look at Uilliam. "Would you give me leave to try my hand at it?"

Helen came out of the tower door again and came toward them, another bucket of ashes in her hand. She smiled at Nicholas as if she was a knowing party to his plan and he made sure Uilliam saw him grin at her.

"Go fishing, lad."

Nicholas forced himself to appear torn between staying and going. "I do not know. Is there gear I can borrow?"

"You can *have* mine if you will but leave me be."

"Fair trade."

"Hmph."

Nicholas followed Uilliam to the hut near the damaged wall site where he had sheltered from the rain yesterday. He stood outside making a point to keep Helen in his sight just to poke the man a bit more to insure he wanted Nicholas gone from the castle.

"You need not watch Helen so intently," Uilliam growled as he shoved a fishing pole and a basket into Nicholas's hands. He gave Nicholas a mighty shove toward the gate. "Walk a mile along the lochside that way"—he pointed straight through the castle gate—"and you'll find a pile of boulders reaching out into the water. 'Tis a good place to spend a long day."

Nicholas clapped Uilliam on the back and did as he was bade before the man realized he had sent him without Duncan as chaperone. He quickly covered the distance from the gate to the loch, then continued until he found the place Uilliam had recommended. He checked to make sure he was not followed by anyone, then found a downed log to hide the fishing gear behind. He grinned to himself. Uilliam had given him the perfect alibi for slipping away for the whole day.

# CHAPTER EIGHT

IT DID NOT TAKE MUCH WORK TO FIND THE PONY'S TRACKS ON THE path that skirted the edge of the woods, though Nicholas took care to keep within the shadowy verge and out of sight of any who might be watching from the castle wall. Once the trail turned up the ben it was harder to see the tracks on the rocky ground but he could not shake the sense that he was surely following the women.

It was a silly notion, but he followed the instinct nonetheless and every so often he'd catch sight of a pony track, or the less distinctive print of a soft leather brogue that assured him he was indeed on the trail of the MacAlpin women.

He began to relax and enjoy the sounds of the birds around him, the distant rough calls of at least three carrion crows, the nearer warble of some small bird high in the treetops. A red squirrel scolded behind him on the trail, drawing his attention. Red squirrels were the clarion of a forest, alerting all and sundry when something was amiss in their territory, yet none had fussed with the women's passing, not too far ahead of Nicholas's position, nor at Nicholas's passing, so why now?

He erred on the side of caution and slipped off the trail into the dense undergrowth, crouching low in the deep shadow of a large bush. Moments later a hooded man came up the trail and stopped just where Nicholas had stepped into the wood. He looked left, then right. He studied the ground for a moment, then stepped into the woods. Nicholas struggled not to grind his teeth, not wanting to give himself away with any sound.

After a long moment the man dropped the hood of his cloak back on his shoulders, revealing close-cropped hair the color of dull copper. Archie.

"I know you are here, Nicholas. Show yourself."

Nicholas rose slowly, grinning. "I am off my game if you found me so easily."

"I know all your tricks." Archie grinned back at him. "How fares Nicholas of Achnamara? Have you found the prize yet?"

Had he? Nicholas knew he should report the possibility that the sack Lady Elspet carried might be important to them, but the bloody echoes of his dream and the unexpected feelings for Rowan kept him silent. "I have found nothing of worth yet."

Archie watched him, the grin replaced with a scowl. "Time grows short. I have sent word to the king where we are, and that the castle wall is breached. He will be expecting the successful completion of our mission soon."

"It has only been a sennight. I am being watched carefully."

Archie's face blanched. "I saw no one following you."

"Not at this moment, but this is the first time I have been unsupervised since the wall fell."

"And how exactly did rescuing those wenches help our cause? We had a plan, yet you acted rashly, suddenly. It was not what we had agreed to."

Even though what Archie said was true, Nicholas found his ire rising. "I could not watch Rowan and Scotia be crushed when it could be helped."

"Rowan and Scotia? You speak of them as if they are friends already."

"Nay, not friends, but useful." He told Archie who they were and how his deed had gotten him the grant of hospitality, even if it was cautious hospitality.

Archie nodded his head slowly, but his face didn't agree.

"Which one have you tupped so far?"

Nicholas once more worked to keep from gritting his teeth. It was not as if they hadn't both used such methods many times in the past to get information or access to someplace they couldn't otherwise get to. Many a mission had been won thanks to pillow talk. But the idea of using Rowan so . . . it did not sit well. There was something about that woman that awoke his long-dormant conscience, but Archie need not know of Nicholas's sudden weakness where Rowan was concerned.

"I have not singled one out as of yet, and as I said, I have been kept on a short leash until not an hour past."

Archie nodded again. "And where were you headed, now that you have been released?"

There was something in his voice that set alarms off in Nicholas's gut. Surely Archie had seen the women heading up the mountain. It was almost as if he was fishing for a lie. The unexpected anger that had been simmering cooled abruptly as suspicion replaced it. Nicholas didn't know what had changed with Archie but he must keep his wits about him until he could figure it out, for they had learned their trade together and no one could read Nicholas better than this man.

"I was following the Lady of the castle and her daughters up the mountain. It seemed odd that they would leave when the Lady is ill," and without a proper escort, nor even the knowledge of Uilliam that she had left the castle, he thought but did not say. "So I thought to discover what they were about. Plus, it seemed a good opportunity to rendezvous with you, if you were back." That last hadn't even crossed his mind, though he knew it should have been a priority.

"Well, this is done. Let's find the women and see what they are up to," Archie said, the tiniest hint of a challenge in his attitude.

Nicholas quickly sorted through his options and found he had none. "Aye, let's, but you must not be seen. I can explain away my following them, especially if I take no pains to keep my presence secret from them, but it would be suspicious if I showed up with you."

"Fine. For now I'll keep out of sight, but I'll not spend the rest of this mission huddled in this God-forsaken wood." He rubbed his hands together in a familiar gesture of excitement. "Let us hope the wenches lead us to this Highland Targe and we can be away with the prize this very day."

An odd hollowness opened up in Nicholas's chest at the thought of leaving Dunlairig and Rowan, but the prize was what he was after. The Highland Targe was the goal, and if he had to sever the unexpected feelings roused by Rowan, then that was what he would do. As soon as he must.

ROWAN STOPPED TO LET THE OTHERS CATCH UP. THE TRAIL HAD grown narrow and she knew from many treks to the sacred well-spring that they would soon reach their destination.

"Pray, slow down," Jeanette said as she caught up with Rowan. She held the reins in her hand, the pony, with Elspet atop, following her carefully up the rocky path. Scotia drew up the rear. Jeanette pulled the stopper out of her water skin and took a long drink, then offered it to Rowan.

"Nay, I just want to get there." And back to the castle.

This trip was ill advised. At least, if anyone asked, Nicholas could tell when they had left, and the guard could say what direction they had traveled.

"The wellspring is not going anywhere, Rowan." They were not the first words Elspet had spoken with an edge of irritation. Jeanette handed her mother the water skin, but she refused.

"I ken that, Auntie—" A red squirrel crying warning down the slope stopped Rowan. She placed a finger to her lips and motioned Jeanette to take the others up the path and hide. When they were out of sight, Rowan stepped off the path, melting into the riot of spring growth, and waited, the squirrel still scolding whatever had invaded its bit of forest. Before she'd even calmed her breath, her thoughts flew to a certain dark-eyed man who increasingly occupied both her waking and her sleeping thoughts.

Had he followed them when she'd made it clear he should not? She could not decide if she thought that possibility a good thing or bad, but she found it comforting either way, just as she'd found his presence in the bailey this morning both arousing and comforting. The urge to make her way down the ben to see if it was him was strong, though she knew it unlikely. She forced herself to breathe slowly, and to stay as still as a rock. Another few minutes and nothing had changed except the squirrel lost interest in whatever had set it off. No one had come up the path behind them.

Not Nicholas. Disappointment settled over her.

Saints and angels! If she had not let him comfort her last night, had not kissed him . . . again . . . had not dreamed about him . . . thoughts of him would not be plaguing her. She listened for another long moment, then stepped back on the path and hurried up the ben.

"Well?" Jeanette asked, falling back to walk beside Rowan as they followed the others up the path.

"No one was there. I am just a wee bit skittish, I suppose."

Rowan let Scotia lead the pony a ways ahead as she took another look down the trail they had climbed. The wellspring was no secret so there was no reason she should feel so jumpy today except for Elspet's ill health. 'Twas surely her imagination conjuring up the idea that someone followed them.

"Rowan? What is it?" Jeanette's voice was quiet, nearly a whisper, yet it still startled her from her thoughts.

"Nothing. I am being daft. We are almost there." She reached for her cousin's hand and squeezed it for a moment. "Perhaps, finally, you will be chosen as Guardian."

Jeanette gripped Rowan's hand as if she meant to hold Rowan there. "Mum wishes you to join us this time."

"Why?"

"She would not say, but she was adamant that you be with us at the wellspring. It is not as if you have not been here before."

Rowan had ventured into the beautiful grotto that cradled the wellspring a few times when she had first come to live at Dunlairig Castle but it had quickly become her habit to keep watch. She had not ventured near it since . . .

Another long-buried memory whispered to life, but this one came to her as clear as the water that flowed out of the mountain, and as fast.

She had not ventured near it since she had experienced the same odd sensation she had felt at the blessing. It had not been as strong long ago but the pressure, the sense of something trying to escape through her, *that* had been exactly the same. Gooseflesh raced over her skin.

"Nay," she said, shaking her head. "I will stay with the pony. I shall keep watch, in case we were followed. I would not have anyone disturb Auntie at the wellspring."

"But she wants you there," Jeanette said.

"Nay," Rowan repeated, hating the sweat that was popping out between her shoulder blades and at her forehead. "I cannot."

Jeanette looked at her oddly. "It is not like you to deny Mum."

Rowan could not look her cousin in the eye. "I cannot," she repeated. "I am sorry but 'tis impossible."

Jeanette sighed and hurried ahead to where Scotia was helping their mother down from the pony. She talked quietly to Elspet as they moved along an almost invisible track that led around the side of an outcropping to the hidden wellspring. Elspet started to argue, but Jeanette shook her head. Elspet glanced over her shoulder at Rowan and Rowan couldn't decide if she saw disappointment there or anger, but she could not bear any of it. She grabbed the pony's reins and pulled him back toward the main path where there was a little moss for him to browse on.

She stood by the pony, fretting at her cowardice, but she could not make herself follow the others into that grotto. She could only pray that the ritual her aunt performed this day would finally transfer the mantle of Guardian of the Highland Targe from Aunt Elspet to Jeanette, or even Scotia, though she did not believe Scotia was capable of taking on such responsibility. Maybe someday, but not yet.

The urge to move away from the beautiful grotto, with the slice of pure water flowing out of a crack in the mountainside, had her pacing away from the pony and around the face of the outcropping, but then she would turn, pacing back to her place by the pony, over and over again, drawn back toward the wellspring in spite of herself.

She remembered the first time she had gone there and watched Elspet kneel next to the pool of water fed by the spring. There was a large flat rock that stretched over the pool a little ways, and there she opened the ermine sack, spreading it out flat, laying it leather-side up to display the three faint drawings there. She had placed the Targe stone in the center upon a circle filled with swirls and then she began a series of chanting prayers in that same language of the blessing.

Rowan had not known at the time that each Guardian repeated this ritual in her daughters' presence until one of the younger women was chosen and the . . . power, for Rowan could not think of another way to describe it . . . passed to the new Guardian of the Targe.

She clenched her fists and paced away from the pony again. This would very likely be Elspet's last trek to the sacred wellspring. Rowan swallowed down the grief that threatened. Jeanette *must* be chosen today. Given the times, the political upheaval in Scotland in recent years, and the constant threat of the English king, it was no time to be without a Guardian and no one seemed to know what would happen should Elspet die before the next was chosen.

A chill ran through her at the thought, sending her back in the direction of the pony, and the grotto.

Jeanette must be chosen *today*.

A tuneless whistling threaded through the trees, stopping Rowan in her tracks. Someone *had* followed them up the ben and she had not a single moment's doubt who the whistler was, though she could not say if that knowledge was based upon hope or something more tangible.

She looked toward the pony, but there was no sign that her kinswomen were returning to him. She stood for a moment, trying to decide what to do, as the whistling grew closer. The only thing that was clear in her mind was that she could not let anyone disturb the ritual, not even herself, so she started down the trail to head off Nicholas of Achnamara before he came close enough to do just that.

NICHOLAS KNEW ROWAN MOVED DOWN THE PATH TOWARD HIM BEfore he could even see her, as if they were connected somehow. He grinned at his own foolishness. Who else would it be but Rowan?

Not Jeanette, who wouldn't leave her mother's side. Not Scotia, who would crash through the woods without a thought to anyone else. Only Rowan would come down the ben almost silently, keeping watch over her family, keeping anyone who might bring harm— keeping him—as far away from her aunt as possible.

He rounded a bend in the path and stopped, his breath taken away by the woman who slowed as she spied him. The sun glinted in her hair, casting bright copper lights through the riot of curls pulled loosely back to frame her face and the irritation that gathered in the furrow of her brow.

"I kent it was you who followed us." She closed the distance between them, stopping just far enough away that he couldn't reach out and touch her.

She was a canny lass, for the one thought in his mind now was to take her into his arms and kiss her again. But he wouldn't— couldn't—lest he reveal his growing feelings for this woman to the watching Archie.

"I thought I made it plain you should not follow us," she said, hands on her hips. "Why do you spy upon us?"

For a moment he thought she had found him out, but it was not possible. "Spy, Rowan? Nay. I did not ken you had gone this way."

"Then why are you here?"

She looked tired, worried, and he wished he dared drag her into his arms and comfort her, take the worry from her. He stepped a little closer, not wanting Archie to overhear whatever passed between them.

"Well, let us see." He grinned, hoping to coax a smile from her. "There was no work to be done on the wall today and Uilliam had naught else for me to do so I went fishing, but nothing was biting, so I decided to do a bit of exploring and this trail seemed well traveled so I took it." He made a show of looking about him at the fresh springtime greenness of the forest, once more taking it all in. "'Tis a beautiful place to walk," he said, his voice unintentionally quiet and reverent, as if they stood in Westminster Abbey itself, instead of a wild wood in Scotland, "and a beautiful day to do so, do you not think?"

Rowan smiled a little, and nodded. "This is one of my favorite places," she said, her voice as quiet as his as she lifted her face to the sun filtering through the leaves and closed her eyes. They stood there silently, Rowan basking in the sunlight and Nicholas basking in her company. She sighed and opened her eyes.

"There is little more to the trail"—she waved a hand generally in the direction behind her where he knew something must be going on with Elspet and her cousins—"so you might as well turn round." The softness of a minute ago was gone. She crossed her arms and stood in the middle of the path, blocking the way.

"Where are your aunt and cousins? I thought you were off to visit someone yet this does not look a likely place for anyone to bide in."

"'Tis none of your concern what we are about. Turn round and go back to the castle."

He let her think he was considering her command for a moment, but in truth he wasn't prepared to give up on his quest. "Your aunt looked so frail when I saw her this morning. Is she even well enough to make this trek?"

She pursed her lips and glared at him. "My aunt's health is none of your concern."

Given the stubborn lift of her chin, this might not have been the right tack but his instinct wouldn't let him abandon it. Not yet. "True enough," he said, taking a half step back. "She is no kin to me."

"So why do you care?" The question popped out of her mouth with such force she looked surprised by it.

"Curiosity." He stepped closer to her, close enough that his chest nearly touched her still crossed arms. "She is important to you and your clan and I find myself concerned with what concerns you." It took every ounce of self-control not to reach out and smooth the crease between her brows with his thumb, to run his fingers over skin he knew was soft and smooth. She took an unsteady breath and looked up, and he found himself caught in her gaze.

"So you followed us up the ben?" she whispered.

He nodded slowly, captivated by the darker flecks of green in her eyes he had not noticed before.

"So you *were* spying upon us, aye?" Her voice was sharp, knocking Nicholas out of his reverie. Now she was the one to step back, distancing herself again.

"Nay, I was not." He was nine kinds of a fool for letting the tricky wench lull him into letting his guard down. "I was curious about where you were bound, aye. I was troubled that you took no men with you to keep you safe. I thought it odd that Lady Elspet was going anywhere at all." He took a chance and moved close enough so he could reach out and push a wayward lock of hair away from her face. "And I wanted to see you."

Her expression softened. The truth in his words must have rung through.

"Rowan?" Jeanette's worried voice sliced through the quiet that surrounded them.

"I am here!" she called back. "We have a"—she looked back at Nicholas—"a visitor."

There was silence from above.

She turned back to him and lowered her voice almost to a whisper even though it was doubtful the other women, or even Archie lurking somewhere close by, could hear them at less than a shout. "You shall not speak a word of what has passed between us, aye? They have enough worries without wondering what is happening between . . ." She looked up at him and he could see that she was as confused by the attraction they shared as he was.

"You have my word," he said. "I have no intention of discomfiting Lady Elspet, or any of you."

"Good. Stay here while I tell them you are here and explain why," she said. "Please," she added, clearly afraid he would follow her again.

"As you wish." He hooked his thumbs in his belt and looked at her expectantly. "Go on. I promise I will not leave this spot without your consent."

She arched an eyebrow at him. He flashed a grin at her and was gratified to see a smile light up her face.

Nicholas didn't wait long before Rowan called out for him to follow her. He glanced into the woods where he knew Archie hid, but could not see the man. Perhaps now he'd find out at least what the women had been up to. If he could manage it, he might get a closer look at Elspet's ermine sack and its contents.

When he arrived at the top of the ben he found Jeanette and Scotia scowling at him. A very pale Lady Elspet sat with her back against a rocky outcrop and her eyes closed.

"I do not ken why you followed us," Jeanette said to him, "but Rowan claims it was out of simple curiosity." She looked from him to Rowan. When Rowan nodded, Jeanette turned back to him. "Whatever your reason, it turns out to be a boon. Will you help us get Mum back to the castle, sir? I am very afraid our adventure has been more than she has the strength for."

"Aye, I will," he said, happy that his very real concern, if not his motivation for following them, would lend credence to his being here.

"Can we trust him?" Scotia asked, standing between him and her mother like a bear protecting her cub, her demeanor at odds with the flirtatious girl he had come to expect.

"I believe we can," Rowan said, holding his glance in hers. A mad wish to prove he merited such trust gripped him, though he knew he never would.

Scotia glanced at her cousin, then back at Nicholas before she reluctantly nodded.

"If you will lead the pony," Jeanette said to Nicholas, "Scotia can ride behind to help Mum stay in the saddle, and we"—she nodded toward Rowan—"can brace her on either side."

"Of course."

Rowan whistled and the pony stepped out of a tiny side trail onto the bigger path.

As Jeanette helped her mother to her feet, Nicholas moved around the still skeptical Scotia.

"Lady Elspet," he said quietly to the woman who looked almost transparent. "May I help you onto the pony?"

Elspet nodded and Nicholas quickly settled her into the saddle. Scotia clambered up behind her mother and wrapped her arms around her. "You can lean back against me, Mum," she said. "Rest and I shall make sure you do not fall." Scotia's mouth was set in a line that trembled but everything else about her screamed determination. He would not have expected such from the flighty lass. An odd sort of pride in her actions settled over him.

Nicholas did not want to feel any softness for these women, but he could not help it. They were all so strong in the face of such impending loss. Even Scotia, who was clearly the spoiled babe of the family, fought hard to do what needed doing for her mother's sake, and for the sister and cousin she clearly depended upon. Elspet did not complain, though she was barely able to keep her seat upon the solid little pony. These women had more dignity in this harsh moment than anyone at Edward's court.

"Lead the way, Nicholas of Achnamara." Rowan motioned toward the trail. "We need to get my aunt home to her bed as quickly as we can."

Their eyes locked and the image of Rowan draped across his bed suddenly filled his mind just as Rowan's face betrayed some similar line of thought, going softly pink.

Jeanette looked from one to the other and shook her head. "Lead on, Nicholas."

With immense effort he looked away from Rowan and began the trek back down the ben, the pony's reins in his hand. Loneliness flooded into him, filling all the hollows in his heart and in his battered soul. He had a feeling the loneliness had been there a long time, but he hadn't noticed it until it had, however temporarily, been replaced with a sense of . . . He could not name the feeling he had when Rowan looked at him, when he touched her, but it was unsettling and welcome all at the same time. He knew he should not pursue the woman or the feeling. He knew he could not let what had begun between them go any further if he ever hoped to leave here as anything more than a broken man.

# CHAPTER NINE

FOLLOWING NICHOLAS DOWN THE BEN WAS A MISTAKE. HE WAS leading the horse at a steady pace, not too fast, but not wasting time, either. But that was not the problem. Rowan put a hand to her belly, below her navel, where heat swirled, urging her forward, toward him, toward the strong hands and gentle kisses that kept her body singing like a tightly strung harp.

Rowan tried to focus on the horse, on her cousin's bare foot that hung behind Elspet's foot, shod in her favorite soft leather slippers. She tried to focus on the almost rhythmic gate of the pony as it picked its way down the rough track. She tried to focus on the feel of the fresh spring air as it rushed up the ben rustling the burgeoning leaves—and Nicholas's plaid.

She tried and she failed. She could not help but watch the sway of Nicholas's plaid as he strode down the mountain in front of her and the way the wind made it flap and swirl about his legs. The curve of his calf was just as muscular as other men's, but so much paler, as if he kept indoors or always wore trews. And yet, despite his unseemly pallor she could not help but raise her eyes to his broad shoulders, nor help but enjoy the way his dark curly hair bounced with each long stride down the mountain.

His presence calmed her fears as nothing else had done today, even with the suspicion she'd been forced to consider when she first saw him striding up the path. Jeanette had said it last night. He was a good man, a man she could trust, a man she could . . .

This would not do. She had no interest in a flirtation with a man who was only passing through, no matter how much his kisses awakened every fiber of her body. She dared not let Nicholas of Achnamara distract her from her duties, as Scotia always let the lads do.

The wind rustled his plaid again, drawing her attention in spite of her best intentions. She forced herself to watch her own feet until the path narrowed between large boulders. Rowan was grateful that she and Jeanette had to fall back from beside the pony, putting the whole animal between her and the man she was trying to ignore. At least she was grateful until she realized she could feel her cousin's eyes on her. She dared not meet Jeanette's gaze.

"Do you not have something to tell me, cousin?" Jeanette asked, a true smile evident in her voice for the first time in a long time.

"Nay. Do you have aught to tell me?"

The smile left Jeanette's face. "Nay. I am still not chosen and neither is Scotia."

Rowan wrapped an arm around her cousin's shoulders. "Perhaps that is good. Perhaps that means Auntie will get better, that there is no need to pass the Guardianship along to one of you yet." But neither of them believed that. They walked in silence for a few minutes until Jeanette caught Rowan looking around the pony.

"You cannot seem to keep your eyes off a certain comely man."

"Wheesht!" Rowan shook her head. "You need not speak so loudly, Jeanette."

"I but whispered, Ro. Tell me what is going on between you and"—she nodded toward the pony and the man who walked in front of it—"him."

"Nothing."

"Nothing? Truly? So that is why your face was flushed when you came up the trail?"

Rowan sighed and pulled her arisaid around her. Jeanette was too perceptive and really there was nothing but a couple of kisses to reveal. She glanced at Scotia and Elspet, then back at her cousin.

"Promise me you will not speak of what we say to Auntie or to anyone else."

Jeanette's face went from teasing back to serious in the space of half a breath. "Of course. What did he do to you?" Concern wove through the air binding them together.

"Do to me? Oh, nothing today. He kissed me last night."

"And?"

"And it was not the first time."

Jeanette's mouth made a silent O and then she grinned. "He must kiss well, then."

A giggle escaped Rowan before she could stop it. She covered her mouth before another one could get away from her and nodded. "Aye, very well."

Jeanette giggled, too, as she linked her arm through Rowan's. "Then why were you so serious a moment ago?"

Rowan shook her head. "This is no time to let a braw man tempt me from my duties."

"In truth, it seems a wonderful time to be distracted from them." Jeanette squeezed Rowan's arm and they both fell silent.

As the two of them caught up, the path suddenly widened. The horse stepped on a stone and momentarily stumbled. Jeanette and Rowan both leapt to steady Elspet and Scotia at the same time Nicholas did. His broad hand landed on Rowan's where it rested on Elspet's waist. The shock of the touch was so strong she froze, her eyes on his, all thoughts of ignoring him gone.

Nicholas's eyes went almost black. "'Tis rude to stare, lass" he said under his breath.

Rowan's entire body flushed and Scotia's delighted laugh ensured there would be lots of teasing in Rowan's immediate future.

"There is little else to see when you take up so much of the trail ahead of us," Rowan said quietly as she slid her hand from under his.

Nicholas's grin transformed his face from handsome to boyish and Rowan heard both Scotia and Jeanette sigh.

"Lady Elspet," he said, shifting his focus from Rowan to her aunt, "would you like to stop for a little while? I can help you off the pony and you could rest a while before we continue on."

"Aye," she answered as she shifted in the saddle with a quiet groan.

Rowan was suddenly very grateful that Scotia sat behind her mother, holding on to her lest Elspet lose her grip and fall out of the saddle.

"I am greatly fatigued today," Elspet added, her voice thin and feeble. "I thought I would be fine for a short outing."

Jeanette caught Rowan's eye over the pony's shoulder. Elspet used to walk this trail regularly with no fatigue or weakness. If ever they needed a sign that things had changed, this day's journey was surely it. If only it had been worthwhile.

Rowan showed Nicholas where there was a small clearing just off the trail at the edge of a beautiful fast-running burn. He handed her the reins and reached up to steady Elspet while Scotia dismounted. Rowan held her breath while he gently lifted Elspet from the saddle. He lowered her to the ground but did not let go of her. He wrapped an arm around her waist while Scotia steadied her with a hand under her near elbow. Two wobbly steps and they eased her down onto a blanket Jeanette had quickly spread on the ground.

Jeanette smiled at him as she settled her mother with her back against the rock. Nicholas stood watching Elspet get settled. He rubbed the back of his neck and somehow Rowan knew he was as concerned as they were over her aunt. He had only recently met her aunt, yet he took care with her as if she were someone important to him.

Rowan looped the reins over a low branch, then stood beside Nicholas, close but not so close they touched. She tried to look at her aunt through his eyes, for as hard as she tried she always seemed to see the strong, healthy woman, not the one she knew was dying. Elspet's sunken cheeks and hollowed-out eyes bespoke a deep-seated illness and pain etched deep brittle lines around her lips.

"Scotia, get some water for Auntie." Rowan returned to the pony and grabbed another blanket. She and Jeanette spread it over Elspet, tucking it in around her legs. Scotia managed to get a couple of sips of water into her mother, but no more.

Rowan turned away, needing a moment to gather herself, and found Nicholas watching her. She had been so distract by watching him as they traveled that she had not noticed Elspet needed a rest. Guilt and sadness swamped her, lightened only by gratitude that he had kept his head and minded Elspet's needs. She stepped close, letting her hand rest on his arm, and whispered, "Thank you."

Nicholas nodded. "I could see her face. You could not."

That he recognized her guilty feeling surprised her. "Perhaps, but you saw it and I am grateful."

"Rowan?" Jeanette said. "Is there aught Mum might eat?"

Rowan smiled, though she felt no happiness. "Thank you," she said to Nicholas again, reluctantly letting her hand drop to her side. She went to the pony and dug in the bag she had slung behind the saddle.

She did not know what was coming over her. She had been unable to keep from touching Nicholas. Indeed, she'd really wished he would take her in his arms and comfort her. At the same time she was grateful that he had not. It was folly to wish for anything from him. It was only that she was worried over Elspet and her cousins that her mind wandered to Nicholas and his searing kisses. It was a physical attraction that could, and would, be ignored. There was far too much to be attended to at present that was more important than a fleeting infatuation with an intriguing stranger.

Rowan pulled a small bag of dried berries from the bag. "Do you remember the averin berries last fall, Auntie? I have the last of the dried berries right here." She sat next to Elspet so that she and Jeanette braced her from each side, shoulder to shoulder. "Do you remember the first time you and my mum brought me up here to gather them with you?" Rowan had heard the story many times and knew Elspet liked to tell it.

Elspet reached for the offered fruit but did not eat it. Her aunt admired the berry, turning it this way and that in a ray of sunshine as if it were a jewel she regarded.

"I do." The smile passed swiftly over her face like a wraith, here and gone. She took a deep wheezy breath. "You were only toddling about at that time and Jeanette was still a wee bairnie." She leaned her head on Jeanette's shoulder and patted her daughter's hand where it rested on Elspet's leg. "Rowan ate so many berries her hands and face were stained for days." She took another long, labored breath and patted Rowan's leg. The sensation was like a leaf falling upon her skin. Her eyes welled up at the casual affection in that touch. "Your belly hurt so bad your mum dared not take you far from your bed for a good two days."

"Will you not taste it, Mum?" Scotia asked from her perch atop a large rock.

"I am not hungry, but perhaps later, after I have slept a bit."

Jeanette and Scotia both looked at Rowan, fear and sorrow in their countenances.

"Perhaps we should continue home?" Rowan rose, asking no one in particular.

"In a mo—" Elspet raised a hand to her forehead, gave a strangled sort of squeak and slid sideways like a rag doll, leaning heavily against Jeanette's shoulder.

"Mum!" Jeanette grasped her, pushing her back up, but Elspet's head lolled as if it weighed too much to lift even though her eyes were open and filled with confusion.

"Mummy!" Scotia screeched, leaping off her rock.

Rowan, Scotia, and Nicholas converged upon Elspet and Jeanette nearly instantly. Jeanette cradled her mum against her, speaking quietly and intently to her. Scotia was screeching, "Mummy! Mummy!" over and over again.

Rowan knelt in front of her aunt, grasping Elspet's hands in her own. "Auntie, can you hear me?" she asked, giving a gentle squeeze to Elspet's hands. Her left one squeezed back, lightly. The right one did not move.

Elspet's mouth worked but nothing recognizable came out, only a croak. She looked at Rowan, fear glazing her eyes like a trapped animal, and tried again with the same result.

"Are you in pain, Mum?" Jeanette and the others waited for the answer but again, they could not understand the response.

Rowan shoved away the grief that sliced through her, leaving her nauseous and hollow. She sat back on her heels, knowing without looking that her cousins and her aunt were waiting for her to decide what to do. A strong hand settled on her shoulder, pressing just enough to tell her Nicholas was there, supporting her while she supported her family. She glanced up at him, grateful that she was not alone with this responsibility.

"Do you ken what happened, Jeanette?"

"Nay," she whispered, tears filling her eyes but not falling. She shook her head slowly. "I have seen naught like this before."

"Then we must get her home immediately. We shall have to send for Morven. Surely she's seen such before."

"Perhaps, but Ro, Mum cannot ride like this," Jeanette said. "We shall have to make a litter."

"I will carry her." Nicholas's calm voice washed over Rowan. The warmth of his voice and the heat of his hand mixed together like an elixir, bringing a spark of life back to the hollow place inside her. Jeanette seemed to calm, but Scotia began to sob loudly.

Rowan looked at him over her shoulder, resisting the urge to lay her cheek against his hand and let him take over. "'Tis another mile or more down the ben."

Nicholas urged her up with a hand under her elbow, then he stepped around her and gathered Elspet into his arms, lifting her gently and as easily as if she were a wee bairn. He gathered her close and Rowan saw him palm the ermine sack that hung from Elspet's belt. He fumbled with it and she could not tell if he was examining the contents or was genuinely trying to get it out of his way. Regardless of why it ended up in his hand, the fumbling turned it upside down long enough for the Targe stone to fall out, landing with a thud at Nicholas's feet.

Rowan heard Jeanette gasp even as Nicholas leaned over to look at what sat at his feet: a grey, rounded stone, about the size of a man's fist, flattened on top and bottom with an irregular surface. Before he could get a closer look at it Jeanette scooped it up, untied the ermine sack from her mother's belt, and slipped the stone inside, then tucked the sack into a fold of her own arisaid, keeping it well away from Nicholas.

"Nicholas," Rowan said, drawing his attention away from the stone and Jeanette, "let me tuck this blanket around Auntie so you don't trip over it and she won't get cold. Get the pony, Jeanette," she said. "Scotia, stop that noise. It does not help your mother."

Scotia hiccupped but managed to quiet her sobs.

Nicholas nodded as if he agreed with all her instructions and moved toward the path with sure but careful steps.

"Scotia, you can make better time down the ben than I can with your mum," he said. "Hurry you to the castle and make ready for her. Summon the healer. Have Helen tend the fire in Lady Elspet's chamber. Find your da. He will want to be there. And summon a priest."

"No," Jeanette gasped.

Nicholas looked down at Elspet, his eyes soft. A sad, sweet smile softened his face. "Prayers will not be amiss, will they, Lady Elspet?"

Elspet managed a slight shake of her head, then closed her eyes, her head cradled against his shoulder.

"Mum?" Scotia cried and Elspet's eyes fluttered open again.

"Scotia, let her rest," Rowan said, her voice tight. "Go and do as Nicholas says. We will be along as fast as possible and all must be ready for your mum's comfort when we get home."

Scotia sniffled, kissed her mum's forehead, and raced down the trail. Rowan and the others followed as quickly as they dared with Nicholas's precious cargo in his arms.

HOURS PASSED AND BY THE TIME ROWAN MADE HER WAY OUT OF THE tower into the unnaturally quiet bailey, the sun had set and risen again, casting the castle in the golden glow of early morn. She'd said she needed a few minutes to collect herself while there was a lull in the storm that Elspet's collapse had produced, but if she was honest with herself, she wanted to see Nicholas, to thank him for his aid to Elspet, and to take comfort in his company. She rubbed at the throbbing in her forehead, then kneaded the tense muscles at the back of her neck.

Kenneth was livid that they had taken his wife to the wellspring. He'd raged against the foolishness, the lack of responsibility, the unbelievable risk they had taken with Elspet's life, and the three girls had had no choice but to stand stoically, even Scotia, and take his anger, knowing that he was right, but also that his anger masked a deep grief that weighed them all down. She needed to shore up her strength before she returned to that grief-filled chamber.

The trip down the ben had been blessedly uneventful and she was incredibly grateful that Nicholas had been there to carry her aunt home, but the hours since had been unthinkable. Elspet had yet to be able to speak. She fretted when she was awake, but slept equally as fitfully. Nothing Morven, the healer who had trained Jeanette, did seemed to make any difference save that she had finally given Elspet a sleeping draught, allowing the woman to rest. At least there appeared to be no pain.

Morven had seen this kind of affliction a few times. She would not say how long the souls had lingered in such a state, but Rowan sensed it was not long. It was as if her aunt was suspended between this world and the next and they could do nothing but wait for her to let go.

Kenneth hurtled back and forth between anger bordering on incoherent rage and inconsolable grief. Rowan did not know if he would ever forgive them for not only allowing Elspet to travel to the sacred wellspring, but for keeping that knowledge from him. She feared he blamed himself for not keeping his beloved wife safe. Indeed she feared they all blamed themselves for Elspet's plight, except perhaps for Nicholas.

He was a hero today. Even though he was not supposed to have followed them, she was exceedingly thankful that he had.

She looked about for him, but did not see him anywhere. She closed her eyes and took a deep breath, pushing it past the ball of guilt-spiked grief that threatened to fill her chest.

"Rowan?" She opened her eyes to find Duncan crossing the bailey toward her. "Are you well?" he asked as he neared her.

"As well as can be, given the circumstances."

"How fares the Lady?" She watched his throat work as he swallowed hard and she could imagine his grief was nearly as great as her own.

"She lives." She shook her head and the ball in her chest grew. "No one kens if she will recover, or when."

"Is there aught needed? Aught I can do for Lady Elspet or for the rest of you?"

The man really was kind. She shook her head, then stopped. "Do you ken where Nicholas is? I . . . I wish to thank him for yesterday. I cannot bear to think what would have happened if he hadn't . . ." She blinked rapidly, refusing to let tears fall. Elspet was still alive. Tears could come later. "I wish to thank him."

"He went down to the loch a little while ago. He said he needed to fetch the fishing gear Uilliam lent him yesterday. Would you like me to get him?"

The thought of the loch, of having a moment with Nicholas without the clan or her cousins looking on lifted her spirits a little. "Nay. I thank you, but the walk will be good for me. I need some fresh air before I return to Auntie's chamber." She thought of Uncle Kenneth pacing upstairs. "Perhaps you could send some *uisge beatha* up for my uncle? He is quite . . . I think the whiskey would do him good."

"Of course. I will take it myself."

Rowan gave him a quick hug, then made her way for the gate passage and the loch beyond.

NICHOLAS TRUDGED SLOWLY, RETRACING HIS STEPS OF YESTER-morn, though it seemed much longer than that. He scrubbed at his face as if he could remove the person he was and reveal someone better. He didn't know what had come over him. One moment he had the sack in his hand. Literally in his hand, but he had not been able to bring himself to take it, fumbling it instead when he'd begun to imagine how Rowan would react to his betrayal of her trust. His long-dormant conscience had not allowed him to do something he'd done a thousand times over before he ever came here.

He could not betray her trust.

Damned weakness. He hadn't been bothered by a conscience in a long time, only doing what was best for himself, and the king, which was, after all, in Nicholas's best interest. Even in this assignment he let the king dictate his conscience, or the withered thing that might have once been his conscience.

The truth was a dismal story. Nicholas was not a good man, not a man worthy of the feelings that were growing between Rowan and himself. And yet he had not taken the ermine sack yesterday even though it would have been a simple task, and quite possibly the end of the mission if that lump of stone had anything to do with the Highland Targe. The knot in his chest twisted tighter at that thought. The end of the mission meant leaving Dunlairig, leaving Rowan and the people he respected much more than he'd deemed possible, much more than anyone he'd known before he came here.

Like Archie.

Archie would not understand. Nicholas didn't really understand it himself. But he knew one thing. He could not bring more grief to Rowan and her family when they had so much already.

He reached the downed tree where he'd stashed Uilliam's fishing gear and was just retrieving it when he noticed Rowan approaching. His heart stuttered at the drawn look on her face. He left the gear and slowly moved toward her, almost as if she were a skittish deer.

"How fares your aunt?" He stopped a few paces from her. She looked bruised—not physically, except for the purple shadows under her eyes—but she held herself carefully in a way that spoke volumes about the emotional beating she'd taken since last he saw her.

Rowan sniffed and tried to smile. "There is no real change. She cannot speak. Her breath is labored. Morven says it may pass, but she looks as if she does not think my aunt will see another morn." Her eyes glistened but no tears fell.

"Rowan." He stepped toward her and before he knew what he was about he'd opened his arms for her and she had melted into his embrace, her face pressed against his chest and her arms around his waist. She was silent but there was a telltale dampness upon his tunic and the tiniest of tremors that ran through her body, silently revealing the storm that broke inside her. All he could do was hold her, letting the emotions pour from her until they lost some of their pain. Long after the tears ceased they stood there, arms wrapped about each other, her head resting over his heart.

Finally, she pushed away from him, swiping at her tear-streaked face. He allowed her enough room to look up at him, but he did not release her. He'd never felt protective of another since his mother. The trust Rowan showed by coming to him, allowing herself these moments of reaction that she clearly did not wish to show to anyone, told him he was not imagining the growing feelings between them.

"Is there aught I can do, lass? Anything at all?" He ran a thumb along the purple smudge under her eye, wiping away the last traces of her tears. He hated that he would cause her any more pain, but it was inevitable.

"Nay. There is naught to do but watch and wait." She closed her eyes and sighed. "She is so frail and Kenneth is distraught. I do not ken if he will ever forgive us for taking her up the ben yesterday."

"Does Morven think the trek is what caused this malady?"

"She would not say for sure, but she did say that these sorts of fits happen anywhere and anytime, as if they are ordained."

"So there is no way to ken if it would have happened if she had stayed abed." He cupped her face in his hands, lightly stroking her cheeks with his thumbs. Her eyelashes were spiked with her tears, her eyes blood-shot, her skin blotched with red and yet she was the most beautiful woman he had ever laid eyes on. "You and your cousins cannot blame yourself for helping Lady Elspet . . ." He still did not know what they had been doing on the ben, but that didn't matter at the moment.

"We should have stopped her."

"Have you ever stopped her before when she was adamant to do something? It did not look like even Kenneth could stop her the night of the blessing."

At last he roused a smile in her, a sad smile, but it was an improvement nonetheless.

"No one ever stops Auntie when she gets her mind fixed on something, but it still feels like we let Uncle down."

"Perhaps, but 'tis done now and naught will change that. We need to look to her comfort and care."

"She is as comfortable as Morven's sleeping draughts can make her. She frets terribly when she is awake. She cannot speak except to make those croaking sounds you heard on the ben. She looks so frightened, Nicholas, but at least when we ask if she is in pain she shakes her head nay. I do not think there is much any of us can do for her at this point except to stay with her and try to keep her calm when she is awake. I know she would be more calm if—"

"If?"

She swallowed and would not meet his eyes.

"Rowan, what is it that troubles the Lady? Is there aught I can do to help?"

Rowan shook her head. "There is naught anyone can do. We tried." She met his gaze, her eyes big. "If she dies . . ." She closed her eyes and Nicholas could not decide whether to shake her for what she would not tell him or envelop her in his arms again. He wanted to do both.

Instead he gently kissed her, then rested his forehead against hers, weighing the comfort he wished to give against the opportunity to push for confirmation of his suspicions. She was fragile and clearly trusted him enough to come to him for the comfort she could not find amongst her family. He could almost hear Archie urging him to exploit the moment. He closed his eyes.

"Does her agitation have aught to do with the Highland Targe?" He whispered the question—a compromise lest Archie was indeed near enough to overhear their conversation, exploiting the moment, but keeping it as private as possible. "Is she the keeper of it?"

She jerked back far enough to look up at him again, shock sparking in her eyes and he found himself glad that he'd been able to push her grief aside, if only for a moment.

"Why would you think that?" she asked, stepping out of his reach.

He stopped himself from scanning the nearby woods for a shadow that would tell him Archie listened. He dared not give away his accomplice, though whether it was because he did not want to disappoint Rowan's trust or Archie's he cared not to ponder.

"I heard stories in my travels, and then there was the blessing and bits and pieces of conversation. There is the ermine sack, the stone that fell from it yesterday. I guessed. It is true, then, she is the keeper of the Highland Targe."

"Not exactly. Nicholas, you must not speak of this to anyone."

He nodded and reached for her hand, guiding her away from the trees and down to the loch shore.

"The Targe is real, is it not?"

She did not answer for a long time. Finally she took a long deep breath and squared her shoulders. Turning to face him, she reached up and laid her palm against his cheek. "I have already said too much. It is not something I can speak of. It is not mine to share, but if it were, I would tell you of it. You have aided this clan in ways you cannot begin to understand. If you were of this clan, you would be elevated to the chief's counsel just for yesterday's work. I would see to it."

The look in her eye spoke of pride in him, of tender feelings for him. He swallowed, but before he could respond she dropped her hand and lowered her gaze to his chest.

"But you are not, and that prevents many things."

A chasm opened up between them where a moment ago there had been understanding and connection, leaving him feeling empty and alone as he had not felt since . . . He tried to reach for her, but she stepped away, shaking her head. He watched as a tear fell to the ground before she looked up at him. "You are a stranger here . . . a beloved stranger . . . and I can share nothing with you."

Panic raced through him, making his heart pound and his mind spin. He had pushed too hard, too fast, and now he was losing her. He could not bear the cutting pain that caused him, the wrench in his chest, the writhing in his gut. She was his.

The thought shocked him, rocking him back on his heels.

She was his.

He knew it deep in his heart.

She was his.

He reeled at the ramifications of such a thought, such a desire. Did he really want a woman in his life? Did he want the responsibilities, the commitments? And this woman . . . how could he be true to the king and to her at the same time?

Impossible. Archie would never understand that Rowan was anything other than a pawn in their mission. If he learned of Nicholas's feelings he would see them as either a grand scheme or a weakness that must be cut out. Rowan's life would be in danger even more than it was now. His bloody dreams would come true and he would not let that happen. If there was any way to spare her from what he must do, he would, but her survival was more important than the betrayal she would endure at his hands.

# CHAPTER TEN

ARCHIE HAD FROZEN THE MOMENT THE WOMAN HAD APPEARED. He'd been about to make himself known to Nicholas, to find out what news the "king's favorite" had discovered since yesterday, but then she'd called out to him, startling Nicholas out of whatever thoughts he'd been lost in. Never had Archie seen Nicholas anything but focused. Never had he been able to sneak up on the man, even when he was sleeping, and yet here he was, not six feet away and he'd not even noticed.

But when Rowan had appeared there was a softness to his expression that Archie had never seen in ten years of knowing the man.

Archie pursed his lips. Yesterday he hadn't been able to tell, from his hiding place in the woods, exactly what passed between these two, but today it was plain that Nicholas had real feelings for the woman, not feigned. His focus would be shattered, his loyalty in conflict. Could Archie still depend upon him to complete this task? Could the king?

Was this finally a crack in Nicholas's armor?

Glee crackled through him and he dared not give into the urge to throw back his head and crow.

For years he'd been playing second to Nicholas fitz Hugh. For years he'd been employed because Nicholas saw to it. For years he'd been kept out of the king's regard by Nicholas—master manipulator of the king's esteem.

But if his loyalty was compromised by this Scottish wench, then Archibald of Easton's moment had finally come, and he was not one to let it pass. With the king's regard came wealth, status, power. Nicholas cared only for the status, but there was so much more possible. And Archie was just the man to exploit every single one of those possibilities.

Maintaining his position with no movement, not even allowing himself the grin he could feel fluttering in his cheeks, was the hardest thing he had done in years. But everything he had endured with false smiles and feigned camaraderie by Nicholas's side these many years was about to pay off in a grand way and he could wait a little longer to reveal his true self to Nicholas—but only a little longer.

First, Archie had to make sure. He had to test Nicholas to see if what he had surmised was true. He settled in to watch, and listen, waiting impatiently for his moment.

"I AM BELOVED?" NICHOLAS ASKED, HIS EYES WIDE AS IF HE COULD not fathom such an idea.

Rowan rolled her lips together, damning herself for speaking what should not have been said, what she hadn't even realized about her own feelings. But she had spoken and she would not lie to him. "Aye, you are. I do not ken how it has come about so quickly." She tried to find the words to describe the way he made her feel. "You make me want . . ." Words failed her.

He closed the distance between them, taking her hands in his. "You make *me* want, too." He smiled down at her and a giddy lightness lifted a little of the grief from her heart. "Is this so impossible, lass?" He raised her hand and softly brushed his lips across her knuckles. "If I stayed here at Dunlairig, would you have me, Rowan?"

If he stayed? Her breath grew shallow and quick as she tried to understand exactly what he was saying, tried to decide if he spoke his true feelings. "You would do that? Stay here? With me? What about your home, Achnamara? What about the life you left behind?"

"I have never been so much at home as I have been since arriving here, since meeting you. I do not wish to leave." Winding through his words was a sense of wonder, as if he was only just realizing this himself. "Would you have me, Rowan?" he repeated.

She studied him for long moments, weighing his words, his expression, and the unwavering sense that he spoke the truth. She knew it was possible, likely even, that she trusted him because he said what she wished to hear, but she had always been a good judge of character, as if she had some other sense she was not aware of. It had always served her well.

"If you stayed, and if my family agreed, I would have you, Nicholas of Achnamara."

A brilliant smile burst upon his face as he pulled her into his arms and kissed her. Every rational thought she'd been struggling to have fled, leaving only Nicholas and the feelings he awoke in her.

She sank into the feel of strong arms about her, tender lips upon her own. She let the scent of Nicholas surround her as completely as his arms did. The man wrapped her in a cocoon of sensation that flooded her mind and her limbs, focusing every thought and feeling on him. Only on Nicholas.

She wanted him as she'd never wanted anyone before. She pressed her body to his, needing to get closer. Needing. She pushed up on her toes and wrapped her arms around his neck, deepening the kiss as he'd done when they kissed before, letting her tongue dance with his.

Her body came alive beneath his lips. He trailed his hands down her sides, up her back, crushing her to him. She whimpered as her breasts brushed against his chest with every ragged breath she took, and nearly cried out in pleasure when he slid a hand between them, lifting her breast and running a thumb over her nipple until her knees went weak. Without thinking, she pressed her hips against his, trapping his need between them. A thrill raced through her, tightening into a restlessness deep in her belly. A low growl rumbled from him as he went absolutely still.

"Rowan, we must not," he said, his lips barely moving against her own. "If we do not stop . . ." He rested his forehead against hers but did not move away. "You tempt me beyond reason."

Rowan smiled. "I could say the same about you." She shifted enough to rest her head against his shoulder, turning her face into his neck, letting the spice and musk of the man soak into her, letting the wonder of the moment enfold them in this time apart from everything and everyone else.

"I did not mean to let that go so far." He ran a hand up and down her back, slowly, as if comforting her . . . or himself.

She could hear the smile in his voice. She kissed his neck and he tilted his head to rest against her crown. An unexpected joy spread through her.

"I did not intend for that to happen," she said, "but I do not regret it."

"I could never regret it, love."

The endearment slid into her heart, warming her.

She looked up at him and laid a palm against his cheek. "I meant only to thank you for helping my aunt yesterday. I don't know what we would have done if you had not been there."

"You are all strong women, Rowan." He smoothed her hair back from her face, the warmth of his hand lingered against her skin. "I doubt not that the three of you would have managed quite well without me." He stopped her reply with a finger to her lips. "But I am glad I was there to help."

The lightness of the past moments fled, leaving only the flicker of Nicholas's desire deep in her heart, protecting her from the darkness of the grief to come. He pulled her back into his embrace. She rested her head over his heart, the quiet thump-thumping soothing her.

"What was so important yesterday that she had to go up the mountain?" he asked quietly.

She stared into the nearby woods, yesterday's trek dominating her thoughts. "'Twas the future of the clan at stake," she said, more to herself than to him. "But it was for naught."

A man-shaped shadow in the edge of the woods shifted, drawing her attention. She stepped out of Nicholas's embrace and moved toward the edge of the wood.

"Who are you?" she demanded.

NICHOLAS PEERED PAST HER INTO THE DEEP SHADOWS. ARCHIE stood next to the downed tree that still hid the fishing gear, barely in the shadow of the trees. His head was cocked to one side, his arms crossed, and a knowing sneer sliced across his face.

Nicholas narrowed his eyes. The man had seen too much, he was sure. Nicholas had let his feelings for Rowan cloud his mind. He knew Archie was likely lurking somewhere nearby, yet the need to touch Rowan had made him careless and now his weakness had been revealed. As much as he wanted to believe Archie would not exploit that knowledge, he knew better.

The ginger-haired man gave them a leer thinly veiled by a grin. "I am Archibald MacGregor of Keltie, mistress," he said, stepping out of the shadows and into the sunlight. "I did not mean to interrupt your tryst"—he winked at her and Nicholas fisted his hands to keep from dragging the man back into the woods and thrashing him—"but then I heard you speak and you sounded so sad. I thought to see how you fared and if this man had aught to do with it."

"You heard us?" Rowan's voice wobbled. Nicholas desperately wanted to throttle the man, for he could well imagine the embarrassed flush that washed across Rowan's fair face even though he could not see it. Unable to stop himself, he reached for her hand and pulled her away from Archie, putting himself between the two of them.

Archie's mouth was a straight line, the jovial-stranger act gone. "Aye. It would have been hard not to hear. Before and after such a fervent kiss."

Nicholas scowled. He did not like the tone Archie took. He would have needed to be barely concealed by the forest to overhear their conversation, to know just how much Rowan meant to him. That was a weapon he had never meant to give anyone.

"She is fine. There is nothing you are needed for here," Nicholas said, hoping to convey his ire at this interruption with his expression, if not his words. "I would ask that you not embarrass the lady by speaking of what you saw or heard."

"I would not dream of embarrassing Mistress Rowan." Archie moved slowly closer to them. "I'm sure her family would not think well of such wanton behavior . . . oh, but there is another in the family that is just as wanton. Or perhaps the fair-haired one would be interested in trysting with me."

Rowan growled behind him. "You will leave my cousins alone, Archibald of Keltie." She stood beside Nicholas. "You will leave this land lest I send my uncle after you."

"Oh, I think not, mistress. I think your uncle would be most interested to learn of your behavior with this man, this *spy* who dallies with you to learn your secrets in order to find the Highland Targe."

Nicholas couldn't move. He dared not look at Rowan. Why would Archie expose their mission like this? He put everything in jeopardy, including the mission and the growing feelings between himself and Rowan. Never again would she trust him. Never again would she look upon him softly, laugh with him, tease him.

Archie's betrayal struck him in the gut like a newly shod horse's kick, knocking the breath out of him. The man clearly had no intention of working with Nicholas to find the Targe. When had that changed? Understanding came to him in an instant. It had changed when Nicholas had gone to rescue Rowan and Scotia from the falling wall. Everything had changed in that moment even though he had not realized it until just now. He had chosen sides, at least as Archie saw it. Whatever trust Nicholas thought the two of them had shared after so many years of working together had been an illusion.

And now that Archie had found a weakness in Nicholas, his feelings for Rowan . . . A cold sweat trickled between his shoulder blades.

"I am sorry," Nicholas said, turning to find her staring at him as if he were something she had never seen before. His dream, that bloody, bloody dream, punched into his mind. It wasn't enough that King Edward would rip this clan to pieces, and with it this woman. Archie would start without their monarch.

"This is true?" Rowan's voice was flat, hollow, matching the look in her eyes, and it tore at him. "You do not deny it?"

It was a measure of how far he had fallen for this woman that he had not even thought to lie to her, to claim that the story Archie wove was a fabrication. He shook his head.

"You are working together?"

"I would not hurt you, Rowan, not if I could help it."

"That is a lie," she said, looking away from him, toward Archie, as if looking for verification from him.

"It would have been a lie a sennight ago, but not now." He reached out to touch a lock of her hair and was grateful she didn't flinch. "Not now."

She slapped his hand away. "No. Lies! If what this man says is true, then you have come to harm my clan and that will hurt me, no matter what."

"I would change this if I could, Rowan. You must believe me."

"I could never believe you." She was looking directly at him and the anger and hurt that he found in her eyes were profound, but so much better than the flatness of a moment ago. "I was a fool to think I could trust you. I am no better than Scotia after all, letting my head get turned by a little attention from a braw man. I thought . . ." She shook her head. "It matters not what I thought. I was wrong."

"And yet you told him much we need to know." Archie was beside them, grabbing her arm, pulling her away from Nicholas.

"Release her, Archie!" Nicholas took hold of Rowan's upper arm in an effort to wrest her away from this man he once thought of as a friend, but Archie yanked her harder, drawing a stunned cry from her as she was pulled out of Nicholas's grasp.

"I think I shall keep her close, Nick. There is much at stake here and I am beginning to think you are not as clear in your duty as you once were. Yes, I will keep her here, close." He pulled her against him in a mockery of the embrace Nicholas and Rowan had shared minutes ago.

White-hot rage burned through Nicholas. No matter what he had to do, this man would not hurt Rowan.

Rowan struggled but Archie had her pinned to his chest, her arms caught between them.

"Now one of you will tell me: Is Lady Elspet the keeper of the Highland Targe?" He looked at Nicholas, a rusty-colored eyebrow raised.

# CHAPTER ELEVEN

FURY GRIPPED ROWAN EVEN TIGHTER THAN ARCHIE DID. SHE HAD to warn Kenneth, warn the clan about the English rats in their midst.

"Let her go, Archie. She knows nothing useful."

She could see naught but Archie's chest but it sounded like Nicholas was moving closer, circling around them.

"That is not what I heard," Archie said, pulling her around, keeping her between him and Nicholas, she was sure. "She would not tell you anything useful. It does not mean she does not have the information we need."

"Rowan, tell him nothing." Nicholas's voice was a low growl behind her.

"Answer me, girl. Is Lady Elspet the keeper of the Highland Targe?" Archie demanded, stepping backward and dragging her with him. "Answer me!"

He loosened his hold on her enough for her to look up at him but when the only answer he got was her glare, he shook her so hard she bit her tongue and the metallic tang of her own blood trickled down her throat.

She took the moment to lift her knee hard, but he shifted quickly, taking her knee in his thigh with a grunt.

"Bitch!"

He spun her in his arms, so her back was to him, and once more pinned her in his iron embrace, backing them up. Nicholas followed them, step for step, his face a mask of concentration, his eyes focused on Archie as if she weren't even there.

Archie stopped at the edge of the loch. "You have been keeping this feisty wench all to yourself, Nick. You used to share."

Silence. She could tell Nicholas's teeth were clenched by the way a muscle jumped in front of his ear. His mouth was hard, his eyes flinty. He stood a few feet away, his hands fisted by his sides, clearly poised for a fight. This fierce man was a stranger to her, so unlike the charming, gentle man she'd thought him to be.

"Perhaps I should tup her, see if she is worth turning your back on the king." Archie ran a hand down her stomach, shocking her as he cupped her between her legs hard. "I hope she likes it rough."

The menace in his words was clear, accented by the tightening of his arm around her waist and the pull of his other hand between her legs. She wanted to retch.

"Let her go, Archie." The fire in Nicholas's eyes and the determined set of his chin promised retribution and for a fleeting moment she thought perhaps he did care for her as she thought.

"Nay, that I will not do. How many times have you interfered with me and my fun? How many, Nick? Too many. Tell me what I want to know or she'll suffer the consequences of your betrayal."

Archie shoved Rowan's head down, bending her over his arm, and began to pull at her gown. Rowan struggled, screaming, unable to see anything but her own feet, even as she heard the thud of fist on flesh. Archie spun, but did not release her.

When she caught her balance the edge of a cold blade rested below her ear.

"I would rather bed her than kill her, Nicholas, but I will not hesitate to slice her pretty neck if you do not tell me what I wish to know."

"'Twould be best you kill me, then," she said between clenched teeth, feeling an increasingly familiar headache building rapidly. "He knows not the answer." Instinctively she reached for the power she had experienced during the blessing, pulling it into her, almost laughing as it rushed up her legs, pooling under her skin, pulsing with her headache as if it were a living, breathing thing awaiting her command. "And I will not tell you anything." She flung the power from her with her final word.

Archie roared, pulling her backwards, but releasing her at the same time. She stumbled, not realizing at first that she was free.

There was splashing behind her and a string of words so foul even Uncle Kenneth had never uttered them. She whirled to find Archie struggling to his feet in knee-deep water, his nose streaming blood. She finally understood why men got such pleasure out of beating each other up.

Nicholas charged past her, shouting, "Run, Rowan! Run!" as he tackled the ginger-haired man, the two of them going down in the icy loch.

Every hair stood up on Rowan's body as the two men clashed, Nicholas's command echoing in her head.

She scrambled out of the clearing and into the familiar woods as fast as she could, running without stopping, as if her feet had wings. Her years of experience in these woods lent speed and direction to her flight—up the ben into the thickest part of the sheltering forest.

Only when she began to stumble over the downed trees and slippery, moss-covered rocks did she slow. She searched for a cave that she knew was nearby, but then thought twice about hiding in a place with no escape route. She pushed into a thicket of juniper crouching low in the deep shadows as she desperately tried to quiet her breathing and slow her heartbeat. It was only then that she discovered tears flowing down her face, leaving wet trails over the top of her gown. She wiped them away, stemming the flow immediately. She would not cry. She'd not give English spies the satisfaction of seeing a Highlander laid low by their betrayal—by his betrayal.

Her hand on her lips kept a moan from escaping. She was a Highlander. She might have allowed herself a moment of weakness with Nicholas—several moments, if she was honest with herself— but now Rowan knew the truth, and she would do whatever it took to make sure neither Nicholas, nor Archie, got any information to Edward Longshanks in England.

And that meant getting back to the castle immediately. She had to warn Uncle Kenneth. They had to hunt down the two traitorous spies. She could not think about what the punishment for spying would be. It was earned, deserved. She rubbed the heel of her hand against her chest, trying to ease the ache that burrowed there.

She needed a plan. If she went straight back to the castle one or both of the spies would likely be waiting for her, recapture her . . .

She wouldn't think about that either.

She knew these woods and bens better than either of them did. She had the advantage there. She knew the castle, its people, and the rhythms of their days better than either of them, too. Another advantage. She glanced up, peering at the sky through the dense foliage of the spring forest. It was not yet midday. Her best chance was to approach the castle under cover of night. It would be daft to think at least one of the spies wouldn't be keeping watch and easily see her if she tried to return during daylight.

But she couldn't stay here. She'd run quickly, but she had no doubt she'd left a trail behind her for them to follow. She needed to move, and she needed to cover her tracks.

And this was where her years of exploring the bens would come to her aid. She quickly oriented herself. There were several burns that ran down this face of the ben and one was not too far to the west of her hiding place. She listened carefully, not just for the footfalls or voices of men, but for the creatures of the forest whose hearing surpassed hers. When she was sure no one was close by she stood and made her way to the burn, carefully avoiding as many things that would betray her passing as possible. When she got to the burn she stepped into the water and quickly made her way up the ben.

NICHOLAS'S FIST POUNDED INTO ARCHIE'S FACE, SENDING HIM spinning deeper into the water, flailing and spluttering as he found his footing. Nicholas backed out of the loch onto dry ground, then quickly scanned the clearing to make sure Rowan had done as he'd told her and run. She was gone, and relief mixed with remorse in a thick band about his chest.

"I knew you were hiding something from me." Archie charged out of the water, hatred etched on his pinched face. Nicholas stepped to the side at the last minute and swept a foot out to trip the man, sending him sprawling face-first in the dirt. Nicholas knew Archie was more brawler than disciplined fighter. In this especially, his early training in the ways of Highland warriors served him well.

"We were partners." Archie stood, brushing bits of gravel from his scraped-up face. "But no, you've gone soft on that Scottish whore."

"She is no whore." They circled each other, each looking for an opening.

"You are a stupid man." Archie's eyes shifted left, then right. He pivoted and sprinted for the forest.

Nicholas sprinted after him, diving and grabbing him about the legs, the two of them tumbling to the ground. Archie bucked and twisted but Nicholas did not release his hold.

"You are the stupid man. You told her everything!" Nicholas managed to straddle Archie. He grabbed the man's hair and pulled his head back until Archie went stone still. "You betrayed our mission, you betrayed the king." His conscience crackled in his head. Archie had done what Nicholas was contemplating, betraying his partner and his king for the sake of a woman, but he'd not tell the man that. "It is done and 'twill be your head on a pike, not mine." He had to take the position of loyalty to the king if he had any hope of getting out of this alive.

Nicholas shoved Archie's face into the ground and leapt to his feet, putting himself between the man and the forest, protecting Rowan as best he could. Archie carefully got to his feet, swiping at the blood that trickled from his nose.

"Not if I take your place inside the castle, another traveler in search of a dry bed and a warm meal. Not if 7 retrieve the Highland Targe and take it to the king myself."

All the ramifications of this ran through Nicholas's mind, all settling on one certainty.

"You would kill me and then Rowan? Do you really think Kenneth will welcome a stranger into their midst after his own niece has been murdered?"

"If the two of you disappear they will think only that you have taken their woman, and if I claim to have seen the two of you together . . . well, I will be the only one who can set them on the right path to track you down and they will be overjoyed to take me into the bosom of their castle."

"What makes you think you can kill me?" He filled his voice with all the derision and hatred he held for this man, goading him to attack again. "You were not even strong enough to keep hold of Rowan."

Archie tilted his head and narrowed his eyes. He stilled, focusing inward instead of on Nicholas. His head lifted and he rocked back on his heels as he often did when he was thinking hard. "She threw me off without so much as touching me. One minute I was about to take her and the next I was flying backward into the water."

Nicholas took a step toward Archie, but the man was so focused on what had happened he didn't even flinch.

"Perhaps there is more to Rowan than you have told me, old friend. A weak, mewling woman has never thrown me off before. She defended herself without a weapon." Archie took a deep breath and a smirk spread over his battered and cut face. "*She* has the Highland Targe. I did not believe the stories, but how else to explain what she did? It must be small, not a true shield at all, but some symbol, some relic. She must have it on her person to throw me off so forcefully. You have had the Targe within your reach, within your embrace, and you either did not know it, or could not bring yourself to do your duty to your king, lost between the lusty wench's thighs."

Nicholas took a slow breath. Rowan had thrown the man off . . . he'd known it, but hadn't stopped to consider how she had managed it. Regardless, she was not the keeper of the targe, he was certain of that—as certain as he could be with no real information—but his instinct and what he had observed told him Elspet was the one. Regardless, he could not let Archie believe it or Rowan would be in even more peril than she was at this moment. His dream seemed more prophecy now than simple nightmare.

"Nay," he said slowly, clearly, "Rowan is not the one we seek. Lady Elspet is."

"You lie to me again!" Archie snorted. "I am not blind, Nick. You wish to keep her for yourself? The question is: Are you really addled by this woman?" His face hardened, his brow a solid line over suspicious eyes. "Or were you planning on cutting me out?" He drew his dagger and lunged at Nicholas, aiming for his gut but Nicholas spun away, grabbing for his own dagger and preparing for Archie's next attack.

"You know I am better at this than you are," Nicholas said, circling the other man.

"No, but perhaps Rowan will be the judge." Archie slashed at Nicholas again, feinting right, then slicing down, drawing blood from a shallow cut along Nicholas's arm.

Nicholas engaged Archie in feints and lunges, moving back toward the loch, away from the forest edge, letting the man think he had the upper hand. When he reached the rocky verge of the loch, he struck fast, again and again, parrying Archie's moves with ease, and turning the fight until Archie's back was to the dark waters. The two of them stared at each other, their breaths coming fast and hard with their efforts.

As Nicholas looked upon Archie, he stared at his past, the greed, the violence, the betrayal he had handed out again and again in service to the king. It was a life he'd been proud of.

But not anymore.

Something about this place, these people—Rowan—had reminded him of who he wanted to be so long ago: a Highland Warrior who protected those who could not protect themselves, who put family and clan above all else, a man of honor. He had not thought he'd had a choice in leaving that behind, in learning to survive in less honorable ways.

But he did. He had a clear choice in this moment. Archie was all he had been. But not all he would be. Archie had already spoiled the trust that had been building with Rowan but that didn't mean Nicholas could go back to his old life. He wasn't the same man he was a fortnight ago. He didn't want to be that man anymore.

He'd not let Archie take Elspet or Rowan. He'd not allow the Targe to fall into Edward's grasp.

His choice was made.

Nicholas attacked, moving quickly, forcing Archie out onto the narrow peninsula of rocks that Uilliam had said was good for fishing. He pushed and struck, drawing blood from cut after cut until Archie stood at the end of the spit of land. With a quick feint and a backhanded attack, Archie's dagger flew out of his hand and into the water. Nicholas shoved his own dagger into its sheath as he lowered his head and rammed it into Archie's chest, sending them both flying into the loch.

The shock of icy water broke the anger that was driving Nicholas. He pushed away from the grasping, flailing hands of Archibald of Easton, only then realizing how deep the loch was even this close to shore. Archie couldn't swim. Nicholas knew he should let the man drown. It was the best way to solve this problem, but something would not let him swim away from the man who was the closest thing Nicholas had to a friend all these years. He knew, were their situations switched, Archie would have no trouble letting Nicholas drown.

He watched as Archie slapped the water, coughing, and crying out to Nicholas to save him. Nicholas sighed, shoved his dripping hair away from his face, and knew himself for a fool.

He neared the floundering Archie, avoiding the man's grabbing hands. Nicholas grabbed Archie by the collar of his tunic and dragged him back to shore with sure, strong kicks that pulled them both through the inky water.

When he could touch the bottom, he stood, still dragging a now limp and coughing Archie up onto dry land. He dropped the man facedown on the rocks, planted a knee in his back, and grabbed his dagger from its water-filled sheath. He held the point of it to the back of Archie's neck.

"One move and I'll drive this into your spine. If you don't die immediately, you'll lie here unable to move until someone finds you or I push you back out into the water to drown. Do you understand?"

Archie started to nod but instead gave a strangled grunt.

"Good. I have a new mission for you." Nicholas gritted his teeth and forced himself not to slide the dagger home as he considered the best way to appeal to Archie's pride and avarice, the best way to get him to leave Scotland and conceal the truth from anyone else, especially the king. "Go to the king and tell him—"

"Tell him what?" Archie croaked out the words. "That you have thrown him over for the favors of a Highland barbarian?"

Nicholas ground his knee into Archie's back, eliciting a startled groan from the man.

"If you convince the king that you found the targe, and that you found it somewhere far away from Dunlairig, you will have the king's reward, you will not share it with me, and, if I am out of the way, you will be the king's favored spy."

"Bollocks. He'll have my head on a pike. Why would I lie to the king for you?!"

"Because if you do not, you will die here. Now."

Archie was silent, considering his options, no doubt.

"You would not kill me," he said, his voice full of bravado. "You could have left me in the loch to drown but you did not."

"I'm finding that was a poor decision on my part." Nicholas let the point of the dagger pierce Archie's skin just enough to let a pearl of blood well up, then run down the side of his neck.

"I do not have the Targe," Archie said. "How am I to take it to the king when you do not even know what it looks like or where it is?"

"I will find it and get it into your keeping."

"All this for a wench?" Archie spat the words out.

Nicholas pressed the dagger in a little more. Blood now ran in a steady stream over Archie's neck.

"I'll do it," Archie whispered. "I'll do it," he said louder.

"Your word."

"You would trust my word?"

"Nay, but I would have it anyway."

"My word. Release me and I will do as you wish."

"You will await me in Oban," Nicholas said, trying to figure out what he could give Archie that would make for a believable Highland Targe if the man kept his word.

"Oban, fine, but you only have a fortnight at most before I must report to the king."

"And you will tell the king?"

"I shall tell him your lies convincingly, you can be assured. If I dared tell him what has passed here he would have my head for not killing you on the spot."

"Aye, that he would. I fear he will be very disappointed with me but if you tell him I am dead—convincingly—he will reward you for completing the mission."

"Indeed. Now let me go. You have my word I will do as you wish."

Slowly, Nicholas rose, leaving his dagger in place until he could step out of reach of Archie's long arms. Archie pushed up onto his hands and knees, then stood slowly, wiping blood and dirt from his face. He looked about him. "My dagger?"

"At the bottom of the loch, no doubt."

Archie pressed a hand to the back of his neck and winced. "Sending you here was a bad idea. King Edward will not be happy."

"King Edward had better think me dead. If I find out otherwise, I promise you I will hunt you down and you will die. Now go!"

Nicholas knew he should have killed the man, that he couldn't trust Archie, but he had never had a stomach for cold-blooded murder. And yet he knew it likely the man would return for the Targe himself. The rewards would be far greater if he could lay Nicholas's betrayal before the king, along with the prize. But at the very least Nicholas had bought a little time while Archie licked his wounds and fetched his reinforcements. The king's men-at-arms were encamped near Oban, at least a hard day's travel there and another back. He could only hope it was enough time to regain Rowan's trust, at least enough to protect her clan from what Archie would bring down upon them.

He watched until Archie disappeared from sight, then turned and sprinted into the forest. He had to find Rowan.

# CHAPTER TWELVE

ROWAN STRUGGLED OVER THE SLIPPERY ROCKS IN THE BURN. HER breath burned in her lungs, and her feet had long past turned to blocks of ice, but she dared not return to the relative comfort of dry ground. She dared not stop.

She tried to stay focused on the sounds around her, though the burble of the water splashing over the rocky streambed made it hard to hear much else. She tried to stay focused on where to place her feet, on taking one more step, on finding a hiding place that did not entrap her. And yet again and again she found herself overwhelmed by the dueling emotions that blocked out everything else, that she could not control: desire and betrayal.

One moment she was scrambling for her life, the next, reliving the moment Nicholas took her in his arms and the passion that burned through her at his touch. The next she could barely breathe as she relived the moment that villain Archie exposed Nicholas's lies.

Was it all a lie?

The things she'd heard from that ruffian, Archibald—Archie, as Nicholas had called him—had betrayed the true nature of Nicholas of Achnamara. She stumbled over a branch, hidden by the water, barely catching her balance. She stopped, pressing her palms to her face for a brief moment before forcing her frozen feet to move up the ben again. How could she be so trusting? He was not Nicholas of Achnamara. He was Nicholas, King Edward's spy, sent to destroy everything she loved.

And yet . . .

Though she had managed to free herself from Archie's grasp— she still did not understand exactly how she had done that!— Nicholas had attacked the other man, helped her escape, and from the sounds that she had heard in the first few moments after she ran, he had fought Archie to keep him from following her.

But Nicholas had betrayed her, betrayed her trust.

She stumbled again, falling to her knees in the cold water this time, drenching the few parts of her skirts that had not already suffered that fate. Her eyes burned but she refused to give in to tears again. She had failed to recognize the danger. She had let herself be swayed by his dark eyes and the passion that flared between them.

"Rowan?"

As if summoned from the maelstrom in her head and heart, he stood at the top of the embankment that flanked the burn, looking down at her. One eye was already showing signs of bruises. He had a scrape along his left cheek as if he'd met the gravel face-first. Blood trickled from a cut on his left forearm.

And he was as drenched as she was. More so.

Concern for him flashed through her, curbed immediately by a steely resolve. She could not trust this man. She would not trust this man.

She scrambled up the steep bank across the burn from him and ran as fast as she could into the dense trees and undergrowth.

Nicholas couldn't miss the flash of warm concern in Rowan's eyes. Nor could he miss the brittle pain there. He would give anything not to have hurt her but it was inevitable. No matter how this mission had played out, the moment he touched her after the wall nearly fell upon them her disappointment and hurt were written in stone. Now he must find a way to regain her trust, at least enough to let him help protect her and her clan from Edward's covetous goal of adding Scotland's conquering to Wales's and ruling the entire island of Britain.

She darted into the darkness of the wood across the burn. He scrambled down the embankment and up the other side, following her as quickly as he could.

"Rowan, stop! Let me explain!"

She glanced back at him but didn't slow down. Nicholas pushed himself, closing the distance between them until he was close enough to hear her ragged breath.

"Please, stop."

She tripped and fell, catching herself with her hands on the ground. He almost stepped on her, but sidestepped at the last moment. She stayed there on her hands and knees, her sides heaving, her head hanging down, the tangles of her hair obscuring her expression.

He stooped down next to her and reached to move her hair away.

"Do not touch me." The words were low and menacing. "Do not dare touch me."

Nicholas stepped away from her, the words drawing old wounds to the surface, childish hurts battled with the need to cradle her in his arms and comfort her. He put more distance between them. Drawing on experience with his mother, he knew that was best.

"I won't touch you, unless you ask me to."

"I will never ask that of you."

"I do not blame you for that," he cleared his suddenly tight throat, "though you will understand if I hold out hope that you will change your mind."

"Hah." She flung her hair out of her face as only women seemed able to do and sat, resting her arms on her bent knees, her breathing still labored. He watched her carefully, ready to chase her again if she bolted.

"You shall never get the Targe."

"Aye, I ken that. We need to keep King Edward from getting it."

"Why would he want the Targe? It only protects those who live upon this land."

Nicholas soaked that information up, adding it to the little he'd gleaned so far. "It is said it protects this route into the Highlands, that it is a shield against invasion."

She laughed then, that husky sound that filled him with an odd joy he'd never experienced before he'd met her.

"You have been misled. If it was that powerful, do you not think the English would have been rebuffed by now? Last I heard, the southern vermin have overrun this land, Lowland and Highland, spreading pain and suffering everywhere they go."

He watched her for a long moment. "I am sorry, Rowan. I . . ."

"You what? Did not come here to my home as a spy for Longshanks? Did not try to seduce me for your own purposes? Did not plan to steal something that doesn't belong to you or your damned king?" Her voice rose with each question until she launched herself to her feet. "What did we ever do to you?!" Anger animated her face bringing high color to her cheeks and lightning to her eyes. She stomped toward him and poked him in the chest with her finger. "What did I ever do to you?"

He started to reach for her but remembered his promise. He hooked his thumbs in his belt but couldn't stop the sigh that escaped him. "You smiled at me. You beguiled me with your sweetness, your fierce loyalty, with your trust."

"With my stupidity."

"Nay, Rowan. Never. You gifted me with something no one else ever had, not even the king. You gifted me with your trust and I regret, more than you shall ever know, that I am unworthy of such a gift."

She looked away for a moment, as if collecting herself. "What are you going to do with me?"

That was a good question and one he didn't know the answer to. "For now, I have bought us a little time. With some persuasion, Archie has 'agreed' to return to Oban and wait for me there."

"Until you bring the Targe to him, no doubt."

"That is what I told him, but in truth, I do not believe he will sit passively and wait for me, so we must prepare for his return. He will not return alone."

"And if he waits for you in Oban?"

"Then I will take him a false Highland Targe. King Edward will have the Targe for his own, and to keep it from him will only stoke his ire and that is never a good thing, but neither Archie nor the king, nor even I, know what it looks like nor even what it is. I can give them a false shield, and give you and your clan some time to prepare. Wales resisted and lost. Scotland will fall, too, whether the king has the Targe or not, but I would not have you and your family suffer"—he had to look away from her as the bloody images from his dream overlaid the woman he faced—"suffer because fate handed you the keeping of the Targe."

"Fate? It is not fate, Nicholas, or whatever your true name is."

Her words knifed through him, cutting at a pride he'd thought long gone. "My true name *is* Nicholas of Achnamara and I truly do not remember exactly where Achnamara is." He looked up at the forest around him . . . so familiar. "I think it cannot be far from here, though, for it is as if I have come home when I look about me. I *am* Scottish." At her lifted eyebrow he added, "Half Scottish. My mother. My father . . . not."

"English." Her voice was flat, a statement, not a question.

"Aye."

"How can you choose the English over the Scots? Were you raised amongst Highlanders? Or did your English family make you who you are?"

"I have no English family," he snarled, then closed his eyes and struggled to calm the rage that ate at him at the mere thought of his English "family." "I went to England when I was ten and two. I thought . . ." He clenched his fists. "I thought my father would welcome his son, so I found him . . ." He paused. "He beat me and told me he would kill me if I dared show my face to him again. The man who ravaged my mother when she was barely become a woman refused to acknowledge her son, though it was clear to look at me who had done the deed. If I had been older, more worldly-wise, I would not have been surprised. But I was."

He met Rowan's wary glance.

"My Scottish family." A muscle jumped in his jaw. He gripped his belt tightly in his fists, but did not look away from her. "I would have stayed there if I could, but my likeness to my sire . . . as I grew, my mother could not bear to look at me. As I reached a man's height, she feared me." He had not ever spoken of this to anyone. "I could not stand to be the cause of such terror in anyone, especially my mother. When she could no longer be near me without quaking, without flying into a rage, or throwing herself into a corner and crying, I had to leave. I could not be the source of such terror in my own mother's life. So I left. I vowed never to return."

"Yet here you are, in the Highlands."

"Not from my own choosing."

"Why are you telling me this?" she demanded, viciously pulling leaves and bracken from her hair. "Is it to gain my sympathies so you can get closer to the Targe?" Anger and hurt radiated from her.

"Nay, love. I am telling you this because coming back here, to the Highlands, coming back to where I was born and raised, has changed me . . . or maybe it has changed me back, to the way I was before I left here." He looked away from her, trying to figure out how to put into words the shift that had taken place deep within him in just a sennight. "Rowan, I am not the man I was when I left England bound for this place to take the Highland Targe for King Edward.

"In England, I am the king's favorite spy and even though few know who I am or what I do, there was pride in that status. I had made something of myself, rising from the ashes of my parentage." He looked back at her. "I found a place where I was valued, not thrown away like so much dung, where I was accepted, not reviled for who I looked like." This was the longest speech of his life but he dared not stop now, not if he had any hope of securing Rowan's future. He needed her to see the truth in the words he was about to speak.

"And then I came here. I met you and your clan. I walked the forest, climbed the ben"—he looked down at his still damp clothes— "fell in the loch. I remembered what it was like to be a Highlander, to wrap oneself in the loyalty and comfort of one's clan. I remembered how it felt to know that this is a place I belong, that these are people I belong to, and that I would do anything to keep them, to keep *you*, happy and safe. I remembered who I wanted to be so long ago."

She didn't say anything for long moments but she didn't look away from him, either, and he counted that a good thing. He could see her battling with herself, softness creeping into her regard, fighting with the hurt he had inflicted. He stepped closer slowly, not wanting to frighten her. He wanted to take her hand in his, draw her back into his embrace, find the peace and the passion they had shared such a short time and such a lifetime ago, but he didn't.

"It is because of my years in the king's service, Rowan, because I have come to know and understand him as I think few do, that I know, beyond any doubt, that he will not stop in his quest for the Highland Targe. If you want your clan to be safe from him, we must send him something he believes to be the Targe immediately and he cannot know from where it came, not precisely. And then we must all disappear so there is no chance he can find us when he does invade."

"Disappear? You understand nothing." She rubbed that spot between her brows that he knew pained her at times like this. "The Targe is not just a thing. It is not just a stone with cryptic runes carved upon it. It is a person. It is a place. It is tied to Dunlairig in ways no one understands, not even Elspet."

"So she is part of the Targe?"

Rowan glared at him but did not answer.

"And the stone in the ermine sack—is that, too, part of the Targe?"

She shook her head, but he didn't think it was an answer to his question. She strode back through the forest toward the burn where he'd found her.

"Where are you going?"

She did not stop. She did not say a word. She kept up her rapid pace until he had to jog to catch up with her. He grabbed her arm, swinging her hard to face him.

She struggled to be released but he did not let go.

"I see you cannot keep even so simple a promise for more than a small space of time." She glared pointedly at his hand on her arm.

"You gave me no choice."

"You had a choice. You always have a choice. Good. Bad. Scottish. English. Keep a promise. Spy for Longshanks. They are all choices."

"And my choice now is to do what I can to keep you and yours safe from Edward."

"By making your king believe he has stolen the Highland Targe, rendering us weak and unarmed? By having us *disappear* from our home so that Edward can run riot into the Highlands?"

"Aye. By removing you from his path. He is not a man any of you wish to come to blows with."

"Oh, aye, he is. He is exactly the man we wish to come to blows with. We will not run like cowards into the bens, quaking at the anger of Edward Longshanks." She jerked her arm free of his grip only because he allowed it.

"Then your clan will be decimated by the English soldiers, whether you have the Targe or Edward does. Edward will not allow anyone who thwarts his rule to live. If you try to protect your castle from him, this route into the Highlands, your family will die. Dunlairig will burn. Is this relic really strong enough to protect you from that?"

"That relic is the key to preventing Edward from attacking us. 'Tis the only hope we have of keeping him from running up the great glen and taking over everything. Elspet would never allow it. I choose not to allow it."

"It will happen anyway. Rowan, I do not want to see your head upon a pike."

"'Twould be better than your friend breaking my will with his abuse."

Nicholas shoved a hand through his water-tangled hair. "You must believe me, I would *never* allow that to happen. Not to you. Not to any woman."

She nodded, studying him. "I know. I do believe you, though I should know better by now, but it changes nothing else."

"So what would you have me do, Rowan? Would you have me walk away and let Edward trample over you and yours?" he asked, afraid of the answer.

"If there is any honor in you, Nicholas of Achnamara, you will come to the castle with me and tell my uncle everything that you know."

"Love, I cannot. Your uncle would—"

"Nicholas, Jeanette said you were a good man. I believed it. Do you? Do you believe you are a good man? Do you really have no heart, no feelings for me, for this clan that has taken you in? Would you exploit Elspet's illness, and my feelings? Duncan's friendship? Kenneth's trust—all for Longshanks's cold regard? Would he embrace you if you fail in this task? Would he offer you a second chance? Would you keep *his* trust?"

Each of her words sliced deeper and deeper, cutting away any shred of doubt about which way his future lay. Nicholas didn't know if he was a good man—he suspected he was not, not after all the things he'd done in his life—but for the first time since he was a boy he wanted to be. He wanted to be what she saw in him, what he had once seen in himself.

"There is no way this will turn out well, Rowan, unless we abandon Dunlairig. None. The king will have his prize."

"Perhaps, but he shall not get it without a fight and you do not ken the fight we can mount." She faced him, fists on her hips, stronger than he'd yet seen her. "Will you fight with us or against us? That is the only question that needs answering."

His choice was simple, clear. "With you, lass. I will fight with you, though I think it a losing fight."

She considered him in silence for long moments, her back rigid and her fists still on her hips. At last she said, "Very well. Come. We must tell Uncle Kenneth everything."

# CHAPTER THIRTEEN

As they neared the castle Rowan kept looking behind her to make sure Nicholas was still there. Sweat beaded her brow and trickled down her back even though the air was cool and soft and her clothes were still damp from her race up the burn. Her breath rasped against her throat. She wanted to trust him but she knew she couldn't. He was a spy. An English spy. And in spite of what he had shared with her about his parents, his choices, his feelings, she did not know if any of it was sincere even though her instinct told her it was. But she couldn't let any soft feelings that had begun to grow between them alter her duty. He was a spy. Uncle Kenneth must know. Anything else was not important.

It helped that Nicholas said nothing as they walked. His silence made it easier to keep her duty foremost in her thoughts, for she feared, if he said anything, touched her, she'd be lost.

And she would not allow that.

They neared the gate passage and Denis was there in his usual guard post, outside the gate, warming his bones, as he liked to say, in the midday sun.

"Whatever happened to you two?" he asked. "It looks as if you tried to drown each other." There was a tenseness in his voice that was unusual.

"A misstep, 'tis all," she answered. "Where is my uncle?"

Nicholas stopped behind her, his presence clear, but he wasn't crowding her.

Denis glanced over her shoulder at her companion, then back to Rowan. "Is aught amiss, lass?"

"I need to speak with my uncle, Denis. Do you ken where he is?"

The old man nodded. "Aye, he is with Lady Elspet." He shifted from foot to foot. "Scotia was looking for you not long ago. She is also there, as is Jeanette."

Rowan's breath hitched. "My aunt?"

"She had another spell from what Scotia said, like yesterday on the ben."

"Go, lass," Nicholas said behind her.

His voice sounded full of concern but she could not trust that. Could not trust him.

"I will find Duncan or Uilliam and tell them everything."

She could well imagine what Uilliam would do when he heard that Nicholas was an English spy, if she could even count on Nicholas doing what he said.

"Nay." She turned to look at him. "Nay. You will come with me. If Elspet is asleep, we shall tell Kenneth together. If she is awake, we will wait for her to sleep. She thinks well of you and I will not do anything to upset her right now. Besides, you have taken one beating today. I do not want you dead by Uilliam's hand before Kenneth has his chance with you."

"Shall I accompany you, Rowan?" Denis asked, his demeanor suddenly prickly.

"I will be fine, Denis." She laid a hand on his arm. "Nicholas will not hurt me"—she glared at Nicholas over her shoulder—"nor anyone else here." Not physically anyway. Emotionally the damage was done.

"Are you sure, lass?"

"Aye. Stay here, Denis. All will be well." She tapped his arm three times with her forefinger and he lowered his chin just enough to indicate he understood there was trouble she could not speak of in front of Nicholas. Rowan finally took a full breath, assured that the watch would be doubled as soon as Nicholas was out of sight. Kissing the old man on the cheek, she whispered, "My thanks."

They left Denis scowling after them and crossed to the tower. Rowan worked to keep her mind blank, her thoughts empty, for if she dared imagine what was about to happen she would not be able to climb a single stair.

Kenneth had prepared them all for trouble and now trouble had found them in the form of a dark-haired stranger who awakened a need in her she'd never known existed. A stranger who had seduced her and betrayed her. A stranger who intended harm to each and every one of the denizens of Dunlairig, to her family and her home regardless of what he thought his motives were.

As they crossed the bailey, Rowan fought to get her emotions under control. Her feelings for Nicholas were all mixed up with the quiet strength and calm attention he had shown when Elspet had been stricken on the ben, with the way he had comforted Rowan—had kissed her—with the laughter and passion they had shared.

And around everything she was choked by his betrayal of her, of her family, and all the implications of danger that treachery brought to those she loved.

She would not allow him to harm her family.

They approached Elspet's chamber and Rowan quietly tapped on the door, unwilling to bring Nicholas into this place without her uncle's permission. Scotia opened the door, looked at the two of them, but oddly said nothing. She opened the door wide enough for Rowan to enter but put her hand out, stopping Nicholas from entering.

"Not you," she said, her voice a choked whisper. "Not now."

Rowan started to object but Nicholas looked over Scotia's head and met her gaze. "I shall wait right here, Rowan. I will not go anywhere."

Torn between trusting his word and seeing what had happened with her aunt, she finally turned to the room and let Scotia close the door on him.

Kenneth sat on one side of the bed, holding Elspet's hand in both of his. Jeanette stood next to him, her hand on her forehead as if she had a headache or was thinking very hard. Scotia sat on the opposite side from Kenneth and took her mum's other hand.

Rowan made her way to Jeanette's side, laying one hand on her uncle's shoulder and the other on her cousin's. "How fares she?"

Jeanette's lips tightened and she swallowed hard but she did not speak. Rowan squeezed her shoulder, understanding all too well the pain of losing a mother. Saying the words would only make it more real.

"What will happen if she dies?" Scotia whispered, sounding like a small child. Rowan's heart lurched. She closed her eyes as the emotions of the day she lost her own mother hovered close, though not the actual memory of it. She had never been able to remember that day.

"We will persevere," Kenneth said. "We must. It is what she would want."

Except for the wheezy rattle of Elspet's labored breathing, there was silence for a long time.

"But what about the blessings? The Targe?" Scotia looked up at Rowan and Jeanette. "How will we protect the clan if neither of us are chosen to replace her?"

A moment of pride warmed Rowan. Scotia was thinking beyond herself for once, but her question was troubling. It would be hard enough to fend off the English with the Targe and its Guardian at full health and strength. Without a Guardian, though . . . would the stone Targe be anything other than a stone?

"What happens if the Guardian of the Targe dies without a successor?" she asked.

Jeanette shook her head slowly. "It has never happened, at least not in any of the Guardians' records I have found. This might be the end of the Highland Targe."

"Jeanette." She drew her cousin to the hearth, far enough away from the bedside to speak quietly without being overheard. "How does the new Guardian of the Targe get chosen? I know you have gone to the wellspring with your mum, hoping to be chosen, but what exactly happens? How does it work?"

Jeanette stirred the full kettle of broth hanging over the fire for long moments. At last she glanced at the bed, and her mother lying there looking more transparent by the moment, her each breath growing louder.

"I am not supposed to speak of it, but I confess I know not what to do." She laid her hand against her forehead again. "Rowan, the power is supposed to seek out the new Guardian. It finds the next lass with a natural gift and chooses her. Mum said it was like she had been empty and felt a sudden upwelling within her, as if she was filled with light and energy. She said it made her dizzy at first, and then had settled within her with an ease and comfort that calmed her and settled her restlessness. It gave her a sense of purpose such as she had never felt before."

The tiny hairs on Rowan's body all stood, the description so close to what she had felt during the blessing . . . and today, when she had purposely called upon whatever that energy was to throw off Archie. She swallowed. It wasn't possible. She wasn't of the line.

"Is there some ritual that must be performed, or some sacred place that must be near for this to happen?"

"I do not ken. For Mum it happened on a late fall day when she and her mum were at the wellspring on the ben. That is why she took us there, hoping that the place was important."

"Her mum was the Guardian before?"

"Aye, and her mum before that. It is not always the eldest daughter, but 'tis most usual. Mum thought since I have a natural talent for healing that I should be the one chosen."

"What was Elspet's natural talent?"

"She had a way with animals. Not a healer exactly, but when she was near, the birthings were easier, injuries healed faster, the cows grew fatter, and the sheep's wool was softer, longer. It worked with crops, too, and people. You've seen her blessings. Whatever power comes to her for that purpose, that is what the power of the Targe made stronger, greater. It made her gift not a weapon but a defense. I have my healing, but it would seem that is not strong enough to make me the Guardian of the Targe. Scotia . . ." She shrugged. "I do not think high emotions are a gift that would serve the safety of the clan."

A long, low moan came from Elspet and she grew suddenly restless in the bed. Jeanette and Rowan made haste to her side. Her eyes opened, a wild-eyed look there as her gaze careened from one person to another.

"Mum," Jeanette said, kneeling and brushing her mother's hair off her face. "Are you in pain?" Jeanette's voice cracked on the last word.

Elspet didn't respond but shifted her stare to Scotia who sniffled as a single tear ran down her cheek. "Mummy?"

Elspet shifted back to Jeanette as if she expected something from her.

"Auntie, are you thirsty?" Rowan said, lifting the cup that stood filled by the bedside.

Elspet finally looked at Rowan, glaring at her, shaking her head rapidly. She pulled her hand from Kenneth's and flailed it in the air until Jeanette took it, shushing her agitated mother. Elspet pulled her hand away again and reached for Rowan.

Rowan could feel the weight of her cousins' and uncle's eyes on her as she stepped closer and took Elspet's hand in hers. "I'm here, Auntie."

But Elspet didn't calm. She grew more agitated, her hand gripping Rowan's with a strength Elspet hadn't had since she had been stricken on the ben yesterday. She gripped it so hard her nails bit into Rowan's skin but Rowan had the strangest sense that her aunt was trying to let go, that some other power made her . . .

"Nay," she whispered. "Nay, Auntie." She tried to pass her aunt's hand into Jeanette's but Elspet would not let go.

Elspet's breath grew harsher and harsher, as if she were running a great distance . . . or fighting something. Fear filled Rowan just as she was hit with a maelstrom that forced its way inside her, pushing through her skin from every direction to fill her. Her skin crawled. Her muscles cramped painfully. It was a stronger, brutal version of what she had experienced at the blessing. She tried to push it away, but the pain of fighting it was almost more than she could endure.

"Nay, Auntie, I do not want it!" She dropped to her knees on the cold wooden floor, but Elspet still would not release her hand, or perhaps Rowan could not let go. Through the blackness that threatened her sight, and the bright, sharp pain that ran underneath her skin, she heard a high keening sound like a banshee let loose in the room. Shouts tangled around the keening, but Rowan was so lost in the pain and the fear, so lost in the determination that she would not take this into her that she could make no sense of anything but the battle she waged.

Nicholas crashed open the door and stopped, stunned at the scene that confronted him. Wind filled the room, whipping the fire into a frenzy of writhing flames, throwing ashes into the air to sweep around the people huddled about the bed. The people.

Jeanette and Scotia crouched over their keening mother, sheltering her from the debris that was caught up in the wind. He looked to the window for the source, but it was closed. Kenneth gripped a huddled Rowan by the shoulders, pulling her away from the bed, away from where her hand and Elspet's were clenched. Above the wind was a sound like a wounded animal, high, piercing, full of pain and fear, and lower were the shouts of the MacAlpins, the crying of Scotia, the entreaties of Jeanette, the bellowing of Kenneth.

"Let her go!" Kenneth shouted over and over again but Nicholas could not tell if he was shouting at Rowan or at Elspet. "Let her go! You are hurting her!" Again, he could not tell which woman Kenneth spoke to.

And then he realized Rowan was the only silent person in the room. She pulled against her aunt's grip. She sheltered her head with her other arm, and he realized her silence wasn't absolute. Whispered words spiked through the chaos: "I do not want it. I do not want it."

He did not know what was going on, but he knew from Rowan's posture that she was in pain, that she feared whatever was happening to her. In the next breath he was by her side, shoving Kenneth off of her, cradling her against his chest as he slid his hands along her arm toward Elspet's hand.

He ignored the odd snapping sensation that leapt from Rowan's skin to his and worked to free her from Elspet's remarkably strong grip. When he finally slid Rowan's hand free she slumped against him. Elspet's keening immediately quieted and the MacAlpins all froze, their eyes on him and Rowan.

"What happened?" he demanded of the trio that quickly formed a shield between Rowan and Elspet.

No one answered.

"What happened?!" he shouted. Rowan tried to push out of his lap, but he was not prepared to let her go until he knew what they had done to her. He sat back on the floor and pulled her tight against him. He settled his arms tightly around her. "What did Lady Elspet do to you?" When Rowan didn't answer, didn't even meet his gaze, he looked from Kenneth to Jeanette, then to Scotia, but they were all wide-eyed and breathing hard as if they'd just fought a battle.

And perhaps they had.

He looked down at Rowan, pushing her tangled hair off her face and lifting her chin so she would look at him. "Are you all right, love?"

She was dazed, her eyes wide as if she'd been through some terrible ordeal.

"I did not want it," she whispered to him, but turned her attention to her family, still standing guard between her and Elspet.

"What, lass? What did you not want?" he asked quietly.

"Mum's power." He looked up to find Jeanette staring at her cousin.

"Power? You mean the power of the Highland Targe?" he asked before he realized he should not know anything about the Targe.

Jeanette's gaze moved from Rowan to him, her eyes narrowing. Suspicion rolled off of her like waves crashing ashore in a gale.

"It should not have happened this way. She is not of the blood. She is no blood relation." Jeanette turned back to her mother, though Nicholas still could not see the Lady. "Why, Mum? Why Rowan?"

A raspy croak was all the answer she got.

"Wheesht." Jeanette sat on the bed, her palm against her mother's cheek as if she wiped away tears. "Do not fash yourself. 'Twill be fine." He heard her heavy sigh. "I can teach her what you taught me. There will be another Guardian after all . . ." She glanced over her shoulder at Rowan, her face shuttered as surely as a window against a winter's storm. "Just not who we thought."

Another raspy croak answered her.

"Wheesht. Sleep now. Your work will be continued."

She turned to Rowan and Nicholas. Rowan, still held captive in his lap, pushed to her feet, swaying slightly until Nicholas slid an arm around her waist and steadied her.

"I am sorry, Jeanette," Rowan said.

"Take her out of here," Jeanette directed her cold, emotionless words to Nicholas. "Take her to her chamber and wait with her. I will attend her shortly."

Jeanette had been nothing but sweet, quiet, almost docile, since he had met her a sennight ago. Now she was hard and commanding, and still no one had explained what had happened between Elspet and Rowan.

Slowly he led Rowan to the door. As he passed close to Kenneth he stopped.

"There is something of great importance we must speak of," he said to the chief.

"Not now."

"Agreed, but it cannot wait long."

Kenneth glared at him, his gaze softening as he reached out and touched Rowan's shoulder. "I shall find you as soon as I may."

ROWAN STOOD IN THE MIDDLE OF HER CHAMBER, GRATEFUL THAT Nicholas was there. He sat quietly on her bed, hands on his knees, watching her but not pushing.

She had to move. She went to the window, but that wasn't far enough so she paced to the door, and back to the window, over and over, her mind a whirling mess. She couldn't stop her thoughts from caroming through the events of the last few hours any more than she could stop her feet.

She turned back from the door again, stopping short of crashing into Nicholas. She stepped around him and kept going.

"Rowan, stop," he said. "Tell me what happened to you."

She reached the window, placed her hands on the sill and leaned into the fresh air. What *could* she tell him? How could she share with this man, this stranger, this spy of King Edward, that she was now the Guardian of the Targe? How could she give him the information that if he or the hateful Archie were to complete their mission, they would have to take not only the Targe stone, but her, too?

She could not tell him that. No matter how much she wanted to trust him, how much her instinct said she could, she dared not give him that much knowledge or that much power over her and the clan.

But she had to tell him something. He had seen too much. Knew too much already. But what?

"Lass." He came up behind her and gently turned her to face him. "Something happened in there. Lady Elspet sounded like she was dying. You were in pain. And I felt crackling along your skin when I helped you let go of her hand. You kept saying you did not want 'it,' but I do not ken what 'it' was."

Instinct warred with logic. She wanted to explain it all, knew she needed to, that he would help her, but . . .

"Tell me what you ken of the Targe," she said.

"Ken is a strong word."

She stared at him, waiting to see how far down this path he had already travelled.

"I think the stone Elspet carries in the ermine sack is the Highland Targe, a relic, not an actual shield. I believe there is real power associated with it, though it is beyond my ken what it is or how 'tis even possible. I know I felt something pass over us when Lady Elspet performed the blessing in the bailey, and I know you felt it even more powerfully than I or anyone else did. And that leads me to believe that Elspet is needed to invoke whatever the power is that comes from the Highland Targe."

He knew everything, or almost. Rowan waited, letting him hear his own words, letting him put the truth together for himself. One breath. Two.

His eyes grew large. "You."

Still she stared at him, telling him nothing herself.

"Whatever Elspet's role was, it is now yours. That is what happened in her chamber, is it not? She gave the position to you. You are the keeper—"

"Guardian," she corrected him.

He cocked his head, reached out to cup her cheek in his palm. "You did not want to be the Guardian," he whispered.

"I should not be."

"Jeanette? It passes from mother to daughter?"

"Usually, but not this time."

"I should not know this," he said, concern gathered in his eyes, though she knew not if it was for her or for himself.

"Aye, you should not. It would be far better for you if you did not."

"We cannot let Archie or Edward learn any of this." Now he was the one to pace to the door, turn and pace back to her. "Archie already suspects there is something special about you after you threw him off." His gaze leapt to hers. "Was that from the Targe?"

All the turmoil in Rowan went still with that question. "It could not be," she said, thinking out loud. "I was not chosen yet." Her pulse jumped. Such an ability, though she didn't understand exactly what it was, enhanced by the Targe would be a formidable defense for the clan.

She knew far too little about the Highland Targe to do more than guess that this was why she was chosen, but Jeanette had been taught to take up the role since she was born. Jeanette would have the answers Rowan needed.

Jeanette and Scotia cleaned their mum's solar while Kenneth stood at the end of his wife's bed, as if he were afraid to take his eyes off her. Elspet still lived, though Jeanette was truly surprised by that, but Elspet was diminished even more than before. She looked so tiny in the big bed, and so frail, as if the slightest touch would shatter her bones. Somehow ashes had ended up everywhere leaving a thin layer of grey powdery dust on everything, including all the bed linens and Lady Elspet. Helen had tended the fire and helped wipe down the chamber. Jeanette and Scotia changed the bedding and at last, Jeanette took a scrap of linen and dipped it in the bowl of fresh water Helen had fetched for them.

"Scotia," she said quietly as she wiped the ashes from her mother's face as gently as possible, "get some broth and bring it here. Mum? Can you hear me?"

Elspet's lids fluttered open and after a moment she focused on her daughter's face. Regret swam in her eyes and Jeanette had to take a deep breath to keep from letting the same emotion show in her own. She didn't know what failing had made her unfit to follow in her mother's footsteps, or what gift Rowan had that made her an acceptable Guardian, but the Targe had chosen and it was too late to make whatever amends might have shifted the choice to Jeanette.

"'Twill be all right, Mum." She blinked hard. "I am sorry I let you down, but all the preparations you gave to me, Rowan will have. I will do whatever I must to make sure the clan stays protected. I promise you."

Still, Elspet looked at her eldest daughter with sadness and regret.

"Will you take some broth, Mum?" Scotia stood next to Jeanette with a small cup in her hand. Elspet closed her eyes and turned her head away. Jeanette leaned her head against her sister's arm.

"So Rowan is the one?" Scotia asked.

"Aye, 'twould appear so."

"But why?"

"Why, indeed?" Kenneth said, the first words he had spoken since taking up his vigil at the end of the bed.

"I do not ken," Jeanette said. "'Twas not how Mum said it would be when the Targe chose a new Guardian. It should not have hurt either of them."

"Could it have hurt because it was not meant to be?" Scotia said.

Jeanette closed her eyes and tried to remember everything that she had seen and heard in those long moments when the power had been taken from Elspet and . . .

"It was forced on Rowan and she did not want it," Jeanette whispered.

"What?" Kenneth asked.

"She did not want it. Rowan. She said she did not want it. She must have been fighting it." She rose and looked at the room, remembering how things had been tossed about the room by an unnatural wind. Suspicion rose in her like a thunderhead sparking with lightning.

"I must speak with her," she said more to herself than to her father and sister. "Scotia, you stay here. If she wakes, try to get her to drink some broth but do not speak of what just happened. She is upset by it and she should not spend her strength on fretting over what cannot be undone."

"Are you sure it cannot be undone?" Scotia asked. "It is not right. It should be you."

Jeanette agreed, but for the sake of her family she could not indulge herself in such feelings. "'Tis done. Now we must determine why so Rowan can be taught how to use the Targe."

She picked up the ermine sack that held the ancient Targe stone that focused each Guardian's unique gift. It belonged to Rowan now, but Jeanette would not give it to her until she was sure that Rowan would accept the duty that had been bestowed upon her this day, however unexpectedly. Though if she did not . . .

"I shall be with Rowan. Fetch me if Mum needs me."

Scotia took Jeanette's place at the edge of the bed, settling the cup on the table where the ermine sack usually sat.

"Da." Jeanette waited for him to react. When he didn't, she said his name again, but still he stared at Elspet. She stood next to him, wrapping her arm around his waist and leaning against him. "Come with me?"

He looked down at her then, his face ten years older than it had appeared that morning. "I will stay here," he sighed and his shoulders sagged. "Nicholas said there was something important to talk about. Ask him what it was and if you think it needs tending, find Uilliam."

Jeanette wished she could stay here, too, holding their family together with her will alone, but she knew her duty lay in preparing Rowan for the tasks before her. And in order to do that, she had to find out what secret her cousin had been hiding from her, from them, for all these years.

# CHAPTER FOURTEEN

NICHOLAS WATCHED AS ROWAN'S PATIENCE FRAYED. HE KNEW SHE did not wish to return to Elspet's chamber, or she would have done so already. He had considered fetching Jeanette himself, but decided, given his uncertain position at the moment, that was not a good idea. He knew there was more than one confrontation with Rowan's family ahead of them and he would do whatever he could to take their anger onto his own shoulders, sheltering her from at least that much.

Rowan rubbed the spot between her brows and reached for the door latch just as the door swung open. Jeanette stood there, staring at Rowan, as if she were a stranger, before she scowled at him.

"You may leave."

"Nay." Rowan stood almost nose-to-nose with her cousin. "He must stay. We must speak to Uncle Kenneth and then I must speak with you."

"Da said to call Uilliam if I had need, but not to disturb him. The . . . What happened . . . Mum is very weak. He will not leave her side."

Rowan seemed to fold in on herself. "I am so sorry," she said, reaching for Jeanette's hands, but Jeanette stepped around her into the room. "My being chosen should not have been possible."

"Unless you were keeping something secret, something important, powerful."

"I am not keeping anything from you, Jeanette. I had no idea I had any gift until Nicholas helped me to see . . ." Her gaze flickered to him, then back to her cousin.

Jeanette's gaze had followed Rowan's and now rested on him. "We should not speak of this in front of him."

"He kens—not everything, but enough."

There was more he did not know?

Jeanette's shoulders went rigid and her hands fisted by her side. For the first time Nicholas noticed the ermine sack she gripped. "He kens? How? Why? It is forbidden."

"Do you think I do not ken that? I did not tell him. He figured out most of it on his own." Rowan stepped between Nicholas and Jeanette. Nicholas leaned a little to the right so he could still see the blonde woman. "He was sent here to steal the Highland Targe."

Jeanette cocked her head and her eyebrows rose, as if she had not heard correctly. "Steal?"

"Aye." Rowan seemed to hold her breath while she let that information sink in.

Jeanette's chin went up and she moved the sack behind her, holding it so Nicholas could no longer see it.

Nicholas rose and faced the women. "I was sent by King Edward, but—"

"'Tis too much." Jeanette turned and strode to the door. "Rowan, do not say another word to this man." She wrenched open the door and shouted for her father.

Rowan started forward. "Jeanette, you must—"

"Wheesht, Rowan. You have said too much already." She screamed for her father this time and Nicholas heard the door at the far end of the corridor bang open, followed by heavy footfalls coming toward them.

"I told you not to—" Kenneth said as he came into view.

Jeanette held up her hand to stop her father, both physically and verbally. Then she pointed at Nicholas. "He was sent here to steal the Targe."

Kenneth's shaggy brows drew down as he looked from Jeanette to the pair in the room. "Is this true, Rowan?" He stepped in, leaving Jeanette out in the hallway and very effectively blocking the only way out.

"'Tis, Uncle, but—"

"For who?" Kenneth said, cutting her off.

Rowan glanced at him and was about to answer but Nicholas stepped forward. "For King Edward," he said.

"Jeanette, fetch Uilliam and Duncan. Now!"

"Uncle?"

Kenneth glowered at Rowan. "You would bring him into our midst, into your aunt's chamber, when you knew this about him?" It was a question, but it was also a condemnation.

"We were coming to tell you. There is another spy."

"Another? Within these walls?!"

"Nay, sir," Nicholas said as he moved away from Rowan, hoping to draw the chief's anger with him. "Not within these walls, but he will be back, and he means to have the Targe for Edward whether I deliver it or not."

"And you will NOT!" The bellowed words were matched by the menace in Kenneth as he strode further into the room.

Nicholas said nothing.

"You will not," Kenneth repeated, shaking his head. "Rowan, you would go to Longshanks with this man?"

"Nay, Uncle."

Emptiness unfurled inside Nicholas.

"Then you cannot take the Targe to Longshanks," Kenneth said to Nicholas. "You shall not have my niece now that she is . . . She was not supposed to be—" The man scraped his fingers through his hair. "You shall not have my niece."

"I ken that." The emptiness spread, hollowing him out at the thought of all the reasons he could not have Rowan for himself, her lost trust heading up the list.

Kenneth stared at him for a long time. "He does not ken it all though, does he?"

"Most, Uncle, but not all." Rowan said.

Confusion. *He does not ken it all?* There was definitely more to the Targe than he had sorted out. There was the stone, there was power, and there was the Guardian who called upon that power, but there was something about the passing of the Guardianship to Rowan, beyond that she was not Elspet's daughter, which was not expected. He still had so many questions—but this was not the time to ask them.

There was a thick silence in the room as the men faced off. Rowan sank down on the bed.

"Do not hurt him, Uncle. I do not believe he means us harm any longer, but there is the other, Archie, a ginger-haired man, who does. Let Nicholas help us defend against whatever trouble that one will bring upon us."

Kenneth said nothing and never took his eyes off Nicholas's.

"Uncle?"

"Your uncle cannot take any chances that I will bring harm to you and yours, Rowan, intended or not." He saw a glimmer then in Kenneth's eyes and thought, perhaps, it was respect—a little at least.

Uilliam and Duncan pounded down the corridor then, skidding to a halt at the open doorway.

"What is it, Kenneth?" Uilliam asked, taking in the tense scene.

"Take Nicholas, if that is his real name, and restrain him."

Duncan looked shocked at the instructions but said nothing. Uilliam grunted as he grabbed Nicholas by the arm, but before he could be dragged from the chamber, Nicholas reached for Jeanette's arm, stopping his forward motion.

"Be easy on her, mistress," he said to her quietly, "she looks strong, but she is much bruised by all of this. She would never do anything to disappoint you if it were in her power not to."

Jeanette stared at him as she wrenched her arm free of his grip. Uilliam marched him out of the chamber, Duncan following behind.

JEANETTE ONCE MORE STOOD IN THE DOORWAY, THE MUSCLE IN HER right cheek working as Rowan knew it did when she was angry.

"Why would you bring him into the castle when you knew he was a spy?"

Rowan winced. Jeanette's words stung as if they were tiny daggers thrown one by one. Rowan had been asking herself the same thing, over and over again, and the same answer came to her over and over again. "'Twas the right thing to do. He agreed."

Jeanette stared at her a long moment, her mouth opening and closing as if she tried to speak but couldn't, until finally she said, "But you let Da take him away."

Rowan nodded her head slowly. "We knew 'twas likely when we decided to come and tell Uncle about the plot."

"And you are all right with that?" Jeanette took two steps into the room Rowan had shared with her and Scotia ever since she'd come here, an orphan, eleven years ago, as if she were both afraid of and angry at Rowan.

"Do I have a choice?" Anger crackled through her, shoving her heart to a rapid pace. She leaped to her feet and faced her cousin. "Do I have a choice about any of this?"

They stared at each other a long moment until Jeanette broke eye contact and looked down at her feet. "'Twould appear none of us has a choice about anything."

"'Twould," Rowan agreed, roughly jerking her gown to straighten it. "I ken you are hurt that I was chosen as Guardian, but you must believe that I neither wanted it, nor called it to me in any way."

"If calling it worked, 'twould have been mine long ago."

The sharp edge of bitterness cut through Rowan's anger, making her suddenly aware of just what not becoming the Guardian meant to Jeanette. Her cousin had been trained to use the Highland Targe her whole life, steeped in the legend and lore of the stone and the prayers that Elspet had painstakingly taught her hour after hour until she knew them each by heart, what each was useful for, the symbols to be made in the air, the rituals to call the protective energies.

"Exactly. So the question is: Why did it choose me? I am not of Elspet's bloodline. I have no training. And until this very day I had no idea I had a gift—" The feeling of pulling that odd flowing sensation through her and throwing Archie off with it made her breath hitch.

She could see the moment Jeanette switched from hurt to curious. Her eyes narrowed and her attention focused completely on

Rowan. Her right cheek no longer jumped in anger, but she chewed on the opposite side of her bottom lip.

"You have a gift? That explains some of this mystery. What is it?"

"That I cannot say. I know I can use it to repel dangerous things, but I know not what to call it or even exactly what I can do with it."

"'Repel dangerous things'? You had need of this today?"

"Aye."

"Nicholas?"

"Nay! The other one, Archie. He grabbed me. I felt something flowing into me so I pulled at it, then pushed it out from me. I threw him off." She thought back to that moment. "I threw him quite a ways into the loch." She smiled, pleased with herself.

Jeanette sat on the end of her bed and Rowan sat beside her.

"But that still does not explain why I was chosen," Rowan said. "'Twas supposed to be you."

"Never in any of the lore Mum has taught me has the Targe ever chosen a Guardian without some form of unusual gift. Some see visions, some have an attraction to water, scrying the future in it. Some are able to focus emotions and use them to protect the glen and the clan. Some, like Mum, have an affinity for growing things and a knack for keeping them healthy and safe." Jeanette sighed. "It seems each Guardian's gift was needed in her time. Which means your ability to repel danger . . . well, it seems likely 'twill be needed to keep the English out of our glen and out of the Highlands, aye?"

"The Highlands? I thought that was but a tale. I denied such a possibility when Nicholas mentioned it."

"It is part of the lore, but the stories of the Targe are steeped in history and it would seem that this may be what you are called upon to do."

Rowan considered the ramifications of what Jeanette said. It was a heavy burden, one she did not want. She squeezed her suddenly trembling hands together, ashamed of her fear. She was the Guardian. There was no choice. She would do whatever she must to protect her family, her clan, and very likely this route into the Highlands.

"You will help me?" she asked Jeanette.

"I will. Of course I will. You must learn how to focus your gift with the Targe stone in order to protect us from the troubles Nicholas and the other spy have brought into our glen. I am the only one now who can teach you that, as well as all the other things required of the Guardian."

Jeanette hiked one leg up on the bed and turned to face Rowan. Curiosity warred with sadness in her cousin's eyes.

"This day you were in peril when you called upon your gift, and this was before the Targe chose you."

"True."

"Are you certain this was the first time you accessed this ability?"

"I felt the flowing sensation during the blessing."

Jeanette pursed her lips. "That would make sense. When Mum called upon the power of the Targe, it found you. Other than that?"

Rowan rubbed her forehead and searched her memory. "Headaches."

"What?"

"Headaches. I had one start as Elspet began the blessing. That is what I felt just before the curtain wall fell. And after"—she dropped her hand from her forehead —"'twas gone, as if the pressure had been released." Rowan closed her eyes and tried to remember the details of the wall falling. "Do you think I made the curtain wall fall, Jeanette? Is that possible?" She rubbed a sudden chill from her arms.

"You were arguing, right?"

"Aye. Scotia had snuck off to meet Conall instead of spending time with your mum. I was angry, frustrated, and so was she."

"And she was making it worse, right? Making you angrier?"

"Aye, but there is no way my anger made the wall fall—is there?"

Jeanette paced away to the far side of the room and back before she spoke again. "Rowan," she said as she knelt in front of her cousin and took Rowan's hands in her own. "There was another time a wall fell—can you remember, the day your parents died?"

Rowan trembled. It was the memory Elspet had tried to get her to recall. The memory that Rowan had not been able to grasp, but that filled her with panic and grief. Even now, at merely the suggestion she remember, her heart hammered and her palms grew sweaty.

"Rowan, look at me. Your parents' cottage—Da said it looked as if it had been blown apart from within. Your parents were inside. You, he found wandering in the forest not far away, without a scratch upon you. 'Twas not so different from what happened with the curtain wall, save this time it was Scotia and Nicholas who emerged without so much as a scratch or a bruise."

Rowan pushed at the dark place in her memory, trying to imagine what Jeanette described, and suddenly it was all there, so fresh it might have happened yesterday. Her parents inside the cottage, shouting at each other, growing louder and louder and louder until young Rowan had left her post by the door and retreated to the burn that burbled at the edge of the clearing where the cottage was set, deep in the forest, far away from any other families or homes. She had stood in the middle of the icy water, wishing the sound of the water spilling over rocks and tree roots would drown out the angry voices. She'd crouched, almost sitting in the water, covering her ears but staring at the cottage, wishing they would stop, that the arguing would end. She had whispered, "Make it stop, make it stop, make it stop," over and over again, until her voice was almost as loud as those in the cottage, when suddenly, her mother had screamed and the walls of the cottage had exploded. Stones sailed out in every direction. Rowan had ducked her head to her knees and thrown her hands out in front of her as if her scrawny arms would keep her safe from the large stones and splintered wood that flew toward her.

After long moments of stones thudding, wood splintering, and Rowan's own shrieks of fear, there was silence, but she dared not look . . . not yet. At length a jay landed near her, slicing through the quiet with its raspy cry and Rowan decided the bird wouldn't be there if it wasn't safe.

It was no wonder she had not wanted to remember what she saw that day. The house looked as if some great force had blown it apart from the inside, pushing all the walls away and sending bits of the roof out in every direction . . . except for where Rowan crouched.

It was as if Rowan had forced all the materials flying toward her to fly back to the cottage. A great void in the debris sat between her and the remains of her home.

And then she'd remembered her parents had been inside.

"Mum!" she'd screamed as she ran to the cottage. "Da!"

It had not taken long for her to find their mangled bodies, pinned beneath the large stones that should have flown away from them.

"What did you remember, Ro?"

The strength of Jeanette's grip pulled her back from the memories.

"Saints and angels." Rowan swallowed hard, the images of her parents, pinned and broken by the stones that had once been their home, still falling through her mind. "Jeanette"—she looked up at her beloved cousin then—"I turned the stones away from me, back upon them. I killed my parents with this . . . this . . ." She could not call it a gift. "I must have made the curtain wall fall."

"You just said you turned the stones away from you when you were little. Do you think you caused them to fly toward you first?"

Rowan looked inward to the devastation that was now so vivid in her memory. She remembered the pattern of stones, as if the house had thrown itself in every direction so that the stones and thatch and broken bits of wood had spread out from the cottage evenly . . . except for that odd void between Rowan and her home. If she had made it explode, wouldn't it have all flown away from her? A new understanding occurred to her and she spoke slowly, carefully, putting pieces together as if she were re-assembling the stones from that horrific day.

"I think my mum did that. They were arguing about living so far away from everyone. Da wanted to move nearer to his family but Mum was afraid what his family would do if they learned of her feyness, of her odd ability to move things with her thoughts. She was afraid they would call her a witch, or do something worse."

She listened to the argument in her memory, something she'd long since thought she'd forgotten but it was there, waiting for her to rediscover it. "Her own family had not wanted her. She once told me that her mother, who I learned then was not her real mother, had found her at the mouth of a barrow when she was only three or four. Her real family had probably left her there for the fey to take back to their realm. I do not think she had a happy childhood, for it was her wish to live away from everyone and when her foster mother died, she did just that, moving away from the clan that barely tolerated her, out into the forest where no one would bother her. I remember them yelling. I remember Da saying there was nothing to fear, that she was as normal as the next woman, and Mum said . . ."

Jeanette let her cousin be silent for long moments before she urged her to continue. "It's in the past now, Rowan, but we need to understand your gift."

Rowan closed her eyes, letting the memories become vivid pictures behind her eyelids. "Mum screamed, 'Truly?! Is this normal?' and then the house exploded."

"And why do you believe you killed them, not your mother?"

"Because they would have been fine, with everything blowing away from them except . . . except for the parts I blew back at them."

"Rowan, look at me."

Rowan let her eyes open, replacing the horror of that destroyed grove with her cousin's serious expression.

"You were a child and you were protecting yourself. Do you think your mum could have lived with herself if she had lived and you had died from her temper? Can you imagine my mum living with such a thing?"

Rowan shook her head and a single tear broke free from her lashes and trickled over her cheek. Jeanette quickly wiped it away.

"You were a child. Clearly your gift is triggered by high emotion—fear for your life, anger with Scotia . . ."

"I understand the fear triggering it, but why that time with Scotia?" Rowan asked, happy to focus on something that hadn't ended in anyone dying. "The wall should have fallen away from us if I caused it, but it did not. It fell toward us except for that one part. Could someone else have a similar . . ."

"Gift, Rowan. I know you do not see it as one now, but I am certain 'tis a gift. We must learn how you can use it with the Targe."

"But the wall . . ."

"It did not fall away from you, into the bailey. Hmm, I wonder if there is anyone who saw it actually fall?"

"Denis was at the gate. He might have seen it."

Jeanette was nodding, one finger tapping her lips. "We need to speak with Denis. We need to understand exactly how that wall fell in order to determine if that was you, or something else at play." She jumped to her feet and was out the door before Rowan could say anything. Jeanette leaned back into the doorway. "Are you not coming?"

Rowan recognized Jeanette was on the hunt for knowledge. She looked down at the dirty and still-damp clothes she wore, shrugged, and followed, pleased that Jeanette's anger had dissipated but worried about what they would learn.

Nicholas allowed the silent Uilliam to drag him out of the tower, and across the bailey. He did nothing to rile the man any more than he already was. He needed Uilliam to calm down enough to listen to him, to understand that he was not the risk facing them, to convince Kenneth that Archie and King Edward were the immediate danger. They stopped before one of the small outbuildings built against the curtain wall. Duncan opened the door and Uilliam shoved Nicholas inside.

"You can rot in here for all I care," Uilliam hissed at him. "Longshanks will not see his blasted spy again, 'tis a sure thing."

Duncan glared at him and Nicholas's stomach dipped. Duncan had been quickly becoming a real friend, not like Archie, and Nicholas was surprised how sad he was to lose that. At least Rowan had not severed their relationship . . . not completely, anyway.

The thought of Rowan had him pushing off the wall he'd landed against, reminding him of just how much was at stake if he could not make them understand.

"There is more danger here than me, lads," he said. "There is another spy, Archibald of Easton. He knows about the Highland

Targe. He was sent here with me to find it, to take it . . . or destroy it." That got their full attention.

"Destroy it?" Uilliam stepped into the still-open doorway, blocking out most of the lingering twilight so that Nicholas could not make out his expression, though the waves of anger and distrust rolling off the man were not to be mistaken for anything less than mortal danger.

"He kens it is kept here. He kens that I suspected that Lady Elspet controlled the Targe. He will come for it, for her."

"How does this Archibald of Easton ken this?" Duncan's wary voice came from behind Uilliam. Duncan shoved his way next to the bear so he could see into the chilly, damp hut.

Nicholas wanted to look away, to lie, to revert to his old slippery self and find the way out of this. But that would take him away from Rowan, away from these good people who deserved better than to be expendable pawns to Edward's greed. It would take him away from the man he wanted to be. He met Duncan's gaze and spoke the truth. "He learned it from me."

Uilliam charged him, grabbing him by the collar of his tunic and slamming him against the back wall of the tiny building. "I— Ye—I should—"

The punch to his gut, like an iron ball flung from a trebuchet, would have doubled him over, had not Uilliam still held him up with one hand. Nicholas tried to breathe but couldn't pull any air into his lungs. He tried again. At last Uilliam let go and Nicholas bent over, hands on his knees, desperately gasping for air.

When he could breathe again, he looked up from his bent position. "I did not do it on purpose. He overheard Rowan and I—"

"Rowan would never speak to a stranger about the Targe." Uilliam stood very close still, his feet spread and his fists clenched at his sides.

"She did not." He held up his hand to stop the growl that was coming from Uilliam. "I came here knowing some about it—not exactly what it was, nor did I have any understanding that a specific person had any part in its function. We thought it would be something like the Stone of Scone—an ancient relic that was held in great reverence, but that was really a symbol, something to hang beliefs upon. But then . . ."

"But then?" Duncan asked, silencing the renewed growl from their companion.

Nicholas took a shallow, careful breath, testing to see how much damage Uilliam's fist had done him. So far, 'twas not bad. He was not naïve enough to think it would not be worse on the morrow. When he was sure he could both stand and breathe he continued

"But then Lady Elspet performed the blessing and I felt it, felt the power in the blessing. Rowan was quite literally stunned by it, though she says such a thing had not happened before. It became clear to me that it was not just a legend, not just a relic. It became clear that there really was power in the Targe. 'Twas later that I saw the stone and 'twas not until this day that I understood"—he suddenly realized these men did not yet know that Elspet was no longer the Guardian. No one had told them and it was not his place to reveal the news—"about the Guardian."

"And this Archie kens this?" Duncan asked when Uilliam did not.

"Some of it. Enough to know that taking the Targe to King Edward will ensure that nothing will stop the king's men from sweeping up this valley and into the heart of the Highlands. Enough to know that the one who delivers it will gain great wealth and the monarch's regard."

"You." Uilliam's voice was flat, dangerous.

" 'Twas to be me and Archie but things changed."

"Rowan." It was Duncan now.

"Aye." Nicholas held his breath, waiting to see if they would believe him, though he knew if the situation were reversed he would never believe the story.

"You ken there can never be anything between you?" Duncan said, a curious softness taking the hard edge off the words.

Nicholas looked Duncan in the eye—the man deserved that. "I ken it is difficult, but I hope . . ."

"Does she feel the same?" Duncan asked again.

Nicholas nodded, his own hope that somehow they would find their way through this mess to each other, clogging his throat. "She did before she learned why I came here. I hope she will again."

"I will be damned if I allow such a thing." Uilliam's voice was a low snarl. "Kenneth will agree."

Nicholas refused to let hope slip away, though he knew the road ahead of him was fraught with many obstacles.

"I understand," he said, "but I am determined to keep Rowan and this clan safe from Edward's machinations. Know this for the truth it is: Archie is dangerous. I have known him for years, and was not unlike him . . . until recently. He feels nothing for those between him and his prize. Plus he feels betrayed by me and that will fuel his desire to take the Targe and win the reward Edward dangles in front of us like a worm to a hungry fish. You ken Edward's drive to conquer Scotland, to be king of all the islands. Archie is a mirror of his master and he will not stop until he has his prize."

"So you tell us this out of the pureness of your heart?" Uilliam clearly did not believe him.

"Nay, for there is no pureness in my heart except where Rowan has taken up residence within it." The warmth he'd drawn from her, the caring, the beginnings of love, filled him, hardening him to his task: the betrayal of not only Archie, but King Edward.

If he succeeded in thwarting the taking of the Targe from these good people his life would be forfeit. King Edward would never let such a betrayal stand unanswered. One way or another, it would surely be Nicholas's head upon a pike outside the Tower. But if he could contrive to keep Rowan safe from such a fate, and her clan, then perhaps he would be worthy of the trust she had given him before she knew the truth. Perhaps he would earn it back.

"I would not see Rowan," he said, "nor any of those she loves, hurt because of my past and my belated conscience. Keep me here if you must. Bar the door. But warn Kenneth. Send out scouts to find Archie before he returns here to take the Targe, for I guarantee that he will not rest until he has it."

The two men stood before him, distrust rolling off them as they assessed his words. It was clear that any trust he had built with these two was destroyed.

"Ask Rowan if what I say is true."

"Rowan has met this Archie?" Duncan's voice was pure surprise.

Nicholas shoved his hair back from his face, wincing at the memory of what Archie had tried to do to Rowan. "She has," he said. "Ask her and do not tarry. Go find her now. Archie must be stopped *before* he gets here. 'Twill take little effort for him to find his way into the castle with the curtain wall laid low. He has no conscience. Everyone who bides here is in mortal danger if they get in his way."

Uilliam glowered at him from beneath his bushy eyebrows, his fists still clenched so hard that even in the dim light of the hut the man's knuckles shown white. A frustrated "arrrg" burst from him as he pivoted and left the hut. Nicholas took a long, deep breath.

"Will he speak to Rowan?" he asked Duncan, who still stood staring at him.

"Aye, he will. I shall see to it."

"My thanks. If I had this to do again, I would not have brought such danger to your door."

Duncan stood stone still for a moment before answering. "I do not ken why, but I believe you. I have seen you with Rowan and she with you. Your affection for each other does not feel feigned. She would not have brought you into Lady Elspet's chamber if she did not trust you."

Nicholas did not correct the man, for he had not been taken inside the chamber by Rowan, only to it, but he would take what advantage he could if it meant Duncan would help stop Archie.

"Duncan, I know Archie better than anyone. I know the man's habits, his strengths. I know his weaknesses, too. I need to speak with the chief. None of you know how Archie thinks or what he is capable of. I am the one to stop him *before* he gets back to the castle."

Nicholas could see Duncan weighing his words. "Naught good can come of this situation," Duncan said. "You will not be released, of that I am certain, but I will see that your warning is heeded."

Duncan pushed the heavy door closed, taking what light there had been with it. As the lock snapped shut Nicholas slid to the floor, bracing his back against the wall. He doubted not that Duncan would do his best to make Kenneth listen to reason, to prepare the castle for Archie's inevitable return, but Nicholas could not simply sit there and wait.

# CHAPTER FIFTEEN

Dawn was breaking as Rowan finished dressing. She perched on the edge of her bed and pulled her hair into a tight braid, determined that at least this one thing would be fully under her control today. Tendrils sprang loose about her face before she'd even secured the end with a leather thong.

Nothing was in her control, not even her own hair.

She cradled her head in her hands, fighting the urge to climb back under her blankets and hide from the day. But that would be cowardly and the clan had no time for her to give in to such weakness.

She pushed up from her bed, threw her braid behind her, and straightened her back. She was the Guardian of the Targe. The clan would look to her for their protection. They would need her and her gift if they were to thwart Archie, and ultimately his king. They would need her to be strong.

And in order to be strong for them, she must learn to call upon her gift, to focus it through the Targe. She closed her eyes, trying to feel the flowing pressure, trying to summon it, coax it to her. But there was nothing but the aches and pains from her run through the forest yesterday.

She had so much to learn and no time to waste.

She shook Scotia awake. "You must attend your mum this morning. Jeanette and I have work to do."

Scotia's eyes slitted open. "'Tis just dawn. Jeanette will not need me for several hours."

"On a typical day, aye, but this is not a typical day. Get out of bed. Attend your mum. We all have responsibilities this morn we did not have a day ago."

Scotia grumbled, but did as Rowan asked.

"Tell Jeanette to meet me below in Auntie's old bedchamber as soon as she may." Rowan picked up the ermine sack from the stool by her bed and left Scotia grumbling about how she was always the one who had to do as she was told and how someday that would all change.

Rowan couldn't help but laugh as she descended the stair to the floor below. It was the same complaint Scotia had been muttering about for years. At least some things hadn't changed yesterday.

As she let herself into the neglected bedchamber she and Jeanette had agreed was as safe a place as they could find within the castle for the work they did this day, she mulled over the information they had collected from Denis last evening.

He had seen the wall fall, first bowing outward then bursting, except for the section nearest the gate. It, too, had bowed outward then seemed to be pushed back upon its foundation before it had finally collapsed upon itself, sending part of its stones down the hillside and the rest piled upon themselves. He cast it off as fancy on his part, old eyes, imagination, but Rowan knew deep inside that he was right. Something had pushed the wall outward. She had pushed back, somehow holding it long enough for Nicholas, Scotia, and herself to escape the devastation. She had felt the pressure give, though at the time she had not noted what she did.

She'd spent another hour with her uncle, Uilliam, and Duncan, answering questions about Archie, Nicholas, their mission, and what had happened by the loch. The men had been angry and a bit stunned by what had transpired, though she had left out the part where Archie had attempted to despoil her. She had defended herself. Nicholas had kept Archie busy so she could escape. Nothing terrible had happened . . . not physically. Besides, she needed them thinking, not going after Archie in a haze of fury. And finally, she'd been able to bathe and rest, though sleep had eluded her for a long time as worry about Nicholas, Archie, and her own new station in the clan clambered through her mind, tumbling one over the other.

She knew there had been a large band of men who had left the castle before dawn. By now they would be spread out, searching for any sign of Archie in the forest.

What she didn't know was if she and Duncan had convinced the chief that Nicholas should be numbered in that group so they could use his knowledge of Archie in their efforts. She'd been surprised by Duncan's support of Nicholas but then he was a clear thinker. Kenneth valued his mind for strategy, his ability to understand their enemies, so perhaps, if her own argument had not meant anything to Kenneth, Duncan's would.

Turning her attention to her own task this day, she opened the ermine sack and pulled the Targe stone out, balancing it in her palm. Last night she had not wanted to touch it. But now . . .

She tossed the sack onto a chest at the end of the bed and settled the stone between both palms. She felt nothing but its cold weight. She raised it up, as if in offering, as she'd seen Elspet do. Nothing.

Perhaps she must speak the prayers, make the signs in the air.

"What are you doing?!"

Rowan spun, startled. Pressure surged through her, then through the stone, as if a dam had been breached. The door slammed into Jeanette, knocking her off her feet, back out into the corridor, closing her out of the chamber. Rowan wanted to move, wanted to drop the Targe stone, wanted to go to Jeanette. But she could not move. Whatever the force was that her gift called up, it poured through her, liquid and strong, holding her in place, whipping an unnatural wind around her. Fear gripped her. If she had been able to force back stone walls before she had been made Guardian, what could she do to this tower now? To this castle? Goose bumps covered her body. The energy grew stronger. The wind made the heavy bed creak and shiver.

She tried to cry out but her voice was no more than a whisper in a tempest.

JEANETTE LAY ON THE CORRIDOR FLOOR TRYING TO REMEMBER HOW she got there. Her head ached fiercely when she touched it and her hand came away smeared with blood. What had happened to her?

Quickly she surveyed her body for more injuries but other than a tenderness on her backside, and some scrapes on her hands where she must have broken her fall, her head seemed to have the only real wound. She pushed herself up and as she spied the closed door in front of her it all came rushing back.

Rowan. The Targe stone. A sudden fierce pressure like a slap from a hand she could not see, knocking the door into her, shutting her out of the chamber. What had Rowan done?

She got to her feet, pausing only for a second as her vision darkened at the edges, then cleared again. She reached for the latch and pushed but the door resisted.

"Rowan?" she called. "Open the door!"

There was an odd rushing sound from within, but nothing from Rowan. Jeanette pushed the door again, setting her shoulder to it, but still it would not open. The rushing sound grew louder and Jeanette went from irritated to worried.

"Rowan, if you can hear me, try to pull the energy back into you!" she shouted through the thick door. "Try!" She banged on the door with her fist. If Rowan could pull her gift back, even a little bit, Jeanette might be able to get the door open. She banged on the door, harder. "Rowan!"

"Jeanette?"

It was her turn to be startled, but the results were far different.

"You are hurt!" Helen said, dropping her bucket of ashes to the floor as she rushed to Jeanette's side. "What happened?"

"No time to explain." Jeanette wiped the trickle of blood from her brow with the back of her hand. "I need help getting this door open. Is Da above?"

"Aye!"

"Fetch him quickly. Tell him—" She did not wish to reveal that Rowan was the new Guardian yet, not until her cousin could bring hope and confidence to the clan instead of danger. "Tell him I am hurt, and that Rowan may be, too."

Helen sprinted up the stairs without any more questions. Kenneth was roaring down the stairs almost immediately, skidding to a halt by Jeanette's side, Helen on his heels. He reached toward Jeanette's injury but she stopped him.

"I am fine. I need the door opened, Da," Jeanette said to him. "But it will not budge. Rowan is within."

Understanding dawned in his eyes. He tested the door, then put his shoulder to it and shoved. It opened, but only a little and Kenneth was hard pressed to keep it from slamming shut again. Jeanette slid through, quickly getting clear of the door this time. She froze at the whirlwind of destruction in the room, rapidly raising her arm to shield her face from flying debris.

Rowan stood just where she had been when Jeanette startled her, the Targe stone raised to the ceiling in her outstretched hands. Wind battered everything in the room except Rowan. The furniture had been displaced, the mattress cover lay in tatters on the floor. The heather that had filled it tumbled in the air, separating Jeanette from Rowan.

Jeanette waded into the vortex but could not reach Rowan. She backed away, sheltering against the wall near the door.

"Rowan! Look at me!" she shouted. Kenneth's shouts joined hers and finally, slowly, as if she fought the wind, too, Rowan turned her head. Her lips were moving but Jeanette could hear nothing but the raging wind.

Jeanette rifled through all the Targe lore she had in her head but could remember nothing to help in this situation.

"Nicholas," Kenneth said, his face red from his efforts to keep the door open. "Helen," he said over his shoulder, "tell the guard I need Nicholas here now! Then fetch Uilliam and Duncan. Jeanette, come out while I can still hold the door."

"Nay, Da, I shall stay here."

Kenneth reached through the narrow opening and grabbed her arm, jerking her through the door and into the sudden calm of the corridor. He let the door slam behind him. "Wheesht, Jeanette," he said to her, though she said nothing. "We cannot risk your life. You are the keeper of the lore, if not the Guardian of the Targe. Rowan will need you."

"But we cannot leave her in there, Da. She cannot help herself."

"And neither can we help her. But I believe Nicholas can."

"Why?"

"He was the one who was able to reach her when she became Guardian. He was able to break her hold upon Elspet when none of us could. I do not understand it. I do not like it, but if he can help Rowan, then we have no choice but to let him."

Jeanette agreed. "'Tis certainly worth a try."

NICHOLAS HAD EXPLORED EVERY PART OF THE HUT THAT SERVED as his gaol and found no way out. The walls were sturdily built. The door was guarded at all times. It had been a cold night and he had learned to appreciate the usefulness of his plaid, which served as his bed and his blanket quite well. A lass had brought him bannocks and ale to break his fast but he had no appetite for them.

His guard had been relieved by another man before dawn. Nicholas had listened carefully, his ear against the door, as the two spoke briefly, and discovered that Uilliam was leading a group of warriors this morning to search for Archie.

Nicholas itched to get out of the dark, confining space and go with them. But no one had come for him. He was stuck, waiting, captive.

"Let him out! Let him out! Let him out!" a woman's voice screeched, echoing through the bailey. "The chief says let him out!" she said as she arrived outside the door.

"Uilliam said—" The guard looked from Helen to the door he guarded and back.

"Rowan is in trouble. The chief said to bring him to the tower, and you are to come with him! Open the door! 'Tis no time to waste, man!"

"What sort of trouble?" Nicholas asked as the guard rattled the lock and opened the door.

Helen stood there, wringing her hands. "I do not ken exactly, but Jeanette is injured and something terrible is happening to Rowan. Kenneth said to fetch you. Come!" she said racing toward the tower.

Nicholas took a quick look at the guard, who motioned for him to follow the woman. The two men sprinted after her.

Nicholas exited the stair a floor earlier than he had expected and was shocked at the large bruised lump on Jeanette's forehead, a cut right in the middle of it. Kenneth scowled at him even as he motioned Nicholas close to the door they stood near. An eerie sound, like wind whistling on a winter's night, came from behind it.

"Rowan is inside, lad," Kenneth said. "We cannot get to her. You did, yesterday, in Elspet's chamber." He looked over Nicholas's shoulder where Helen and the guard stood listening, then he looked back at Nicholas with raised eyebrows. Nicholas understood all too well what Kenneth did not want made public.

"I did," Nicholas said. "I shall do so again."

Kenneth put a shoulder to the door and shoved with all his might, tendons standing out underneath his skin, his teeth clenched, and a mighty grunt escaping him. The door barely budged.

"Is it barred?" Nicholas asked as he joined Kenneth against the door.

"Not exactly," the chief said.

With two of them the door moved, but not much.

"Again," Nicholas said, pushing harder this time. The door opened just far enough for the sound of the wind to hit him. Debris flew through the crack, hitting him in the face. His curiosity turned to fear. "Again!" The door opened further, almost enough for Nicholas to squeeze through, already far enough for him to see the chaos inside the chamber. "Again!" and it opened further still. He squeezed through and let the door slam shut behind him.

Immediately he was battered by wind and bits of he knew not what.

"Rowan!" he called to her. "Love, you must stop!"

He realized the wind was circling her, leaving her in a calm in the center of the storm. He set his back against the wind and fought against it as he sidled toward her, speaking to her all the time. "Rowan, love, you must fight this. You are strong. You are the Guardian. It is your place to command the Targe. Take command now. Calm this wind." He repeated himself as he drew closer to her until he thought to step into the calm only to find the chaos stayed upon him, closing in around her, too, sweeping both of them up in the wind until Nicholas could neither see nor hear anything but the windstorm engulfing them.

"Rowan!" he reached for her, pulling her rigid body hard against him, trying to ground her in the physical world. The force she drew scared him, for she seemed lost in it or perhaps even held captive by it.

"Rowan, look at me!" He found her face with his hands and held her nose to nose with him. "Open your eyes! Rowan, you must stop! Do not let it control you." He kissed her, hoping to rouse her from her trance. "You. Must. Control. It. Open your eyes, love. Look at me. Look at me!"

His fear was mounting with the ferocity of the wind. The door began to shake, banging against its frame. The sharp sound of a window shattering skated on the wind. He ran his hands up her arms, still raised over her head. He tried to pull them down but for all his strength she did not budge. He ran his hands out to hers, but when he tried to touch the stone pain seared through his fingers, throwing him away from her.

He battled the wind back to her side and took her face in his hands again.

"You must not bring down these walls, Rowan. You would not survive and then where would the clan be? Where would I be?" He kissed her again, a veil of her hair falling between their lips. "I have only just found you. I need you to come back to me." He would not let whatever this force was have her. She was his and he would not lose her.

"She is mine!" he finally yelled into the chaos. "You cannot have her!" He wrapped his arms around her, and tucked his head next to hers, holding her close to his pounding heart. "You are the Guardian of the Targe, Rowan. Your clan needs you. I need you to come back to me, love."

He did not know what else to do so he held her close, sheltering her from the maelstrom, slowly running his hands up and down her back, hoping, praying, that she would be comforted by his presence and find her way out of whatever darkness she was lost in.

"Rowan?" he whispered, his lips next to her ear. "Rowan? Do not abandon those who count on you. Do not abandon me. I do not ken what I will do if you do not come back to me."

As if a candle had been snuffed, the wind ceased. All of the airborne debris fell to the earth like raindrops. Rowan collapsed, her arms falling to her sides finally, the Targe stone clattering to the floor. She would have fallen had he not already been holding her tightly against him. He sank to the ground and pulled her into his lap, cradling her there, murmuring nonsense to her as he smoothed her tangled hair away from her face to find tear tracks over her wind-roughened cheeks.

"Kenneth!" he called. The door slammed open, banging against the wall as the chief and Jeanette surged into the chamber.

"Holy mother of God," Kenneth muttered, taking in the destruction. "Does she live?" he asked, hunkering down next to Nicholas and reaching to touch Rowan's face. Jeanette knelt on the other side of Nicholas.

"She is breathing," she said.

For that Nicholas was immeasurably grateful, but Rowan still had not opened her eyes. He could not say how long he sat there, rocking her, talking to her, begging her to awaken, not caring at all that Kenneth and Jeanette were witness to his weakness.

ROWAN HURT ALL OVER, AS IF FIRE HAD LICKED EVERY PART OF THE inside of her skin. Her head pounded, her joints wept in pain. She dared not move, not so much as an eyelash, for she was certain it would only hurt more.

And yet there was warmth, a gentle rocking, a singsong voice that soothed the pain. "She is mine!" The words rang through her head and her heart, though she could not recall where she had heard them or even who had said them.

"Rowan, you must wake up. Please, love, open your eyes. Come back to me."

She heard those words, and the feel of Nicholas pressed against her in the heady kiss they had shared by the loch rushed through her, damping down the pain, making it but an echo of a moment ago. She hung on to that feeling, that pleasure, but she dared not move yet.

"Open your eyes." A soft kiss on her brow, a gentle hand running up and down her arm. "Rowan. Please."

The remembered pleasure washed through her again, pushing the pain even further away. She sighed at the relief and forced her eyes to open.

Nicholas stared down at her, a sad smile lighting his handsome face—his scratched face. "There you are. I knew you would not leave me forever."

She reached up and stopped just shy of touching a cut on his cheek. "What happened to you?"

His smile stayed on his mouth but his eyes grew somber. "You did." He leaned down and placed a feathery kiss on her lips. "Do you remember?"

She didn't remember, not for a moment, and then it all came back to her on a gasp. "I could not control it. I hurt Jeanette."

"I will live, Rowan," Jeanette's voice came from close by.

Rowan craned her neck and found her cousin sitting close to Nicholas, her hands on Rowan's head, a large angry goose egg on her forehead. "I am so sorry. I would never —"

"We know, love." Nicholas said. "You did not do it on purpose."

"I was trying to call the energy but I could not . . . and then suddenly it was there, rushing through me as if it had been imprisoned, as if I was a door suddenly flung wide and there was nothing I could do to stop it, to control it."

"I can help you learn that," Jeanette said.

"It hurt," she told them. "Will it always?"

"I do not ken," Jeanette said, "but I have not ever seen anything to indicate being the Guardian of the Targe brought pain. You fought it again, didn't you? It frightened you when it leaped through you and you fought against it."

Rowan thought about that split second when she had turned to find Jeanette in the doorway and the energy had surged through her. Panic had gripped her . . .

"Aye, I fought it. I had to control it."

Jeanette seemed to be culling through her knowledge, lost in thought. Nicholas ran a hand up and down her arm, calming her like a fussy bairn.

"I do not care to think about it anymore," Rowan said.

She heard Jeanette rise from the floor, could feel her standing over her. "You have little choice in this matter, Rowan MacGregor, Guardian of the Targe. You must protect the clan. It is what you are meant to do."

Rowan pushed out of Nicholas's lap and stumbled to her feet. "You saw what happened, Jeanette! I was helpless against it, though I fought it. I did not want to hurt you, or Nicholas. I do not want to hurt anyone. I fought it, tried to stop it, but I could do nothing against it."

"But it stopped."

She swallowed and nodded. "It did. I do not ken why. Was it finished with me?" *For now*, she added silently. She looked at Nicholas where he still sat on the floor between the two women. "Did you do something to free me from it?" Another memory whispered up from the pain she had been in. His voice, calling to her, railing against whatever held her hostage. Over and over again. Claiming her. "She is mine." Tears threatened at the tenderness she had felt underlying that fierce claiming, the loneliness, the longing.

"It was you that stopped it." She rubbed her aching forehead. "You stopped it."

He rose and took her hands. "Then I will stop it again, and again, until you discover how to control it, to fight it, to stop it yourself."

She shook her head, remembering the fear, the terror, the pain when she had not been able to move, had to endure the flames that burned through her, the wind that scraped and pushed at her, nearly suffocating her. How could she allow that to happen again?

"Perhaps that is the problem," Jeanette said quietly. "Perhaps the Targe does not want to be controlled or fought. Perhaps 'directed' is a better way to think about it." She looked around the demolished chamber, then moved toward the nearest wall, retrieving the Targe stone. The ermine sack was caught on the remains of a chair that had been smashed against another wall. "Mum said it was an odd, but pleasant, feeling when the energy flowed through her. She never spoke of controlling it, nor fighting it. She welcomed it, guided it. The next time, do not fight it."

Jeanette placed the stone in the sack, pulled the cords tight, and held it out to Rowan.

Nicholas lifted it from Jeanette's hand and placed it in Rowan's, wrapping her fingers around it when she did not do it on her own. "You must learn to use this and I promise I will be there with you, helping you, calling you back."

She could only hope that would be enough.

# CHAPTER SIXTEEN

"I will take him back to the gaol," the guard said from the doorway.

Rowan stared at the ermine sack in her hand, its softness belying the hard truth of what lay within it. She was the Guardian. She must learn to . . . What was it Jeanette had said? Guide it? Aye, that was it. And she would not do that without Nicholas by her side to keep his promise.

"Nay, Myles," she said, looking up at the guard, a lad she'd known since he was a toddler. "He stays with me."

"But the chief, he said—"

"He is not here."

"As he left," Myles said, "just afore you awoke, he said I was to take . . ."

She held the sack up in front of her so the guard could see it. "I am the Guardian now. I need Nicholas's help. He stays."

"Rowan," the guard said, staring at the sack, "I . . . I . . . I cannot ignore the chief's command."

"Nor can you ignore the Guardian's." She felt a small twinge of empathy for the young man as he glanced from Rowan to Jeanette, to Nicholas and back to Rowan. The feeling passed quickly.

"Perhaps," Nicholas said, "he could stand guard outside this chamber? 'Twould satisfy both the chief's requirement to keep me under guard and your requirement, Guardian, to keep me close enough to help you."

Rowan allowed herself half a smile. "Will that do?" she asked the guard.

He nodded rapidly and backed through the doorway. "I shall be here, outside the door."

Jeanette took pity on him. "Fear not, Myles. I will tell Da you had no choice in the matter."

He nodded rapidly again and took up his post.

Rowan turned her attention to her cousin. "Is Morven still here?"

"Aye. She did not want to leave until Mum . . ."

"Find her and have her tend your head." She sighed. "I am truly sorry. I did not mean to hurt you."

Jeanette ran a hand down Rowan's arm. "I ken that, cousin. Nothing is as anticipated right now and you are caught in a place you did not expect to be." She gingerly touched the lump on her forehead. "You will see that she does not try anything with the Targe until I return," she said to Nicholas.

"I will do my best, but she is the Guardian. It seems the Guardian is not to be denied," he said with a wink that had both women smiling. "Hurry back, mistress. I fear we may need Rowan's gift before much longer."

Jeanette left. Rowan shut the chamber door behind her, irritated by the guard still standing in sight. When she turned back to the room she realized that she was suddenly alone with Nicholas. An unaccustomed shyness overtook her.

"Did I hurt you?" she asked.

"A few scrapes and bumps, nothing serious."

Neither moved and silence fell between them, thick as the walls that surrounded them.

"Were you hoping for more injuries, Rowan?" His words sliced through the silence.

"Of course not! Why would you think such a thing of me?"

He slid his fingers into his hair, pushing it back, revealing a cut along his temple.

"You have reason to hate me. If I were in your position, I think I should like to do some damage to the man who threatened my clan."

Rowan closed her eyes for a moment and settled her jumpy emotions. "I do not hate you, Nicholas," she said quietly. "My feelings are complicated and confusing but hate is not amongst them."

Rowan took a deep steadying breath and moved toward him. "Thank you for helping me, not just today, but with Archie. That could not have been easy to turn against a man you have worked with for so long."

He reached out to her, running the backs of his fingers down her cheeks. She leaned into his touch, needing so much more of him than that.

"I would do anything to keep you safe, Rowan, to keep you happy. My fate is here now." He hooked his hand under her hair, cupping her neck, and gently pulled her to him. "With you," he whispered against her lips.

The touch of his lips was like a drink of cool water cascading through her, quenching a thirst she hadn't been aware of; diminishing the gut-twisting fear that she hadn't been able to conquer on her own. His groan as he wrapped her fiercely in his arms, tilting his head to deepen the kiss, calmed her and heated her simultaneously. The slide of his tongue against hers, the taste of him, the scent of him, and the feel of his hands pulling her so close she could feel the rapid beating of his heart against hers. She pressed against him. Deepening the kiss even more, she reveled in the pulsing of her blood in her veins, the heat of his desire that pressed against her belly, and knew that he must feel the same way she did even if neither of them would speak the words.

A quiet tapping on the door drew them back from the brink. "Rowan, Da wants to see you in his chamber," Scotia said, her voice muffled by the door. "Only you."

"Of course," Rowan said quietly. "Tell him I will attend him presently," she called loud enough for Scotia to hear.

"He is in no mood to wait," Scotia replied.

"Rowan, I—" He rested his forehead against hers but did not let her move any further away from him yet.

"Wheesht." She nuzzled him with her nose until he let her kiss him again, gentler this time, a promise of things not said, things that could not be said yet.

When Rowan arrived in her uncle's chamber Jeanette was already there, along with Uilliam and Duncan. The chamber was not large. A fire burned brightly on the hearth behind Kenneth. The rest of them stood in a loose semicircle around the chief, Rowan taking her place amongst them next to Jeanette.

Kenneth leaned back in his chair, a wooden tankard in his hand. His hair stood in tufts at odd angles as if he'd been pulling on it. He glanced from Jeanette to Rowan and back several times before he said, "What sort of gift is this, exactly? It is nothing like my Elspet's."

Rowan had expected Nicholas to be the first order of business.

"'Tis not unusual for different guardians to draw from different gifts," Jeanette said. "Mum draws from the energy that flows around all living things. Rowan appears to draw from the energy of the air, fueled by strong emotions."

"Nay, Jeanette, I do not understand why the wind accompanies it, but it always feels as if there is energy flowing up from the ground, filling me, looking for a way out, a way to escape. I think the wind is pulled to me by that energy."

Jeanette looked surprised. "Why did you not say so before?"

"Because I had not put it all together in my mind until this very moment."

"And what emotion fueled the maelstrom I witnessed?" Kenneth demanded.

"I startled her. The power surged and frightened her. She fought against it," Jeanette said.

Kenneth blanched. "A simple startle caused that?!"

"I was holding the Targe stone for the first time, trying to call my gift."

"You held the Targe stone?" The shock in Duncan's voice had them all turning to him.

Rowan lifted the ermine sack where it hung from her belt.

"But . . . I do not understand," Duncan said. "'Twas supposed to be Jeanette . . . or Scotia."

"None of us understand," Rowan said, letting the sack drop back by her side, "but 'tis done. I am the Guardian."

Uilliam pulled on his beard but said nothing. Duncan started to say something else but Kenneth stopped him.

"It is as she says and I have seen evidence of it myself." His face was drawn, worry etching deep lines across his brow. "Can you harness this gift, Rowan? Can you control it for the good of the clan?"

"Not at present, Uncle, but," she reached out and grabbed Jeanette's hand for strength, "with Jeanette's guidance, and Nicholas's help, I hope to."

All three men went stiff at the mention of Nicholas.

Kenneth took a long pull from his tankard. He rubbed a hand over his face, then scratched his scalp, rearranging the tufts of unruly hair. "I did not wish to call upon him, but it seemed the only way."

Rowan relaxed. "I do not understand why he is able to summon me from the grip of my gift, but I thank you for trusting him to help."

"Trust is not what I feel about the man," Kenneth said.

"But you trusted him enough to have him help me."

"Aye, but it was trust born of necessity."

"It is a start," she said, content that someday, perhaps, Nicholas might win back the trust of all of them.

"Jeanette, you will help her in whatever way is necessary," he said. "It is important that the blessing be made over the wall again as soon as possible. It falls to Rowan to protect the clan. And this route into the Highlands." Kenneth looked at Rowan. "You will have to learn how to do that, as well. The responsibility of the Guardian is bigger and more important than just this clan and this castle, but it starts here."

"I promise to do whatever is within my power." She swallowed and steadied her shaking hands by grasping her skirts as if they were a lifeline and she were bobbing in the vast ocean all alone. "But I need more help than Jeanette can give me."

Kenneth glowered at her, but she continued, confident that he would see reason.

"I need you to do two things for me, Uncle." She relaxed the death grip she had upon her skirts. "I need you to free Nicholas of Achnamara."

"I will not promise such a thing. I care not what he did for you this day, he is a spy. He will hang."

Rowan's breath hitched and pressure once more rose within her. An ominous rattle started at the window and the door. Jeanette grabbed Rowan's hand and glared at her father.

"Emotion, Da. Emotion is what drives her gift—a gift that allows her to move things with her mind. To threaten him so will not help her control her gift!"

A wind had begun to whip around the edges of the room, even though Rowan was trying with all her might to resist it. She took a deep breath, trying to calm the lurching of her heart.

"I need him, Uncle." She closed her eyes and tried to will the wind and the rattling to cease. After a long moment, she managed to calm her heart, her fears, and the wind. The rattling still continued, though quieter now.

When she opened her eyes she realized that Jeanette still held her hand, both of them in fact. Duncan and Uilliam had stepped away from her and Kenneth was slowly shaking his head.

"If he hangs . . . If harm comes to him what will happen?" Kenneth slowly asked.

Rowan looked to Jeanette for the answer, as did everyone else.

Jeanette sighed. "Until she learns to control the gift, I believe she could destroy this entire castle with her grief. 'Tis clear she cares for him, Da. You ken Rowan. You ken what a good judge of character she has always been, seeing into the heart of people as none of the rest of us can." Her delicate eyebrows drew down and she pulled her bottom lip between her teeth. "Perhaps that is a facet of her gift. I need to speak to Mum"—her voice caught. "I will see what I can discover," she finished, her voice tight and a little higher than usual. It was Rowan's turn to squeeze Jeanette's hand in support.

Kenneth ran his hands over his scalp again.

"There was another thing you wished to ask of me," he said to Rowan.

"There is." She tried to determine if he had acquiesced on her first request but the man gave nothing away. "We all need Nicholas's help if we are to keep the clan safe from Archie and whatever mayhem he brings with him. He kens the man as none of us do. He kens what Archie is capable of, what he is likely to do next. We need Nicholas's help in protecting us long enough for me to learn how to use my gift."

"We cannot do that, my lassie," Kenneth said, holding up a hand to stop her from reacting. "I ken you trust him and believe that he intends no harm to us anymore. But I cannot trust him with the lives of all my people, the welfare of my family and my home. I would not deserve to be chief of these good people if I gave my trust so quickly and so easily to someone known to be an enemy."

Rowan clenched her teeth together to keep from interrupting him. She took great long breaths to try to keep her heartbeat and her emotions steady, even, calm.

Kenneth rose, taking Rowan's hands from Jeanette's into his own.

"I would not do anything to bring you grief if it were within my power."

"But, Uncle, this—"

"Wheesht, lassie, let me finish."

She nodded, swallowing around the lump in her throat.

"I promise you this: I will bring no harm to Nicholas of Achnamara, or whatever his true name might be, but . . ." It was Kenneth's turn to gulp in a great breath and let it out slowly. "But, I cannot let him move freely about this castle or this glen and I cannot entrust him with knowledge of our plans to defend ourselves. He is to stay locked up, under guard." He tipped Rowan's chin up so she had to meet his steely gaze. "Do you understand?"

She forced herself to remain calm and was gratified that even the quiet rattling of the door ceased. "He can help us, Uncle."

"That may be true, but I canna risk that he may not be the man you believe him to be. Not right now." He slumped back into his chair. "Let us begin with the blessing. I suspect that the protections my Elspet put in place collapsed when the Guardianship shifted to

Rowan. We must get that protection back as soon as may be done. I want it in place by sundown."

Jeanette agreed.

"I will do my best," Rowan said. Surely she could do at least that.

"We should keep the news to ourselves for a little while, until you have had a chance to learn a bit about being the Guardian and how to use the Targe. Once you can protect the castle and the clan, then we will reveal this strange twist of fate that has befallen us."

"I fear the news will spread before then," Rowan said. "Myles, Nicholas's guard, and Helen both witnessed what happened. You ken how news spreads like fleas through the clan."

Kenneth sighed.

"And Nicholas? What will be his fate?" she asked.

"I do not ken," Kenneth said, but did not look her in the eyes. "We will take it one day at a time and see what unfolds."

"You promised you will not harm him."

"I did. And for now, that is true, but in the end . . ."

"Nay, Uncle. I am the Guardian. It is my place to protect the people of the clan. He will not be harmed."

"He is not clan," Kenneth said, glowering at her, but she did not back down. In this she would not back down.

"You granted him hospitality. He has proven himself true to us. He went against his compatriot to keep me safe. He risked his own safety to help me calm my gift, a task that protected the entire clan. He would gladly help us defend ourselves against Archie if you would but accept that help. He will not be harmed."

"Yet he is here to steal the Highland Targe. He is an agent of Longshanks. He is English. I am chief of this clan and I will not allow the man free range of this castle or this land! He will remain under guard!" Kenneth roared, surging to his feet, but Rowan did not flinch. "On that point I will not bend."

She met his glare and did not blink. "Very well, but he will stay in the tower. Auntie's old chamber will suit with some cleaning up. A guard can keep watch there, and follow the man around when he leaves the chamber."

"He shall not leave the chamber." Kenneth's fists were on his hips, ire snapping in his eyes.

"He will if I need him to." Rowan mirrored his stance, fists on her hips, her chin raised. She hid the surprise at her own actions. Never before would she have gainsaid her uncle in anything, but now . . . now it was as much *her* responsibility to protect the clan as his and she would not shrink from her duty.

"Da, it is reasonable," Jeanette said, laying one hand upon his arm and the other upon Rowan's. "'Tis sure I am that Duncan and Uilliam will also keep watch over him if he is about the castle."

Kenneth crossed his arms over his wide chest and glared at his daughter and niece. Finally he nodded, one quick jerk of his head.

IT WAS ALL NICHOLAS COULD DO NOT TO CALL A HALT TO THE TE-dious afternoon. Rowan was exhausted, hungry, and Jeanette made her repeat the same nonsense words and swishy symbols in the air over and over and over again. He was exhausted just watching them.

"She needs a rest," he finally said, pushing off the wall where he leaned next to the window. "She almost had it an hour ago but now she is making more and more mistakes."

"I am doing my best, but he is right," Rowan said, letting her hands fall limply to her sides. "I cannot even think clearly at this point. There is no way I can make the blessing before sunset."

Jeanette stared at her cousin, her face emotionless. "Perhaps we should take a break for a little while. I would like to check and see how Mum fares. You could sleep a little."

"You should get some sleep, too."

"I will sleep when I have to." But the slow blink of her eyes be-trayed her fatigue.

"Soon, then," Rowan said. "I do not wish to upset Auntie or Scotia so I will stay here, but please tell your mum I love her. Do not tell her that I cannot do her duties yet. I would not have her sap her strength with worry."

Jeanette nodded and went to the door. Her hand on the latch, she stopped and looked back at Rowan. "You must find a way to call upon your gift when you need it, Rowan, not just when you are angry or afraid. Until you can do that we are unprotected. It is your duty now."

"I ken that."

Nicholas was surprised to see anger wash across Jeanette's fair features as she left the chamber.

Rowan knuckled her gritty eyes and stared at her bed.

"I do not think I can sleep." She gave him a tired smile.

"At least sit," he said, leading her to her bed and gently pushing her down. He sat next to her and indulged himself by lifting her hand and massaging it.

"Mmmm. That is heavenly," she said, leaning her head on his shoulder.

"You will get this, love. You just need time."

"Which is the one thing we do not have."

He kissed the crown of her head and laid his cheek against it, wondering how he could help her. He felt the telltale dampness of tears on his shoulder as she swiped her hand across her eyes.

He raised her chin with a finger, pulling her back far enough to place a gentle kiss upon her lips. "We will figure this out together, you, me, and Jeanette." Her lips were so close to his, he could feel the warmth of her breath there, like the lightest of kisses. "You are not alone in this." A lone tear escaped over her pale cheek but he brushed it away with his thumb. "We will find a way, together, for you to wield your gift without hurting anyone, including yourself . . . unless you mean to hurt someone." He waggled his eyebrows at her, hoping for a smile. "I think you might not mind hurting Archie."

Her face lit up at that thought. "Nay, I would not mind that at all."

"Are you sure you cannot rest?"

"I am so tired, but inside . . . I cannot rest. I must master the blessing."

"Perhaps . . .," he said, thinking back to how he had learned most new skills in his life. "Perhaps you need to start further back."

"Further back?"

"Aye." He turned on the bed to face her. "When I was first learning to wield a sword I was not handed a claymore and told to kill someone with it. I watched my kinsmen sparring. I was given a small wooden sword to practice with, one that fit my hands and whose weight I could manage. I got the feel for that training sword before I ever was allowed to touch a claymore. It is like Jeanette is handing you a claymore when you need to practice with a wee wooden sword."

"But how?" she asked.

"Have you ever just looked at the stone? Got the feel of it in your hand before you tried to force anything to happen?"

"Nay."

He nodded toward the ermine sack where it sat on the stool next to her. " 'Tis a first step, like a bairn learning to walk."

She grabbed the sack and let it settle in her lap as she pulled it open until it lay almost flat, revealing not only the stone he'd seen when it had fallen at his feet on the ben, but odd decorations stained on the leather interior of the sack. She lifted the stone and studied it carefully, turning it over in her hand, running her fingers over it.

"What are those symbols?" he asked, tracing a snaking line with his finger.

She let the stone rest in her palm as she looked at the symbol he traced. "I do not ken why they are there, but Jeanette tells me that this one"—she pointed at one of the symbols on the leather, and again to the same incised symbol on the stone—"is a mirror but she does not ken what it means. This one"—she pointed to another symbol about a third of the way around the painted part of the sack—"is a broken arrow, but again, what it means has been lost to time. And this one"—she pointed to the third one, closest to her, the one he had run his finger over; it was a simple drawing of three stacked wavy lines contained within an upside-down V—"no one kens."

Nicholas leaned close to get a better look at both the paintings on the sack and the slightly flattened, round stone she cupped in her hand. The same symbols were in the same positions on the stone. "It looks like water, or wind," he said. "That"—he ran his finger over the upside-down V on the stone—"makes me think of the bens, as if the lines are water flowing under the mountains."

"Aye," she whispered. "Wind whips up from nothing when I get afraid." She ran a finger over the rippled lines on the stone, then over the same symbol on the sack, back and forth, thinking hard until she squared her shoulders and reached out for his hand, gripping it hard. "This is the symbol of my gift. I am sure of it. But, if the lines are for wind, why are they below the ben? And if the lines are water, why is it always wind that comes to me with my gift? Somehow my gift draws from the wind, the water, the earth beneath our feet. Wait." She thought hard about exactly what she felt when her gift came upon her. "My gift, it pours into me from below, always starting at my feet, then rising up through me. But what does it mean that these symbols are on the stone, and on the sack?"

He could hear frustration in her voice, feel it in the iron grip she had on his hand. "Wheesht, love, we'll figure it out." He ran his free hand over her hair, down her back in a gesture that seemed to soothe her as much as it did him. "Perhaps Jeanette understands the symbol."

"I think it unlikely. She has not mentioned anything about them. If there was lore to guide us, she would have read it in the manuscripts she has. She would have called upon that knowledge to help me already."

Shock coursed through him at her words. "Jeanette can read?"

"Aye. When she was little and learned of her destiny . . . of what she thought was her destiny," she amended, "she begged her da to find her a tutor to teach her to read the scrolls Aunt Elspet had in her keeping. Kenneth denies Jeanette nothing and so she learned to read and write. She has been adding to the scrolls, keeping a record of everything Elspet taught her, everything Elspet has done as Guardian."

A written record. In the Highlands. Indeed, thought Nicholas, these people were not the barbarians Edward believed them.

"The king must never know of these documents," he said. "We must not let them fall into Edward's hands."

"I had not thought of that. You are right. We must secure them."

She took her hand from his and ran her finger over the circular symbol in the center of the sack. Within the circle were three intermingled circles swirling into and out of each other as if they were all one, though they looked like three.

"Do you ken what that symbol means?" he asked.

She shook her head, studying the painted symbols in front of her and idly turning the stone in her hand.

"Perhaps," she said after a long while, "the symbols show the different sorts of gifts that come to Guardians? But I do not see one here that makes me think of Auntie's gift."

"What was her gift?" he asked. "I ken she blessed things, but what was the gift?"

"That was her gift: the gift of blessing. Everything she blessed thrived. It was a good and gentle sort of gift. She never hurt anyone with it . . . unlike me."

"You are not in control of your gift yet, Rowan. Perhaps yours is stronger because that is what is needed in these troubled times. Elspet was able to ensure the prosperity and survival of the clan. You must defend it against outside attack, against me and the troubles I have brought to your gates."

She turned and looked at him, rather than into some middle distance of thought. "It is Edward that brings these troubles to our gates. If it had not been you, 'twould have been Archie or someone else."

He could not refute that, but still he felt responsible for the troubles coming to her clan.

"Perhaps if I returned to England with news that there is no Highland Targe . . ."

"Archie knows that Elspet is the Guardian. We cannot undo that knowledge, though he does not know that I have taken her place. He will return, won't he?"

"Aye, and with some of the king's men, no doubt."

"Then I must figure out how to use my gift to defend my family and my clan." She turned her attention back to the stone in her hand, turning it about, turning it over, and turning it about again. "This stone is the key to the gifts, mine and these others." She gently touched the symbols on the stone. "Three . . . three symbols, three circles in a circle." She placed the stone on the center circle of the opened sack, turning it until the symbols on the stone lined up with the symbols on the sack.

"Nicholas," she whispered, still staring at the arrangement in front of her.

"Aye?"

"I am going to try to call upon my gift."

"Steps, Rowan." He looked about and spied a well-worn brogue, the leather soft and formed to one of the women's feet. He put it on the stool next to her. "See if you can move that shoe."

She chewed on her lower lip and for a moment he was distracted enough to lean in and kiss her.

"What worries you?"

"I do not want to hurt you, or myself, though I seem adept at protecting myself."

"What do you want me to do?"

She looked from the shoe to Nicholas and back. "If I cannot control my gift, you must stop me. Promise me."

"I promise."

She swallowed hard then closed her eyes and muttered something under her breath that sounded a lot like the blessing prayer Jeanette had been teaching her all afternoon. She raised her hands and moved them through the air as he had seen Elspet do at the blessing and her lips still moved.

And nothing happened.

"What use is a gift if I cannot even call it!?" She shoved her fingers into her hair and gripped her head. "Elspet made it look so easy. Jeanette says the Guardians before me have always naturally called upon and controlled their gifts. Why cannot I?"

"Perhaps you are trying too hard? Or perhaps Elspet's way is not your way? How far back do Jeanette's chronicles go?"

She still held her head in a white-knuckled grip.

"I do not ken how far back, or how many Guardians are part of the record. I do know she found none with anything like what I do."

"Which means that the way you use and control your gift is not in the chronicles either."

"True."

"So what has brought your gift forth in the past?"

"Emotion—strong emotion," she said without hesitation. "Fear, anger."

"And with those the gift was destructive, aye?"

"'Defensive' is a better way to describe it. It protected me."

Nicholas considered that information for a moment. "Then let us start with that." He leapt to his feet, grabbed the shoe and flung it at her. She threw up her hands and the shoe flew back at him. It happened so fast he did not have time to duck. It hit him square in the chest. He burst out laughing at the shocked look on her face. "You did it!" He leaned over and gave her a smacking kiss.

Wonder shined in her eyes. "I did not think, I just acted. 'Tis how Jeanette said the other Guardians wielded their gift, by instinct more than training."

"You, love, have a very well-honed instinct for defending yourself. I imagine 'twill be the same when the clan is in trouble." He squatted in front of her so he could be eye to eye with her. "'Tis a formidable gift"—he rubbed the spot on his chest where the shoe hit him—"if a bit dangerous," he added with a grin.

"Thank you," she said, reaching out to cup his cheek in her palm. "At least now I know I can call upon it under attack, but I still need to be able to protect the clan *before* the danger arises."

He placed a kiss in her palm and stood, looking about the chamber for inspiration until his eyes landed back on the amazing woman sitting on her bed. Other, more emotional activities for a bed sprang to mind. "You said 'strong emotion' drove your gift, aye?"

"So far."

"Strong emotion is not all negative or dangerous, Rowan." He had no intention of bedding her, but there were ways, without going so far, to raise strong emotion in a lass. He retrieved the shoe and placed it on the open windowsill this time. He held out his hand to her. She pulled the sack up around the stone, tying it to her belt as she joined him.

"Face the window," he said, moving up behind her as she did so. He put his hands at her waist and felt a shiver run through her. He stepped closer until he could nuzzle that place where her shoulder met her neck, leaving a trail of tiny kisses up her neck until he reached the shell of her ear. "See if this sort of emotion works, Rowan." He nipped at her earlobe. "See if you can push that shoe out the window."

She took a shaky breath and lifted the ermine sack into her hands. She also tilted her head a little, as if asking for more. He obliged her, kissing along her neck again as he slowly ran his hands up her sides and back to her waist and up again, letting his fingertips lightly brush the sides of her breasts. His own breathing was growing ragged.

"I can feel . . . 'tis different, not sharp but softer, the energy," she whispered. "I cannot move the shoe, though."

"Keep trying," he said. Shifting his kisses to her other shoulder, he gently pulled her back against him, letting his hands brush from her sides to her belly and up, just under her breasts.

Her breath caught and the shoe twitched. "Dear God, 'tis working, Nicholas. Do not stop." The last words were barely more than a throaty sigh.

He smiled, happy to oblige her. He slid his hands over her belly again, brushing lower until she gasped, then up again, this time allowing himself the almost painful pleasure of lifting her breasts in his hands. He could feel the rapid beat of her heart against his chest, could feel the quick shallow breaths she took. And he could feel a breeze growing around them, a breeze that did not seem to come from the open window.

"That is it, love." He caressed her breasts, laid tiny kisses on her neck, and still the shoe did not do more than twitch a time or two.

He did not know how much more he could take of this seduction. His erection ached with his harshly controlled desire. The heady scent of her passion played havoc with his resolve, as did the little feminine noises she made as he touched her, and the way she leaned into him. He moved one hand back down, skimming over her belly and lower. He let the pressure of his hand rest at the apex of her thighs as he rubbed his other thumb over her taut nipple. She moaned and pressed into his hands, her head leaning back on his shoulder. The wind grew stronger, but it was not the angry wind of that morning. This one was more like a warm spring wind, strong enough to keep anyone from disturbing them, but not strong enough to hurt anyone, either.

"The shoe, Rowan," he reminded her before they both became lost to sensation.

She lifted her head from his shoulder with a jerking motion and the shoe went flying out the window as she turned and wrapped her arms around his neck, drawing him down into a fervent kiss.

# CHAPTER SEVENTEEN

As soon as Jeanette had returned to Elspet's chamber she had sent Scotia for fresh soup and wine, as well as food to be brought to Rowan and Nicholas. Elspet slept fitfully, and Jeanette was glad, once Scotia had left, for a few moments by herself.

She closed her eyes, shutting out all the signs of change around her. She sighed around the ache that had been lodged in her heart, growing bigger, more painful ever since Rowan became the Guardian. She wanted to scream, to cry, to rail at whatever it was that chose a Guardian. It was her place. Her blood right. Her future.

But not anymore.

Now she must pass on everything that she knew, everything she'd thought she would be, to Rowan. It was her duty not to *be* the Guardian, but to train the Guardian, to protect the Guardian. It was not fair. But she could almost hear her mother's voice, as she'd said so often to Scotia: Life is not fair.

She pulled the blanket up over her mother's shoulders and left the chamber, carefully leaving the door open. She needed to move, to pace, to let the emotions that she usually managed so well take over. Normally she was the calm one, the serene one, sure of herself and her position within her world, her clan, and her family. She was the one destined to become the Guardian, to take an important place in her mother's line. She was the one who had a calling, a clear path for her life but now . . .

Now she had nothing.

She passed the guard who stood outside the chamber she had shared with her sister and cousin for years. She remembered the rows between the willful Scotia and the protective Rowan. She remembered her place between them as the peacekeeper, the voice of reason, always explaining the motives of one to the other, her place as the future Guardian requiring them to listen, to heed her warnings and her advice. They were so very different from each other, the three of them, and yet they had found a way to fit together. She had bound them together.

That, too, would change.

Jeanette paced further down the corridor to a narrow window and glanced out over the ben, then paced back to her mother's door. She was cold outside her mother's overheated chamber, so cold, but she did not think it had aught to do with the ever-present chill of the thick stone walls.

What was she to do now? Her whole life had been defined by whom she would be when her time came to take up the mantle of the Guardian. Everything she'd ever done, wished for, thought about, was bounded by the knowledge that she would always be here at Dunlairig, would always be bound to the clan. The lore she had studied, postponing her choice of a husband, how she comported herself—all had been founded on her future role as Guardian.

She would do what she must. Tend her mother, guide her sister, train her cousin. What else was there for her?

ROWAN'S PASSION NEARLY DROVE NICHOLAS OVER THE EDGE. HER bed was there. The wind she drew around them would keep anyone from entering the chamber.

He buried his nose in her hair, gripped her backside in his palms, pulling her against him. She moaned and drew his mouth back to hers. Nicholas struggled against instinct, against need, against desire. This was madness. He had promised to protect her, even if that meant protecting her from him.

Once he would have taken what she clearly wanted to give and thought nothing more about it. But this was Rowan. He wanted so much more than a quick tumble from her. He wanted a life with her. He put his hands on her waist, where all this had started, and pushed her gently away, breaking the almost overwhelming contact with her, but she continued to kiss him.

"Rowan," he whispered. "Rowan, we must stop this." Those were the hardest words he'd ever spoken. "Love, this is not the way." He released her and took a small step back. The wind immediately began to die down until it was but a sigh around the edges of the chamber.

A deep pink stained her cheeks and she would not look him in the eye.

"Love?"

"I'm sorry," she said.

"Ah, Rowan, I am not."

She looked at him, her eyes the brightest green he had ever seen. "Nay?"

"How could I be?" He reached for her hand, wanting to lay his heart bare to her, but he could not burden her. She was the Guardian, and no matter how much he knew he had been changed by his time here in Dunlairig, by her, he knew he would never be allowed to have her for his own. And he would have her no other way.

"I was as wanton as Scotia." She looked away from him, toward the window, the charming pink of her cheeks growing rosier. "I did not want to stop." Her attention shifted abruptly. "Where . . ." She hurried to the window. "The shoe. 'Tis gone!"

Nicholas grinned. The sweet torture had been worth it to hear the wonder and pride in her voice.

"I did it!" She leaned out the window, looking downward where the shoe must lay. She looked across the bailey at the same moment the scent hit his nose.

"Saints and angels," she gasped. "Fire!"

ARCHIE JOINED THE STREAM OF PEOPLE FLOWING INTO THE CASTLE. The fire was roaring, just as he'd planned, pulling everyone's attention to the immediate problem of containing it, putting it out. As he entered the bailey he could barely see through the thick smoke that swirled inside the walls as if the wind sought to hold it all there. The sun was blotted out and but a faint glow compared to the golden flames that rose from the great hall. His nose burned and his eyes watered.

Thatch made for great tinder.

He could make out a bucket line forming by the well near the center of the bailey, but he'd set the roof of the large hall aflame and there was little they could do until it collapsed, bringing the fire closer to those who would put it out. He grinned on the inside, carefully keeping concern upon his face.

He kept away from the well and the bucket line, needing to see where everyone was before he moved to the next stage of his plan. A command bellowed from his right. The chief, unmistakable as much from his air of command as from Archie recognizing the steely haired man from that first day here. The day Nicholas made a fool of himself rescuing the women from the falling wall.

The day Nicholas had changed everything.

If the chief was here, his second—that great black-haired man—was sure to be close by. Ah, there he was. Now, where was Nicholas? The fool would no doubt be lending a hand to put out the fire, rather than working with Archie as his loyalty should dictate.

No matter. This way Archie alone would have all the glory of completing the mission. Archie alone would have the goodwill and appreciation of the king. And Archie alone would have the riches such appreciation would provide.

He was better off on his own. He didn't need Nicholas to take what they had been sent for.

But he did not see Nicholas anywhere. A screech from near the burning building had the chief and the bear surging into the thickest part of the smoke. Now was his chance.

He made his way quickly to the tower, grateful for the thick, swirling, choking smoke that cloaked his passing. He eased the door open and slipped inside. Shouts sounded from above, moving toward him. He melted into the deep shadow beneath the stair as Nicholas, Rowan, and another man rushed out the door. As soon as it closed again, he was up the stairs.

The Targe and the woman who kept it would soon be his.

Rowan skidded to a stop halfway across the bailey. Nicholas managed to get around her without knocking her over and when he stopped and looked up she heard him gasp.

The fire had increased in the time it had taken them to alert Jeanette and race down the tower stairs. Flames licked high into the sky, the base of them obscured by thick, black smoke. Rowan dashed by Nicholas, running full out toward the inferno. Nicholas grabbed her arm, stopping her from racing into the chaos.

"Let me go!"

"Wait, Rowan!" he said.

"But Scotia . . . Jeanette said she had gone to the kitchens. The whole hall is aflame. We must find her, make sure she is safe!" Frantic, she pulled the edge of her arisaid up, holding it over her nose and mouth to keep out the choking smoke. "I cannot see her."

Nicholas reached for her hand, and she was grateful for the strength she could feel, the concern that communicated itself in such a simple touch. "Is there aught you can do to stop the fire?" he asked.

His thought mirrored her own. "I do not know, but I must try."

He nodded stiffly, his whole body leaning toward the fire. "I will stay here then."

Gratitude and shame washed over Rowan. She was not a weak person and yet she had forsaken her strength, giving herself to the fear of the power invested in her as the Guardian, and Nicholas was trapped by his promise to keep her from hurting herself and others. How could she do her duty if she was afraid of it?

"Go," she said, pushing him toward the fire. "I will do what I can. Find Scotia, please!"

"I will find her and bring her to you, here." He pointed at the ground. "Do not leave this place unless the fire threatens you." He gave her a quick kiss and sprinted toward the inferno.

Smoke swirled about him, swallowing him like some mythical beast. "Be safe," she whispered, almost like a prayer.

Quickly she pulled the ermine sack into her hand, opening it so that it lay over her palm, the stone exposed, settled over the center symbol. She closed her eyes and reached for the energy, finding it easily this time, pulling it into her as she muttered the blessing prayer Jeanette had tried to teach her, determined that even if she didn't get it exactly right, it might still help.

Nothing happened.

She tried again, and again, nothing happened.

Her eyes popped open. The fire burned hotter than even a few moments before. She had not changed anything. Frustration had her in its grip and Jeanette's words came back to her. She needed to *guide* the power of the stone, not try to control it or force it. She focused on the fire and allowed the energy to flow through her. The wind rose around her, clearing the smoke from the bailey but also fanning the flames that roared over the great hall. They needed rain. She scanned the horizon, spying storm clouds in the distance. Could she bring them here? Clouds moved on wind. She could raise wind.

Holding the stone high, she opened herself to the energy, letting it flow through her without resistance, guiding it through the Targe stone, directing the wind to rise, to widen its reach. She focused on the distant clouds but could not see any change in them. She fed the energy, determined to bring the rain to the fire.

A shout went up, a woman's voice, screeching, sharp with fear. "She is still inside! Mistress Scotia is still inside!"

Rowan looked away from the clouds, to the crowd near the blaze. She stared in horror as Nicholas disappeared into the undercroft that led to the kitchen. Smoke billowed out around him, swallowing him whole.

ARCHIE FOUND THE TOWER WAS EMPTY ON THE FIRST TWO FLOORS. Clearly any able-bodied person who might have been here was fighting the fire. When he reached the top floor he stopped at the top of the stair, hugged the wall, and listened.

A rustling sound came from his right. He carefully peered into the corridor. The door to his right was open and he could see a bed. A frail older woman lay there, her eyes closed. A younger woman moved into view. Her blond hair and slender build told him this was the one called Jeanette, the one who had been summoned to see to Rowan's hurts the day the wall fell. The younger daughter, the hellion, did not appear to be here. He pulled his dagger and slipped into the chamber.

Jeanette was folding a blanket, her back to him. He grabbed her, setting his dagger to her pale neck.

"Do not move or call out or I will slice you open ear to ear."

She did not move.

"Do you understand?" he growled, pulling her more tightly against him.

"Aye," she whispered. "What do you want?"

Everything, that's what he wanted, but for now he would be content with what the king wanted. "The ermine sack, and your mother."

He could feel her swallow but she said nothing.

"Where is the sack?" he demanded as he pushed her to sit on the wooden chest at the end of the bed. He brandished his dagger with one hand while he pulled a length of rope free from where it was wrapped around his waist. "Where is it!?" He shoved his dagger back in its sheath and grabbed her wrists, wrapping them tightly with the rope.

"They are not for you, Archibald of Easton," she said, her voice surprisingly hard.

He backhanded her, flinging her from the chest onto the floor with a crash. She lay there, stunned.

He grabbed her by her hair and pulled her upright. "Where is the sack?"

"Not here!" There was fear in her voice now.

Archie smiled, pleased by her fear. "You lie." He yanked her head backward, extending her neck as he placed his dagger against it once more. An odd grunt sounded from behind him. He pivoted, only to find the old woman flailing an arm toward him, an almost animal growl coming from her. He threw Jeanette to the floor again and turned his attention to Elspet.

"Speak, woman. Your daughter's life is in the balance. Where is the sack?"

She glared at him but said nothing.

"I spoke the truth," Jeanette said. She was sitting up, scooting backward, away from him. "The sack is not here. It is not in my mum's keeping anymore."

Archie looked from one woman to the other, assessing the situation. "Who has it?" He held the dagger to the old woman's throat this time as he pinned Jeanette with his glare. "*Who?*"

Jeanette pushed herself to her feet against the wall. She looked at her mother, as if seeking counsel, though no words were spoken.

Archie pushed the dagger in enough to draw blood. The old woman never so much as whimpered but Jeanette reached her bound hands toward him as if to stop him.

"I must, Mum," she said quietly, then turned her airy blue eyes to him. "Rowan. Rowan has the sack. She left here with your friend just a few moments ago."

Fury sliced through him. Disbelief curdled in his stomach.

"Aaaah!" he screamed. "You lie!" Rage consumed him, turning everything red. It could not be true. Nicholas could not have the ermine sack and its keeper.

Who was not the old woman.

It was Rowan.

Nicholas had lied to him again and again. He'd betrayed everything, taking everything for himself and leaving Archie with nothing. Archie's wrath took over as he plunged his dagger into the useless old woman's chest.

Jeanette screamed and flew at him. He backhanded her once more, flinging her halfway across the large chamber, where she fell hard to the floor and didn't move.

Archie tore the chamber apart, sure that the woman had lied to him, that the sack, and whatever it sheltered within it, was here, that somehow Nicholas had devised this lie and they were so much in his thrall, so charmed by him, that they had conspired against Archie. They lied. The sack must be here.

He opened every basket, every chest, rolled the old woman over in the bed, as he searched for the ermine sack that held his destiny.

At length there was nothing left to ransack, to destroy, nothing left to vent his rage upon. Nothing except Nicholas . . . and Rowan.

Nicholas had forgotten his allegiance to Archie, to his king, because of that barbarian wench. But why? What was it about that woman that could shift Nicholas's loyalties so suddenly, so completely? It must have something to do with the sack and whatever was in it. It must have something to do with riches, power, for the man would not be swayed by something as common as a lusty lass.

Aye, that must be it. She must be connected to the Targe in some way. She was the keeper of the ermine sack now. Nicholas kept her safe, kept her for himself.

But she would be Archie's.

He would deliver her to the king, her and the sack she possessed. He did not yet know what her part in this mission was, but he was certain she was the key to his future, and Nicholas's disgrace . . . Nicholas's demise . . . Nicholas's death.

He would have the pleasure of seeing Nicholas's head upon a pike in London. But first he had to find Rowan.

Rowan's heart was beating so hard she could hear it drumming in her ears. Scotia was inside. Nicholas had gone for her, he would find her as he'd promised. They must not perish!

But what could she do? The clouds were too far away, even if she could bring them here. She searched for an idea, her gaze landing on the large grey stones that made up the foundation and undercrofts of the great hall. She could manipulate stone. She'd done it before she became the Guardian. What could she do now? If she could throw stones, could she hold them in place?

She abandoned the wild idea of drawing the storm clouds to put out the fire and turned every bit of attention she had to focus the Targe on holding up the vaulted ceilings of the undercrofts. The fire leapt as the force of the Targe's energy pushed the wind ahead of it. The roof groaned and collapsed. She gasped, feeling the weight of it press against her efforts. Burning timber crashed to the ground around the great hall. Sparks flew, whipped high into the air. She prayed there were enough people tending the other structures in the castle to put out any new fires the embers were sure to cause but she dared not look. She dared not take her eyes from the place where Nicholas had disappeared. She dared not let her focus be distracted lest Scotia and Nicholas die.

# CHAPTER EIGHTEEN

Sweat ran down Rowan's back. Her eyes stung from the heat and smoke. Her teeth were clenched so hard her jaw ached, but she would not give up. The walls of the upper level were beginning to topple, one by one, and still she held her position, Targe stone raised high, all her focus on holding up the undercrofts until Scotia and Nicholas emerged from the impossibly thick smoke, until they were free.

Suddenly she was hit and sent flying through the air. She landed hard on her side. Disoriented, she realized she no longer held the stone, though the ermine sack was clenched in her fist. She pushed herself up to sit, only then noticing Archie squatting near her, the Targe stone held in his blood-covered hand.

"Is this what you are looking for, witch?"

A deafening roar filled the bailey as the undercrofts gave way, sending overwhelming waves of black smoke, burning timber, and ashes over everything and everyone. Over Nicholas and Scotia trapped inside.

"Nay!" Grief and rage clawed at Rowan even as the ermine sack was jerked out of her hand. The next thing she knew she was lifted into the air and thrown over a hard shoulder. She tried to scream, to kick, to throw herself out of his grip but he held on fast. The smoke was so thick she could barely see or draw breath but she was certain he headed for the gate passage.

She had to stop him. He had sealed the deaths of Scotia and Nicholas when he broke her focus. He could not have her or the Targe stone. He would pay dearly for their deaths.

Stone or no, she had fought off Archie once without it, she could do so again. She gathered the energy to her and let it loose upon him.

The blast threw them both to the ground, but she was ready for it, rolling away from him as fast as possible, crouching low, trying to see under the smoke, to find him. She reached for a nearby rock, the size of her hand, and gripped it, ready to defend herself if necessary.

The smoke cleared just enough for her to see Archie as he looked for her. He gripped the ermine sack, clearly containing the Targe stone again, but still he did not see her.

"I know you are there. You cannot fly away on the smoke." He backed away, though he still seemed to be scanning about him, looking for her. He lifted the ermine sack as he said, "I shall take my victory this day. It was too easy to bring fire and death to a clan supposedly protected by a feeble old woman and her pagan relic. But she is dead, and without this in your possession, you will not be able to protect this decrepit castle from me. I can return anytime I wish to take you, too." He backed up even further, disappearing into the smoke.

Rowan stayed frozen in place, listening for him, sure he would circle around her and tackle her again. As she waited, his words began to filter through the fog of loss in her mind. *She is dead.* How could he know if Elspet yet lived or died? And then she remembered the blood on his hand and the answer hit her, knocking her backwards. Dead. Anguish writhed through her. Not Elspet, too. It could not be!

ROWAN MADE IT TO THE TOWER QUICKLY, MORE BY FORCE OF WILL than by any ability to see where she was going. She pulled the tower door open and sped up the stairs, two at a time.

"Auntie!" she shouted as she rounded the top of the stair and pushed the door to Elspet's chamber open. The scene before her stopped her heart and stole her labored breath. What had he done?

Elspet lay flopped like a ragdoll almost sideways across her bed, a crimson stain spreading beneath her like a ghastly poppy flower.

Rowan stepped through the chaos on the floor. "Auntie?" She brushed grey-streaked hair back from her aunt's face, only to find a blank stare where there should have been a spark of life. "Nay. Nay. Nay," she whispered over and over and over. "Why did he do such a thing, Auntie?" she asked, though she knew she would get no answer.

But she did hear a groan coming from the side of the bed.

"Jeanette?!"

Rowan sidled around the bed and only then saw her cousin lying on the floor amidst the ruin of the chamber. Another groan came from Jeanette as she rolled over onto her back. Blood trickled from her nose and the gash on her forehead had opened again. Her hands were tied, but she was alive. Rowan rushed to her side.

"Rowan?" Jeanette murmured weakly, her eyes fluttering open for a moment before she closed them again.

"Aye, 'tis me." She gently untied her cousin's hands, then grabbed for the cloth and bowl of water they kept by Elspet's bed, only to find the bowl overturned and the water spilled. The cloth would do. She returned to Jeanette and blotted away the blood from her nose, grateful to find it was no longer bleeding. She did the same to the gash on her forehead, though it bled profusely. Pressing the cloth to the cut, she looked about her for anything she could bind around Jeanette's head to hold it in place.

The basket her cousin kept for tending such things lay across the room, its contents dumped on the bench beneath the window.

"Can you hold this?" she asked, taking Jeanette's hand and pressing it against the cloth. "Just for a moment."

Jeanette didn't answer but she kept her hand there. Rowan grabbed the basket and piled what contents were easy to identify back into it. Grabbing a rolled length of linen from where it had fallen under the bench, she took everything back to her cousin.

It took a bit of doing but she managed to bind the cloth in place and get Jeanette sitting up, braced against the wall but still on the floor.

"Archie did this?" Rowan asked, glancing around the chamber that was as devastated as anything she could do in the grips of her gift.

"She is dead, is she not?"

Rowan swallowed and nodded. "I am so sorry I was not here."

"You could not have changed what happened, Rowan. He is a madman and he wants to hurt Nicholas."

"And me. He came here for the Targe." A terrible hatred grew inside her, wrapping all her grief and remorse in its tentacles. "He set the fire." She would not burden Jeanette with the death of her sister and Nicholas yet, though she swore she would have vengeance on the man if it were the last thing she did. "He took the Targe stone, Jeanette. He tried to take me, too."

"I am so sorry, Rowan. I did not ken what else to do."

"What do you mean?"

Jeanette looked over at the bed where her mother lay. Tears ran down her cheeks until the remorse and sorrow began to harden in her eyes, leaving a coldness Rowan had never thought to see in Jeanette.

"I told him," Jeanette said. "I tried to save Mum. I told him about you so he would leave her alone but he flew into a rage." She wiped the tears from her cheeks. "Mum was murdered because she was no longer the Guardian. I am sorry. I had to try to save her from that madman."

Rowan couldn't breathe. "Of course you did." She sat then, reeling from so much loss, so much wasted life at the hands of a single Englishman.

"You cannot let him get away with it, Rowan. You must avenge her death. I cannot wield any power, but you can."

Rowan looked over to where her aunt lay, knowing the bloody, violent image would forever remain vivid in her memory. Grief gripped her in sharp talons. "I will avenge her death, I swear it." She would avenge Scotia and Nicholas, too, and her own broken heart.

"I am depending upon you, Guardian," Jeanette said. She sank back against the wall as if there were no bones left in her body.

Rowan rose. She must go after Archie before he disappeared too far into the forest. "Will you be all right here alone until I can find Uncle Kenneth?" She was not the only one who had lost too many loved ones this day and she hated that she must bring this news to him.

"I will be right here," Jeanette said, pointing at the ground where she sat.

ROWAN BURST THROUGH THE TOWER DOORWAY INTO THE BAILEY, already searching for Kenneth when she heard her name.

"Rowan, there you are!"

She blinked, sure she was seeing a ghost. Soot had blackened his skin and clothes, but his smile and his voice were unmistakable. Nicholas. She threw herself into his arms.

"How? I saw the great hall cave in. I held it up as long as I could but then—"

"You held it up?" He whooped and swung her around just as thunder rolled over their heads and fat raindrops began to fall all around them. "Did you bring the rain, too?" He swung her around again as the cold water began to drench the fire.

"I did . . . I think. Nicholas, you need to put me down."

He did as she asked. "I know I should not be so happy," he said, "but I did not think to ever get Scotia or wee Ian out of there alive. You saved us, Rowan." He held her face between his palms and kissed her softly. "The Guardian saved us."

"Scotia is alive?" She covered her mouth with a trembling hand. "I thought you both dead."

"She is alive, and wee Ian, too. She was trying to carry him out when a beam fell, trapping them. I managed to clear enough of a path for them to get out but it took time. I do not think we would have made it without you holding up the building. I still cannot believe you did that."

She swallowed the tears of relief that threatened. "It is amazing what I can do when people I love are in danger."

His eyes went soft at her admission but before he could say or do anything else, she stopped him.

"Archie started the fire." She had to get it all out quickly. "He killed Elspet and stole the Targe stone from me—that is when the ceiling gave way. I was sure he had killed you and Scotia. He tried to take me with him."

"He killed Elspet? Took the stone?" Nicholas shoved his fingers through his wet, sooty hair. "You fought him off, did you not?" There was a hint of pride this time and it warmed Rowan's heart that he knew that about her. "My God, love. I knew he was heartless but I did not see *this* in him."

"And Kenneth does not know."

Nicholas turned toward the fire and bellowed Kenneth's name, dragging Rowan with him as he yelled for the chief again.

Uilliam emerged from the diminishing smoke. "What d'you want with Kenneth? He is a mite busy!" He was as sooty-black as Nicholas.

"Where is he, Uilliam?" Rowan asked quietly. "It cannot wait. You need to hear the news as well."

Uilliam scowled but nodded at her and bellowed the chief's name until they heard Kenneth mutter one of his favorite curses as he appeared like a wraith in the smoke.

Rowan did not waste a moment telling him what had happened, only then noticing that Scotia stood behind him, hearing everything, too. Kenneth was stunned into an unnatural quiet.

"Uncle, you need to see to Elspet and your daughters. Uilliam, can you spare a few men and come with me to find the bastard who did all this?"

"You are not going after him," Nicholas cut in. "It is too dangerous."

"It is no more dangerous for me than for anyone else today. Look at what he has already done to us. He has no soul. He'll not hesitate to kill you, even if you were once friends." She reached out and gripped his hand. "I do not want to lose anyone else I love this day."

"We were never friends, not true friends. I know that now. But the clan cannot risk you that way."

"Nicholas, I will not be alone. You will be there beside me. You will be my Protector. I choose you to be my Protector." She spoke to him, but looked at her uncle, Uilliam, and Scotia.

Uilliam grumbled. Scotia did not react at all. Kenneth stared at Nicholas, his eyes revealing nothing, then gave a quick incline of his head.

"As the Guardian wishes," Kenneth said formally, if reluctantly. "But the bastard is not to be killed." His voice was like hot iron. "Bring him back to me alive."

"We will," Nicholas said, his voice as hard as Kenneth's.

Without another word the chief went to the tower, Scotia following him a few steps behind. Uilliam left to round up men to find Archie.

It would be far easier confronting the bastard than it was confronting the evil the bastard had wrought.

# CHAPTER NINETEEN

LEFT ALONE IN THE BUSY BAILEY WITH NICHOLAS, ROWAN WAS SUDdenly unsure of herself. No matter how much she wanted to fling herself into his arms or race off after Archie, she knew she could not until Nicholas understood exactly what was required of him as her Protector.

"How fare you, love?" he asked.

"So much has happened, and there is so much to do, to recover from," she began, looking past him to the fire-wrought destruction, before she looked up into his eyes. "But there is something we must speak of before we hunt down Archie." She glanced around them at the people still handing buckets of water down the line, while others beat at the crumbled ruin of the great hall with wet cloths. Too many people present for something best done in private. "Not here."

She grabbed his hand and made for the stairs that led from the bailey up to the wall walk where they had first kissed. It was a fitting place for this conversation.

At the top, she slipped into the same deeply shadowed spot where he'd found her once before. When he joined her, she slid into his arms and kissed him with a desperation honed with the grief she had felt when she thought him dead in the fire and the joy she knew when she found him alive. He ran his hands down her arms, over her back, cupping her face. She leaned into him, running her hands over him just as hungrily. She needed this not to be their last kiss, but that was up to him now.

The possibility that he would not take up the role she offered stilled her, though she held on to him tightly.

"We must talk," she said, hearing the edge to her words as hope and fear laced through them.

"Of what, love?"

She looked up at him. "I named you my Protector but I did not tell you what that means and I will not hold you to it if you do not want . . . me."

"Is it not clear that I want you quite desperately?"

He kissed her, softly now, holding her so close she felt the hard length of him against her stomach. A heated thrill ran through her, but she knew this was not enough.

She smiled. "Aye, but 'tis not exactly what I meant." She tried to step back but he wouldn't release her.

"I love you, Rowan," he said. "I do not think I have ever loved before, but I know I love you."

She touched a hand to his chest, just over his heart where it beat in time with her own. "That is fortunate, since I love you, too." She took a steadying breath. "But that still is not quite the point I need to make clear." She did step away now, putting a little distance between them so she could think clearly.

"I must explain what it means to be the Guardian's Protector, Nicholas. I will not let you accept the position until you understand exactly what it means."

She was wringing her hands now, and he reached out to still them, gently bringing them back to rest on his chest again.

"Tell me."

She nodded and took a deep breath looking him straight in the eye. "It means you would be my husband." She swallowed but did not look away from him, wanting him to see how deep her feelings for him went.

He held her gaze for long moments. She could barely draw breath as she waited to see in what direction her future lay.

"Are you asking me to marry you?"

"Aye. I know it is not the usual way of things, but for the Guardian of the Targe, nothing is usual." She took his hands in hers now, holding them between them. "I am asking you to be my husband, Nicholas, but with that comes as large a responsibility as I have as Guardian. The Guardian's husband is the chief of the clan."

Shock was clear in his eyes and in the tense grip of his hands on hers, but he did not let go and she allowed herself to hope.

"But I am not a MacAlpin," he said, as if that mattered.

"Neither is Kenneth. He is a MacGregor, like me. Elspet chose him as her Protector and he became chief here."

"But he still lives. He is still chief."

"Only until I marry."

Now he dropped her hands. He started to speak, then stopped. He walked away from her, then turned and came back. He started to speak again and she stopped him.

"It is too much I ask of you. I understand." She blinked hard, disappointment difficult to hold back.

"Nay, Rowan," he said, once more taking her hands in his. "Nay, it is not too much to ask. You offer me the world. You offer me your love, your life, a home, a clan, a place to belong, to protect. You offer me the life of a Highlander, something I'd long since given up as impossible.

"But your clan does not trust me. They might accept me as your husband, but they will not accept me as chief. I would marry you instantly, Rowan," he said, "but I would not do so if it causes trouble with the clan, with Kenneth. They do not trust me, and with good reason."

"But if they came to trust you, you would accept all that is required of the Protector?"

"I would embrace it, treasure it, and do everything in my power to be a good husband to you and a good chief to the clan."

She cupped his face in her hands and drew him into a lingering kiss.

"It is my decision alone," she said. "I wish for you to be my Protector, my husband, and the chief of this clan. Kenneth is grief-stricken but he kens how chiefs are chosen. He will still be a valued member of the clan, a necessary counselor for you, as Jeanette will be for me. We have much to learn, we two, but together we can keep this clan from further harm. Your knowledge of the English king, and what he plans, will be invaluable in protecting us."

She closed her eyes for a moment. "I need you," she said as she looked up into his eyes and saw her own love, and need, and yearning reflected there. "I need you here to watch over me, to call me back when my gift consumes me, to love me as no one else ever has. And I need you to let me love you."

He pulled her close. "I would wed you this very moment, if the clan would agree, but I will not come between you and your family. Your first responsibility is to them, not to me."

She smiled at him, her heart lighter than she had dared imagine. "They will do as I wish, but not right away. We have much to grieve this day, much to make right, and I would not take the right of passing judgment upon Archie from my uncle." Her expression turned fierce. "I will love you no matter what anyone else says."

He grinned at her then and swept her into another long kiss. "And I will love you, no matter what."

ROWAN AND NICHOLAS MADE THEIR WAY BACK DOWN TO THE BAIley where they found Uilliam, Duncan, and a knot of warriors ready to leave with them.

"We are leaving sufficient men here to see to the fire?" Rowan asked Uilliam.

"Aye, lass. There was much arguing over who would have to stay here and who would get to hunt down the vermin who killed Lady Elspet, but we settled it." Rowan did not want to know how the argument had been settled, for she'd seen such things before and they usually included much yelling and fists flying before decisions were agreed to.

"Let us get this done," she said, anxiety churning her empty stomach once more. "There is much work needs doing here when we return."

There was a rumble of agreement from the warriors.

"Duncan will track the man," Uilliam said, but he looked at Nicholas. "Do you ken where he might have headed? Was there a meeting place you had agreed to, perhaps?"

The words were surprisingly civil and Rowan realized that Nicholas had been right: He had not been trusted, but now something was subtly different. Uilliam might not trust him, exactly, but he trusted Rowan and her decision to claim Nicholas as her Protector changed much.

"I do not know for sure," Nicholas said.

"He said he would return for me," Rowan said. "I do not think he understands what my role is, but he saw me wielding the Targe when he took it from me. He said he would return."

"Then he has not gone far," Nicholas said, his face as grim at this news as the other men's. "If he suspects Rowan is important he will want to take her to the king with the stone to collect his reward." He looked toward the gate, considering something.

"I do not think he will be alone," he said, his voice measured, thoughtful. "There were English soldiers in Oban when we were there. He was with me when we first came here, the day the wall fell, but he disappeared and I did not see him for at least a sennight. He told me he had returned to Oban to send word of where I was to the king as a token of our efforts, along with news of the breached defenses here. If I had been in his position I would have had the king's soldiers draw close to the glen so they would be nearby if I needed their aid. Archie well knows that we will be hunting him for this day's deeds. I am sure we will find him surrounded by soldiers and they, most likely, would be camped west of here, between us and the sea."

Uilliam was quiet, then grunted his agreement. "That is what I would do, too. Is he so predictable?"

Nicholas thought for a moment. "Archie is a good spy but he acts on his emotions more than logic and careful consideration. Sometimes that serves him well. Sometimes it does not. He is angry and he wants to hurt me for my betrayal. He would not want to make it too hard for me to find him. Aye, I believe he is so predictable, at least in this situation," Nicholas said.

Uilliam stared at him, nodded, and led the group out to hunt down Elspet's killer.

Archie had made it difficult for Duncan to track him, but it wasn't impossible. The ground, where it wasn't rock, was muddy from the rain, making it hard for Archie to completely hide his passing. Some of his tracks had washed away, but Duncan managed to find his trail again and again, first leading away from the loch, counter to Nicholas's expectations, but then eventually winding back toward the loch just as the sun sank behind the western bens, casting fingers of golden light and indigo shadows down the length of the dark water. They smelled the smoke of a cook fire long before they came upon the English men-at-arms' encampment.

From their hiding place in a dense thicket of young trees, Rowan did a quick count—a score of soldiers, plus Archie. Their horses were tethered to a line on the west side of their camp.

The fire was positioned near the base of a rock wall that rose a good fifteen feet or more, leaning out toward the loch. It likely had given the soldiers some shelter from the rain, though judging from the mud that made up most of the area, not much.

"No one is coming," one of the soldiers grumbled loudly.

"Quiet, damn you!" Archie hissed. He was seated on a large boulder, his mud-covered feet drawn up out of the muck. He watched the perimeter of the camp like a hawk watched a field for mice, his head swiveling slowly as he scanned the area.

Uilliam swiftly gave silent orders for the Highlanders to spread out around the camp, sending Duncan and half of their warriors around the stone outcropping to take a position on the west side. Even though the English camp was set back from the lochside, there was insufficient cover to hide the Highlanders' movements.

A quarter hour later Rowan heard the *her-uh* sound of a tawny owl—the signal that Duncan and his men were in position. Uilliam gave the countersignal and suddenly the Highlanders were rushing the camp, claymores at the ready, and shouting wildly. Rowan had been instructed to stay hidden, Nicholas by her side. They had both argued for a different tactic but Uilliam had refused to let the Guardian act as bait when there were plenty of Highlanders ready for a fight. He had forbidden them to move from their hiding place.

They watched as the Highlanders dispatched soldier after soldier, pressing the fight back against the rock face to keep their quarry from escaping. But Archie managed to stay on the edge of the fight, getting pushed closer and closer to the edge of the forest, until finally he sank his sword into one of the MacAlpin warriors, pulled it free, and sprinted into the forest.

"He's getting away!" Rowan said, racing after him.

Nicholas passed her quickly, gaining on the man hurtling through the woods and leaving her trailing behind. She heard a sound like two elk crashing together, followed by a very human curse. She sped up and came upon Nicholas and Archie rolling on the ground, fists flying until they bashed into the wide trunk of an ancient Scots pine. Nicholas grabbed Archie by the hair and pounded his head against a gnarled root until the man lay there, stunned. Nicholas pulled back his fist to finish the man off.

"Nicholas! Stop! We need him alive."

Archie's sword had gone flying, or he'd thrown it at Nicholas, she couldn't really tell, but it lay near her, the point stuck at a shallow angle in the root of a tree. She grabbed it, holding the heavy sword in two hands as she'd seen the warriors do, and moved to Nicholas's side, holding the point toward Archie's throat. He blinked up at her.

"Witch."

Nicholas punched him.

"Why do we need him alive?" Nicholas asked Rowan as he flipped the now unconscious Archie onto his stomach and pulled his arms roughly behind him. He pulled off the strip of cloth Archie wore around his neck and bound his hands with it, leaving him facedown in the mud and last fall's leaves.

"He has the stone."

Nicholas wiped mud from his face. "So he does." He swiftly checked Archie's body for the sack or the stone but found neither. "Son of a whore." He kicked Archie in the hip, hard enough to rouse him.

Archie groaned and Nicholas pulled him to his feet, leaning him against the ancient tree's bole. He grabbed his dagger and held it to the man's throat. "Where's the stone, Archie?"

The ginger-haired man managed to smile and sneer at the same time. "Why should I tell you?"

"Because I shall do to you what you did to Lady Elspet."

Archie shook his head, the smile gone, the sneer left behind twisting the man's face. "You will not do that or your witch will never get her stone back, nor the sack with the pagan symbols painted inside it."

"I am no witch." Rowan stepped toward him, tired of the smirking man. "But you are a murderer and a thief."

"So is Nicholas here. He is the same as me, driven and as free of conscience, are you not, my old friend?"

Nicholas said nothing and Archie grinned, though there was no mirth in his eyes.

"Ah, you think just because this woman lets you between her legs, you belong here? You know better, Nick. You have been between many a woman's legs and none have tethered you before. This one is no different. I have the stone. You have the woman. I saw her in the bailey with it, as if there were some ritual she performed, though I could not tell what she did. You must know how to use them both by now. If we take them to the king, together, as always . . ."

Rowan held her breath, wanting to believe Nicholas was no longer the man Archie said he was, the man he admitted he had been. Nicholas stared at Archie, then started shaking his head.

"Nay, that will never happen. I will never turn Rowan or the stone or any of her kin over to Edward. He would torture her to force her to do his will."

"Or he would kill her to keep her from falling into anyone else's hands," Archie said.

"Then someone else would become the Guardian," Rowan said. "I am but the current vessel for the power of the Targe. If you, or Longshanks, were to kill me, someone else would take my place."

"But Edward would still have the stone."

"Aye, but without the Guardian it is only a stone, useless for anything other than holding down a parchment or propping open a door." Rowan tried not to chew on her lip.

"Enough," Nicholas said. "Let us return to your camp, Archie, and you can return the stone to Rowan."

"And what do I get if I do that, Nick? Will you not kill me instantly?"

"Nay," Rowan said. "That is for my uncle to decide."

"So there is naught for me in this deal."

"A few more hours of life."

"Then I refuse."

Nicholas grabbed the man's arm and hauled him off the tree, dragging him back toward the encampment. Rowan followed as she tried to determine where they had leverage with this horrible man, but found none.

As they neared the camp the sound of fighting was loud. As they made their way into it, they could see many of the English on the ground, dead or dying, and a few of their warriors as well.

"Cease!" Nicholas bellowed, hauling Archie in front of him. "Tell them to cease fighting," Nicholas said to his prisoner.

"Nay, I think not."

Archie's entire person reeked of confidence, cockiness, arrogance, and Rowan hated him for it. He had killed her aunt, set fire to her home, and now threatened her ability to protect what was left of it. She let the anger, the grief, the frustration . . . the hate, fill her as she called upon the energy from the earth knowing that without the focus of the Targe, what happened next would be unpredictable. She pulled hard at the energy, forcing it again, hoping she would have the stone before she lost control. The ground rumbled under their feet and she felt a swirling rise through her, searching for a way out.

"Where is my Targe stone?" she demanded, her voice harsh now, the hatred sharpening the edges of each word.

"It is yours no longer, witch."

The rumbling grew stronger, wind whipped around the clearing, loosening pebbles and small rocks from the stone face.

"Rowan, nay!" Nicholas yelled, but she looked away, losing herself in the sensation of power that surged through her, the battering wind howling about her, drawn by hatred and grief. "Rowan, you must not. It is too dangerous. You would not bury your own."

His words flitted around her, but the hatred pushed them away. She raised her hands, as she had done with the stone, though they were empty of it now. The power burned, but she did not care, she wanted to let it loose, to release the terrible hurt that King Edward's spy had created within her heart.

And suddenly Nicholas was there, his hands on her face, his fingers sliding into her hair. "Rowan, no! You must not let it loose. Not here, not now. Uilliam, Duncan, and the others are too close to the wall. If it comes down you will kill your own, not just the English. You will not be able to live with yourself if you do that."

The pressure of his hands upon her skin, the fervent tone of his voice, forced her to look at him, to remember that she had tasked him with calling her back, that she trusted him, trusted his judgment, loved him.

"It hurts," she whispered.

"I know, but you must pull it back, push it down. Do not let it free." He bent as if to kiss her lips but whispered against them, "Not yet." He kissed her quickly. "Can you do that, Rowan, Guardian of the Targe?"

It was like trapping a million tiny needles within her, each heated red hot, searing her from the inside out, but she nodded. "I can. I am, but I do not know how long I can hold it, Nicholas."

"Not long—" He collapsed at her feet and she was suddenly looking into Archie's wild eyes.

"It would appear the pagan stone is good for killing someone, too." His grin was pure evil as he raised the stone as if to bring it down on her head next.

She flung her arms out to protect herself, and managed to grab the stone, though Archie did not let go. She held on when he would have raised it again and she let all the power that was burning to get out of her race into the stone in one sudden, focused burst. Archie was thrown backward by the blast, halfway across the clearing, landing in the mud near the boulder he had been perched on earlier, but Rowan's hands were empty.

He'd managed to hang on to the stone, damn the man.

She crouched next to Nicholas long enough to determine that he still breathed. Then she stalked toward the stunned Archie, who still lay on his back, blinking up at the sky, his arms outstretched to either side, the stone gripped in his right hand. She stepped on his wrist and bent to wrest the stone from him, when suddenly he snaked his free arm around her, grabbing her, rolling with her in the mud until he ended up on top. He straddled Rowan and pinned her arms over her head with one hand the stone gripped in his other.

"Now you are both mine, witch, and King Edward will be most appreciative of my efforts, killing the spy who betrayed him for a Highland whore, and bringing the 'Guardian' and this hunk of stone to him. It will be the end of the Scots as a difficult, useless people. He will invade. He will be your sovereign, and I will be paid handsomely for making that possible."

Rowan said nothing and kept her eyes on his, but a movement behind him had her ready to act.

Nicholas's arm came around Archie's neck, jerking him off Rowan even as the man tried to beat the Targe stone against his attacker's head behind him. Rowan leaped to her feet and grabbed Archie's flailing arm with both hands, hanging from it with all her weight, but still he was too strong for her to wrest the stone from him. She bit his forearm as hard as she could, almost gagging at the blood she tasted. He howled and began to flail the arm to get her off him until, as suddenly as Nicholas had dropped, Archie went limp. She caught the stone as it fell from his hand.

"MacAlpins, to me!" she yelled, hesitating only long enough for her Highlanders to run toward her before she let another blast of energy escape her through the Targe stone, shattering the ledge at the top of the stone face, and raining it down upon the remaining English soldiers.

# CHAPTER TWENTY

THE BATTLE WAS OVER. NICHOLAS THREW THE LIMP ARCHIE INTO Duncan's keeping, reaching for Rowan as her knees gave way.

"I have you, love. I have you. You did well." He murmured to her as he leaned against the boulder and pulled her into the shelter of his arms. She was as thoroughly mud-covered as he was, but she seemed to be unhurt—just shaken.

Uilliam was busy sending a few warriors off to chase down any of the English who might have escaped. Duncan was trussing up Archie hand and foot. A few of the other MacAlpins were gathering their injured and two dead to take back to the castle.

"Do we bury them?" one of the men asked Uilliam, nodding toward the dead English soldiers, "or leave them for the animals like the carrion they are?"

Uilliam did not hesitate. "We'll bury them right here. Rowan has already started a cairn for us. Pile them up. We shall gather the stone to cover them."

Nicholas held on to Rowan, who was now starting to shiver in her cold mud-soaked clothes, trying to share what little body heat he could generate with her. "I need to get Rowan back to Dunlairig. She needs a fire, dry clothes, and food," he said to Uilliam.

Uilliam looked about him at the industry of his men. "Let me see if any of the horses are lingering nearby. 'Twill be easier to load that one"—he glared at Archie who was beginning to awaken from Nicholas's stranglehold—"onto a horse than to carry him back, and I will not chance an escape by loosing his feet."

"If you find two, Rowan should ride as well."

"Nay." Her voice was stronger than he'd expected. "I am nearly recovered and walking will help keep me warm—warmer." She smiled up at Nicholas. "Thank you, Protector. Thank you, love." She kissed him lightly, mud flaking on both their lips.

When Nicholas looked up he found Uilliam standing there, a scowl so deep that his eyes disappeared under his bushy black brows and his mouth so pinched it was hardly visible either.

"Protector." It was not a question.

"Aye." Rowan stepped out of the shelter of Nicholas's arms but reached for his hand. "But I wish to give my uncle time to bury Elspet first. We must all mourn her before any changes are made."

"There may not be time for that, lass," Uilliam said, the scowl loosening as he pulled on his beard. "I do not believe that this is the end of Longshanks's plans for us and we must be prepared."

Nicholas pushed off the boulder and looked about at the mayhem they had wrought. "I agree, but first we must finish this business and return to the castle before we lose all light. Kenneth will cast judgment. We must bury Lady Elspet. And then I would ask the entire clan's permission and blessing to wed their Guardian, my Rowan."

Duncan returned that moment, leading a brown garron, one of the small sturdy ponies preferred in the Highlands. "What is this about a wedding?" He tried to sound stern, but the smile on his face worked against him.

"All in good time," Rowan said, grinning at him. "Before anything else we need to find the ermine sack. I have the Targe stone." She held it up for all to see. "But not the sack."

Nicholas let go of her hand and strode to a pile of travel bags, weapons, and tools the MacAlpins were gathering together. He searched amongst the bags until he found a familiar, well-worn, tooled leather bag that he knew Archie had traded for with a pilgrim who was freshly back from Spain.

He pulled back the flap and found the Targe's sack balled up inside. He pulled it out and held it up for her to see.

"Let us return to the castle," she said, taking it from his hand and settling the stone within it. "There is much this Englishman must answer to and I would not keep my uncle waiting any longer."

Nicholas grabbed her free hand—she gripped the sack so hard in her other one her knuckles were white—and together they moved off toward the castle. Duncan, with Archie trussed belly down over the garron's back, followed behind.

ROWAN WAS EXHAUSTED, DIRTY, COLD, AND YET THERE WAS A FIRE in her belly that energized her and kept her feet moving until they were within the remains of the castle wall. Denis cried out as they came through the torch-lit gate passage, alerting everyone within the castle of their arrival. Cries went up but Rowan could not tell if they were cries of relief or disbelief, for she was sure they all looked like they had bathed in mud. They stopped and Nicholas let go of her hand long enough to assist Duncan in getting Archie off the garron. Each man held the prisoner by an arm as he swayed between them, shaking his head as if to clear his vision. A roar came through the crowd, which parted, letting Kenneth through. His hair stood out in clumps.

He came to a halt next to Rowan. "Is this the man that killed my Elspet?" he demanded.

"Aye, Uncle, this is Archibald of—"

Before she could finish Kenneth drew his dagger and plunged it into Archie's belly. Archie gasped. Nicholas blanched.

Kenneth roared at Duncan and Nicholas. "Put the bastard on the ground." When they didn't immediately obey, he lowered his head and cocked it a little to the side. "Do you disobey your chief?"

"Nay, Kenneth, we do not," Nicholas said. "But—"

"Down! 'Tis my right to pass judgment on this man and I have found him guilty of murder. The sentence is death by my hand. Do you disagree with my judgment?" He was bellowing at Nicholas and Duncan, but Rowan knew he also dared anyone else to gainsay his right to kill this man.

"Nicholas," she said, trying to speak as calmly as she could when her heart was pounding loud in her ears. "Duncan. Put the man down."

Kenneth moved with Archie as he was laid down, keeping his dagger set deep in the Englishman's gut. "I would put this knife through your heart, bastard, as you did to my wife, but that would be too quick." He twisted the hand that gripped the dagger and Archie could do nothing but let out a strangled gurgle. "I would cut your heart out, as you have cut out mine, but that, too, would be too quick." Kenneth twisted the knife again and Archie managed a grimace.

"This is not over, Highlander," he gasped. "The king will have the stone and the girl." Kenneth pushed the dagger deeper and Archie's eyes started to roll but he fought it, rasping out, "He knows—" A long rattling breath left him and he lay limp in a pool of his own blood. Kenneth stepped away, leaving the dagger in Archie's body as he turned away and made his way back through the crowd, heading toward the tower.

It was only when her uncle left that Rowan was able to look away from the body. Nicholas was pale, but showed no grief over the death of the man. Duncan's eyes were fixed, across the open center of the crowd, on Scotia, who stood expressionless.

Jeanette was not to be seen until Rowan looked up. Her cousin stood in the window of Elspet's chamber looking down at the gathering in the bailey, and even from this distance the grim set of her mouth was plain.

"Betsy, Meg, will you take him and wrap his body?" Rowan said to two of the clanswomen standing nearby.

"You mean to bury him?" Meg asked, her voice disbelieving.

"Aye, with the men who died for him today. Duncan, when they are done you will take him back to the clearing, add his body to the cairn they are making there."

Duncan nodded at her, then reached down and drew Kenneth's dagger out of the body.

Hours later, after Rowan had helped Jeanette into bed, and Scotia after her; after Kenneth had made it clear he was not leaving

Elspet's side this night and Rowan had settled him in a chair next to Elspet's bed, then she managed to change out of her mud-caked clothes and wash most of the dried dirt from her hair and body before she collapsed upon her narrow bed in the chamber with her cousins. Nicholas had refused to leave her and slept upon a pallet blocking anyone from entering the chamber. It seemed only moments after Rowan laid down when she woke with a start.

Looking around to see what must have woken her, she found Nicholas quietly snoring by the door and Scotia standing at the small window that looked out over the bailey. Rowan disentangled herself from her blanket and went to her cousin.

"Scotia," she said quietly, not wishing to startle her. "Sweetling, what is it?" She expected tears but found instead a steely-eyed expression she'd never seen before.

"I wanted to go with you today. I wanted to see the man who . . . who . . . who hurt Mum. I wanted to kill him myself."

Rowan looked at this lass she almost didn't recognize standing before her, not manipulative or coy, but angry, determined, with vengeance on her mind and in her straight back and stiff shoulders. Rowan sighed, sorry that the immature Scotia seemed to have been killed with her mother, but proud that she was not buckling under grief, that she sought action as a balm for her broken heart, not pity. Rowan was sorrier that Scotia would not get vengeance upon Archie except through her father's hand.

"You were needed here."

Scotia scowled but did not take her gaze from the dark bailey. "There was nothing I could do here to change what happened to Mum."

"Her death has been avenged."

Scotia did not reply and now Rowan saw a lone fat tear roll down her cheek. "We will all miss her," she said to her cousin, remembering when she lost her own mother. "It is a pain that will never fully heal, a hole in our hearts that will never completely close, but she died protecting the clan. Even in her state she would not give in to that man's demands. She died as she lived, Scotia, protecting the people and the place that she loved."

"She died too soon." Scotia wiped the tear from her face with a knuckle. "She died too soon."

Rowan tried to swallow around her own grief at losing a mother not just once, but twice, for Elspet had been every bit a mother to her since she'd first come to live here. She hugged Scotia's stiff body to her and laid her head on her cousin's shoulder. "Aye, it is always too soon to lose a mother."

They stood there for a long time and finally Scotia relaxed and wound an arm around Rowan's waist. "What are we going to do without her, Rowan?"

"I do not know. We shall muddle through as best we can. We still have Kenneth, and Elspet taught Jeanette much, so we yet have her knowledge if not her wisdom. We will have to find our way without her."

"I already miss her." It was the faintest of whispers.

"I do, too."

They stood together, arms looped one about the other, watching as the moon set and the sky began to lighten with false dawn. Scotia's stomach rumbled and for the first time Rowan realized that more had been lost than her aunt and a building. Their food stores had been in the larder, below the great hall. It was doubtful any of it had survived the fire and the water. Panic set up in her stomach, sending spikes of anxiety through her chest, constricting her breath. How would they feed everyone?

And then she felt the warmth of a hand on her shoulder, patting it, as if to calm her. She looked around to see who it was, only to find no one stood behind her and Scotia's arm was around her waist, not over her shoulders.

Shaken, she realized the sensation was familiar, exactly what Elspet used to do when Rowan was young and newly come to Dunlairig. When Rowan would get worried, or sad, or angry, Elspet would pull her into her lap and pat her shoulder until she calmed down enough to think clearly. As she got older, she no longer sat in her aunt's lap, but Elspet would still from time to time pat her on the shoulder, reminding her that things were not as bad as Rowan thought.

She smiled at the memory and the panic began to subside as she thought about what her aunt would do in this situation. Elspet would call upon those families who lived up and down the glen to share what they had with those who lived in the castle. She would send out hunting parties for meat, smoking and drying whatever was not immediately needed. She would send the women into the bens and the valley to find what was available to feed a hungry clan. She would have the milk from their cows and sheep made into cheeses.

They were lucky it was not winter and that the gardens and oat field had not been burned. The grassy shielings further up in the bens would provide good fodder for the animals over the summer, as they always did. It would be more work than usual, but not a great deal more. They would survive. By late autumn they would have their stores replenished enough to get the entire clan through the winter, they would have to.

Aye, that is what Elspet would do.

She was sure she would often look to her memories of her aunt for guidance as they all found their way without her. It gave Rowan a warm comfort to know that in this way at least her aunt would be with them always.

As the sky heralded true dawn, Rowan quickly donned a gown over her kirtle, and an old arisaid that she belted about her waist and drew up over her shoulders, fixing it in place with the pin that had been her mother's. She realized that what she had told Scotia about losing a mother was true, the wound never healed, but it did grow fainter with time until it was more a gentle familiar ache than the sharp pain it once was. It gave her comfort to know they would never forget Elspet, but neither would they suffer without end at her loss.

She went to Nicholas, who was still quietly snoring on his pallet by the door. His beard-stubbled face looked younger and unguarded in his sleep. She placed her palm against his warm cheek, stroking her thumb across the smooth skin above the beard. "Love," she said, leaning down to kiss his brow. "The sun will rise soon. We have much to see to this day."

He did not open his eyes at once but a smile spread over his face, and he captured her hand against his cheek with one of his own. "I would wake this way every morn," he said, his voice thick with sleep, "with your hands upon me." He cracked one eye open and his smile turned to a grin until he saw her fully dressed. She watched as the playfulness was replaced by grim determination. "You should have awakened me sooner."

He released her hand and sat up, pushing his hair out of his way as he looked toward the window where Scotia still kept watch. He cocked an eyebrow at Rowan, but she shook her head. Scotia would grieve in her own way and own time.

A WEEK LATER NICHOLAS WAS SHOVELING RUBBLE AND ASHES from the burned great hall, instead of moving rocks from the fallen curtain wall. Duncan worked alongside him and Uilliam oversaw the workers. It was oddly the same as when he'd first arrived at Dunlairig Castle more than a fortnight ago, and yet so much had changed.

He loaded up the cart and one of the older lads struggled to pull it toward the gate.

Elspet had been buried the afternoon after she died. Archie's body had been returned to the clearing.

And now Nicholas and Rowan waited to be together, to be married.

Rowan did not want to rush her family into such a change even though it was inevitable. Truth was, Nicholas still did not think himself worthy of leading this clan so he was in no rush either, except that he desperately wished to wed Rowan, and she him. They had found little opportunity since returning to the castle to be alone together. A stolen kiss here and there was all they had shared and he found his patience growing thin.

"Nicholas of Achnamara."

He turned to find Kenneth striding toward him, and he wondered if now was the time Kenneth would finally seek vengeance upon him for bringing all this trouble down upon Clan MacAlpin.

Kenneth drew near, his face stern. The man was intimidating, even to Nicholas, who had dealt with King Edward.

"Chief," he said.

"I have been waiting a sennight for you to seek me out."

"You have?"

"I have. I have been alone with my grief and that is not a good thing."

Nicholas stared at him, at a loss for what the man was talking about.

"Hmmph." The man shook his head. "My Elspet would not let me sit and sink into such gloom if she were here. She would not sit idly by while the Guardian's chosen Protector does not take his rightful place as her husband . . . and as chief."

Nicholas opened his mouth to say something, but nothing came out. He opened it again. Nothing.

"Are you a fish?" Kenneth asked.

"Nay, it is only . . . we wanted to wait until you . . . until the clan . . ."

"Until we were over our grief?"

"I doubt you will ever be over it," Nicholas said.

"Too true, but all the same Elspet would not wish us to postpone such a celebration as Rowan's marriage to a man who has proved himself her true Protector. You love her, do you not?"

"Aye, sir, I do."

"And she loves you?"

"It was she who asked me to marry her, so yes, I believe she does love me."

"Then it would seem there is little left to be settled."

"Except . . . I will not marry her if the clan deems me unworthy of her, and of the position I will have as her husband."

"Do you think they will judge you unworthy?" Kenneth asked, looking about at the busy folk who had been working alongside Nicholas for days clearing the remains of the great hall.

"I do not ken. Do you think I am worthy?"

Kenneth considered him for a long moment, then slowly nodded. "I do. Uilliam told me of your part in capturing the spy, and in protecting my niece. She speaks highly of you, and goes on and on about how you help her manage her gift. And you—you light up when you so much as look at her. You are a good man, strong, loyal to our new Guardian. You have put the clan above your own self-interests. I can think of no better description of a Protector, and of a chief."

Nicholas didn't know what to say. It was more than he'd ever hoped to hear from anyone, more than he ever thought he could be.

"My kinsmen," Kenneth bellowed, drawing the attention of the folk working in the bailey. "Rowan has chosen this man as the Guardian's Protector and all that entails. Is there any reason we should not accept him as such?"

There was silence and head shaking, and then a voice came from behind Kenneth. "I told you they would accept you," Rowan said, her face alight with happiness. "Do you doubt it now?"

"How can I in the face of so many who do not doubt me?"

"So you will be my husband?"

Nicholas walked to her slowly, took her hands in his, and drew them to his heart. "Will you be my wife?"

Rowan threw herself into his arms and he swung her around and around as laughter and whistles sounded around them. When he stopped, he found Kenneth grinning at them, Jeanette standing by his side.

"How soon may I marry your niece?"

TWO DAYS LATER NICHOLAS CARRIED ROWAN INTO THE BEDCHAMber she had destroyed when she first assumed the role of Guardian. Jeanette had overseen its renovation and it was theirs now that they were finally wed. Preparations for the wedding had been hurried. Neither had been willing to wait. The wedding had taken place that morning. The transfer of the chiefdom from Kenneth to Nicholas had taken place after the midday meal. They had this one night to revel in each other before decisions must be made about how to protect the clan when next Edward sent soldiers after the Targe.

But tonight it was just Rowan and Nicholas and the big bed that stood before them. Nicholas kicked the door closed behind him and let his wife slide down his body until her feet touched the floor. She reached up and kissed him shyly at first, until the hunger took over.

Clothes seemed to shed themselves and before Rowan realized it they were falling onto the soft bed together, hands everywhere. His dark hair fell in waves around the hard planes of his face and she could not stop herself from touching it, touching him.

He turned his lips into her palm, placing a kiss in the center of it, sending tingles through her blood. She closed her eyes and let the sensation play through her body, raising a dangerous need in her. She leaned forward, closing the small space between them, and kissed him. "I want you . . ."—she laid a kiss at the corner of his mouth—". . . to touch me," she said against the other corner of his mouth, "everywhere," then moved to kiss him once more, letting her tongue brush against his lips.

He groaned and teased her lips open, pulling her fully against him until her breasts were pressed against his chest and she could feel the length of his arousal pushing against the apex of her thighs, fanning her own heat to a roaring fire within her. She needed to get closer, to feel him everywhere. She hooked her leg over his hip. He groaned, moving his hand to her bottom and pressing her harder against him, drawing a gasp from her as a wave of pleasure swamped her senses. "Do you ken what you are asking of me, lass?" he asked, somehow kissing her and talking at the same time, the words like a buzz against her neck where he nuzzled her.

"Aye, I ken exactly what I am asking of you." She found his lips, letting her actions speak for her.

Oh, how Nicholas wanted her. She was everything to him: sweetness, challenge, passion. She was unlike any woman he'd known before. He needed to claim her in that most elemental, most primitive way.

Pushing thought away, he reveled in the sweetness of her lips, the taste of her skin, the scent of heather and fresh air that surrounded her. He pulled her riot of silky curls about them, constantly touching, caressing, exploring.

Tentatively, she ran her hand between them, down his belly until she touched the core of his need. Lightly, she ran her fingers over the length of him.

"I am not fragile, love," he said. She looked up at him, a small smile playing over her kiss-swollen lips. "Do what you like." His voice was low, gravelly with his need for her.

She looked down between them as she slid her palm down him, her fingers momentarily brushing his balls, making them draw up. She wrapped her hand around him and he could not help but push himself against her.

"This pleases you," she said, almost to herself, as she tightened her hold, stroking him as his hips pushed at her again. She chuckled at the groan that escaped him and stroked him again, stronger now, more sure of herself. She explored, transfixing him with her inno-cent curiosity until he had to stop her.

"I do not wish this to be over too soon," he whispered, taking her hand from him and rolling her to her back. It was his turn to explore, to learn her body as she was learning his.

Rowan lay back, her body heated, yet the warmth and weight of Nicholas where he lay half over her was welcome. He pinned her hands beside her head and plundered her lips, kissing his way slowly down her neck, lingering over the pulse point at the base of it before he continued his journey down, between her breasts. He released one hand and cupped a breast, running his hand over it, his thumb bringing the nipple to an aching hardness. And then the wet heat of his mouth was there, suckling, pulling, licking, and each sensation echoed in that aching place between her legs. As if he knew that other ache needed soothing, his hand skimmed over her belly and down, cupping her, pressing against her, drawing a moan from deep within her.

She pressed against him as he had pressed into her hand, squirming, not able to ease the ache. Indeed it built so hard and so fast she could not be still. He kissed her mouth, her neck, her other breast, all the while pressing against that white-hot need.

Suddenly, he slipped a finger into the wetness, rubbing her more intimately until he slid it inside her, drawing a gasp from her even as she pressed upward, urging him deeper. He slid the finger out, circling a point of almost excruciating sensitivity before sliding it back in, again and again until her head thrashed and her hips surged and everything shattered within her. And then he was over her, between her legs, and she felt a different pressure where his finger had driven her mad. Instinctively she pushed against it, another long moan rising from her as he pressed into her, then stilled.

"Nicholas." She opened her eyes and peered up at him. She pressed her hands against his back, urging him inside her.

"I do not want to hurt you," he said.

She tried to slow her breathing, to quiet the overwhelming sensations he was building in her body, to listen to him.

"I do not want to hurt you," he said again, his teeth gritted and lines of strain marking his face.

She reached up and pulled him to her, kissing him more gently now. "I ken that there is some pain, but I want you. I want this." She kissed him again, slowly, deeply and raised her hips to his. He groaned and with one swift stroke, filled her. She arched into him, the kiss forgotten with the swift sharpness of her maidenhead gone. Euphoria swept through her as he settled deep within her.

And then he began to move, to surge. He kissed her hard, and she met him kiss for kiss, stroke for stroke, until they both were breathing hard, moans married between them, until every sensation, every sound, every scent gathered into a tight, bright moment and burst forth on a passion-filled cry as he surged one last time, deep within her, going rigid, her name on his lips, at the same moment her world shattered into thousands of blinding shards of light.

Sometime later when she could finally open her eyes she looked about and realized that the room was badly wind blown.

"I suppose I will have to learn to control my gift a bit better." She laughed and felt him grow hard inside her again.

"I suppose we shall have to work on that together." He smiled down at her as he slowly began to bring her to her peak again.

"Aye," she said as a breeze fluttered the bed curtains. "We will have to work on that a lot."

# EPILOGUE

KING EDWARD HELD HIS HAND UP TO HALT THE PROCESSION OF soldiers and camp followers as he moved from London toward Carlisle. A rider was bearing down upon them from the north. The captain of his guard sent two men out to meet the rider. They stopped, spoke very briefly, then returned to the king's procession, riding down the column until they pulled up close enough to speak to the king.

"He has news from Scotland, sire," one of the soldiers said.

Edward eyed the bedraggled man. "What news?"

The messenger looked askance, then said quietly so his voice did not carry far, "From the two you sent to Oban."

Edward summoned the man closer and bade those around him to move away, giving them some little privacy.

The tired man took care to convey all that he had seen and heard before he had escaped the trap the witch called Rowan had sprung upon them, felling the cliff with an outstretched hand. He told of the fire, of the stone in the ermine sack that Archie claimed was the prize they sought, and of his railing against Nicholas's betrayal. He spoke of the battle the man had been lucky to survive.

"I saw it all, your majesty, for I hid in the woods until I was sure there was no hope. The one called Nicholas gave the ginger-haired one—Archibald he called himself—over to the Highlanders as their prisoner. Nicholas supported the witch, calling her 'love,' protecting her from Archibald. He gave her the stone and the ermine sack that Archibald said was yours. He was right, my lord, Nicholas has betrayed you. He has taken sides with the Highlanders and their witch."

Edward let out a vicious roar and backhanded the man so hard he fell from his horse. The king leaped off his own mount and dragged the man to his feet by his tunic. "Can you find your way back to this half-destroyed castle?"

The man nodded rapidly, blood flowing freely from a deep cut on his cheek. "I can, sire."

Edward dropped him to the ground again and tried to calm his raging mind. Betrayed by Nicholas fitz Hugh, his master spy, the one man he had trusted implicitly to do his bidding? It was not possible. And yet, if this man spoke the truth, it *was* possible.

"I will have his head!" Edward shouted, climbing more slowly back into his saddle. He called his captain to his side, giving orders for two regiments to ride hard into Scotland, to take the Dunlairig glen and its decrepit castle into English hands and to hold the traitor Nicholas fitz Hugh and the woman, Rowan, as prisoners.

"When you have them, relieve them of their heads and the stone and send them all to me!" He signaled the column to continue as he spurred his own horse to a gallop, needing to burn off the fury that gripped him.

"These Highlanders are nothing against me!" Edward shouted.

# ACKNOWLEDGMENTS

We writers always moan about how writing is a solitary activity, and in many ways it is. However, I, for one, need a community of other writers to help keep me focused, on track, motivated, and writing.

Huge hugs go to my sisters-of-the-heart Pamela Palmer and Anne Shaw Moran. Plotters, critiquers, life coaches, friends. I don't know what I'd do without you two!

Another big hug to my daily writing compatriot, Phyllis Hall Haislip. Nothing has kept my fingers to the keyboard better than meeting Phyllis every day for coffee and writing.

And a group hug for the fabulous crew at Montlake Romance. Thanks, Lindsay, Eleni, Jessica, Melody, Nikki and all the other talented people they work with. You all know what a fan I am!

# ABOUT THE AUTHOR

MICHAEL TAYLOR

LAURIN WITTIG COMES FROM A LONG LINE OF NATURAL STORYTELLers, so it only made sense that she was a voracious reader, and eventually became a storyteller, too. She was indoctrinated into her Scottish heritage at birth when her parents chose her oddly spelled name from a plethora of Scottish family names. At ten, Laurin attended her first MacGregor clan gathering with her grandparents, and her first ceilidh (kay-lee), a Scottish party, where she danced to the bagpipes with the hereditary chieftain of the clan. At eleven, she visited Scotland for the first time and it has inhabited her imagination ever since.

Early exposure to many cultures led Laurin to study anthropology at Brown University. Her curiosity led her to a long career in the computer industry, first as a trainer, then as a consultant, and finally as a technical writer. When she dropped out of the paid workforce to stay home with her two children, she used those precious napping hours to write her first book, which went on to become a two-time finalist the Romance Writers of America Golden Heart contest.

Laurin's first published book, *The Devil of Kilmartin*, won the National Readers' Choice Award for short historical romance and was a finalist for best first book in that contest and in the Holt Medallion.

Today Laurin lives in southeastern Virginia with her husband (who refuses, under any circumstances, to ever wear a kilt), and Anna the Eskie. She can be found online at LaurinWittig.com.